Acknowledgments

My books are like small children; they take a whole village to get them to a literate state. I want to offer my deep gratitude to my village: my editor, Carrie Feron; my agent, Kim Witherspoon; my website designers, Wax Creative; and my personal team: Franzeca Drouin, Leslie Ferdinand, Sharlene Martin Moore, and Ashley Payne. My husband and daughter Anna debated many a plot point with me, and I'm fervently grateful to them. In addition, people in many departments of HarperCollins, from Art to Marketing to PR, have done a wonderful job of getting this book into readers' hands: my heartfelt thanks goes to each of you.

My Last Duchess

ELOISA JAMES

My Last Duchess

THE WILDES
OF LINDOW
CASTLE

PIATKUS

PIATKUS

First published in the US in 2020 by Avon Books,
An imprint of HarperCollins Publishers, New York
First published in Great Britain in 2020 by Piatkus

1 3 5 7 9 10 8 6 4 2

A CIP catalogue record for this book
is available from the British Library.

ISBN 978-0-349-42901-4

Printed and bound in Great Britain by Clays Ltd, Elcograf S.p.A.

Papers used by Piatkus are from well-managed forests
and other responsible sources.

MIX
Paper from
responsible sources
FSC
www.fsc.org   FSC® C104740

Piatkus
An imprint of
Little, Brown Book Group
Carmelite House
50 Victoria Embankment
London EC4Y 0DZ

An Hachette UK Company
www.hachette.co.uk

www.littlebrown.co.uk

Chapter One

Lindow Castle
Cheshire
October 7, 1766

The Duke of Lindow dropped into a chair behind his library desk, feeling as if he'd taken a
sharp blow to the gut. His hand tightened into
a fist, crumpling the parchment he held, the record of an "Act to dissolve the marriage of Hugo,
Duke of Lindow, with Lady Yvette Mordant, and
to enable the said Duke to marry again."

That would be his second marriage, since he
had lost his much-beloved wife Marie a decade
earlier. His ill-advised marriage to Yvette was
over.

A pulse of anger went through him, and he

shoved it away. Yvette had fled with her Prussian lover a year ago, leaving behind their four children—not to mention Marie's three and his young ward, Parth—with all the concern of a cat abandoning a litter of kittens.

Hearing voices in the entry, he dropped the document in a drawer just as his twin sister, Lady Knowe, strode into the room. She was dressed for riding, wearing a cream-colored habit in the newest style: a huge collar, a great many buttons on her sky-blue waistcoat, and easily twice as many on the jacket. Her wide-brimmed hat was made of the same sky-blue silk, trimmed with white fur.

"Did it arrive?" She pulled off her hat and threw it on a chair.

Hugo's mouth quirked up. "Your wig, Louisa."

"Bloody hell," Louisa said crossly. She plucked up her hat and the attached wig, shook off a few pins, and plopped the wig back on top of her head, adjusting it in the glass that hung over the fireplace. "Don't try to distract me. Prism says that you are brooding over the post, which can only mean one thing."

There was no privacy in a castle, no matter how large.

"I'm a free man."

His sister came over and gave him a whack on the back. "No rest for the weary, Hugo. You should be on the road to London before the end of the week. You need a new duchess—and those children of yours need a mother."

"No."

"What do you mean, no?" Louisa fell back, hand on her heart, looking as shocked as if he'd declared his intention to retreat to a monastery.

His first wife Marie's death had torn a hole in Hugo's chest. He hadn't been able to summon more than mild affection for his second bride, Yvette, and even that had quickly withered in the face of her bottomless need for attention. She had turned to Count Yaraslov, a man distinguished only by his fatuous smirk and yellow hair.

The last thing he wanted was another discontented woman in his household. "No," he stated, just managing to stop himself from growling it. "No, I am not taking another duchess."

His sister shoved over a ledger and perched on his desk. "Feeling bruised?"

"Not particularly."

"Yvette was a weak-headed ninny, and she'll make the count's life hell."

Hugo had come to the same conclusion; he had been married to Yvette for six years, and fathered four children with her, and he still hadn't understood her. Nothing seemed to please her: not him, the title, the castle, the children, nothing.

Even so, she had wanted—she had deserved—more from him.

"She ran off with Yaraslov because I didn't give a damn," he said, meeting his sister's eyes squarely.

Louisa snorted. "Last time I heard, the church hadn't started handing out dispensations for adultery on the basis of a husband's lack of affection. Who *could* give a damn about Yvette? I can't abide a woman who makes an art out of complaining."

"Her children."

"Now, there you're wrong," his sister said cheerfully, getting up from the desk. "The babes hardly knew what she looked like, and they've forgotten her entirely by now. The last time she visited Lindow Castle was two years ago at Yuletide. Did she spend any time in the nursery? No."

"She was great with child," Hugo pointed out.

"Other mothers manage to visit their children during confinement. She deposited the newborn with a wet nurse and climbed into a carriage two days later. About the only thing I can say for Yvette is that she has a constitution like an ox. Six children in four—"

"Four children in six years," Hugo corrected.

Louisa shrugged. "The nursery is so crowded

that I lose track. To return to the important point, you have no need for more offspring, but you do need a mother for those you already have. If I include Parth in the number, since the boy is now an orphan, you have *eight* children."

Hugo nodded. "True."

"You're like that old woman who lived in a shoe, except Lindow Castle is a mighty fine shoe. Luckily, you aren't showing your age—or, should I say, *our* age—so you should be able to scoop up a new duchess without a problem," his twin continued.

"No lady would want to marry a divorced man," Hugo said, keeping it simple. He was not only divorced—an exceedingly rare status granted by an Act of Parliament only in cases of extraordinarily bad behavior—he was jaded, cynical, and completely uninterested in the flimsy, foolish twaddle that passed for polite conversation.

"I'll be damned if another wife of mine takes a lover," he added. "I should have challenged Yaraslov the moment I heard of it." The sad truth was that he hadn't cared enough to duel the man.

"Pshaw, he wasn't worth it," Louisa said, with a dismissive wave of her hand. "Yvette was a hussy. The key is to find a woman with disdain

5

for the bed. Believe me, London is full of ladies in that frame of mind."

Hugo groaned. "A lovely prospect for a spouse."

"You have a fine figure," Louisa said, surveying him from head to foot. "You'll need to order a new suit, of course. That is pitifully passé. Luckily, I have a length of rose silk that I can donate to the cause."

Hugo glanced down at his breeches, waistcoat, and coat, made from somber grey with black buttons. "Rose silk," he said with revulsion.

"Over-stitched with gold thread," his sister said, nodding. "You're disgustingly handsome, even given the Wilde eyebrows, so I'm not worried on that front. No, the real problem is persuading a skittish lady that eight children don't pose an insurmountable burden. I'll definitely have to sacrifice the rose silk; it might be enough to weight the scales of your desirability against your offspring."

"No need for a sacrifice," Hugo said, his tone sharpening. "I employ two nannies, three nursemaids, and a governess. That's enough mothering. What's more, given that Horatius is at Oxford, and Roland, Alaric, and Parth are at Eton, four of the eight would scorn the notion they needed mothering."

Louisa groaned. "Parth is more trouble than the other boys put together. Did I tell you about what he—" She cut herself off. "Never mind that. Ignoring those boys, and the two others, for the moment, you have *daughters* in the nursery. I'm serious, Hugo."

He raised an eyebrow.

"The girls must be taken to London, presented at court, and brought out at balls. That's not to mention the delicate business of steering them away from fortune-hunters and toward respectable young men."

"You—"

She shook her head. "Your daughters cannot wither in Cheshire, going to the local assemblies, living on the edge of a bog, racketing around the castle with no one to talk to."

That stung. "I visit the nursery at least once a day."

"Your children are rarely *in* the nursery so that hardly matters."

Hugo frowned. "They aren't running around Lindow Moss, are they?"

"When they're home, the older boys virtually live in the bog," Louisa said dismissively. "The children love to visit the stables, even the baby. My point is, terrible mother though she was, Yvette knew everyone in London."

"As do I."

"I have trouble picturing you rounding up your

7

acquaintances and putting on a ball in Betsy's honor—which will have to take place in a mere dozen years or so. I don't mind acting as your hostess here, but I rarely leave Cheshire, as you know. I go to London solely to visit the *modistes* and see an occasional play."

"Perhaps Horatius will have married by then," Hugo said, thinking of his oldest son. "I have every faith that he will choose a perfectly raised daughter of a peer, who can do the honors."

"I can imagine," Louisa said, with a shudder. "I'll probably hate her."

"You won't have to see much of her, if you out-live me. Horatius informed me last year that I was neglecting the future of England. He will surely attend every session in Parliament, so he'll have to live in London a good part of the year."

"I adore Horatius, but he's a terrible prig," Louisa said.

Hugo didn't answer, because . . . it was true. Sad but true. His eldest son was best taken in small doses.

"At any rate, you can't lean on the wife that your heir doesn't yet have. Horatius is only eigh-teen. Perhaps he'll rebel and turn into a complete rogue."

They both considered it, and shook their heads

at precisely the same moment, an unintended benefit of being twins.

"Enough," Louisa stated. "You have to take a wife, and that's all there is to it. The girls, particularly Joan, need a noblewoman of unassailable reputation to usher them into society."

Hugo's brows drew together, but before he could speak, his sister planted her fingers on his desk, leaning over and meeting his eyes. "Joan looks like Yvette; I'll give her that. She's going to be beautiful. But she does not look like a Wilde."

"She *is* a Wilde," Hugo growled, surging to his feet.

Louisa drew her shoulders back but held his gaze steadily. "Don't play the fool, Hugo. Whether or not it's true, her golden hair will be seen as a gift from Yaraslov. You need to marry a powerful woman *now*, so that rumors are throttled early, if only because those gossips are terrified of the Duchess of Lindow's wrath."

"Wonderful," Hugo said, deadpan. "You're telling me to marry a dragon with a disgust for bed sport. She'll be a delight to live with."

"You don't have to bed her," his sister pointed out. "Lord knows, you have more than enough heirs. Think of it as taking on a superior governess."

"I don't want another governess, no matter how superior."

Louisa snorted. "I'll let Prism know that you'll be leaving for London tomorrow. Take the silk directly to Grippledon; I think he's the best tailor these days." She headed for the door, scooping up her hat on the way, but stopped and swung about. "Do not, under any circumstances, mention the children during your courtship, Hugo."

"You just said that I need to find a woman precisely because of my offspring," he said. "I should talk of nothing but the children—just as I would when choosing a governess, may I point out."

"No," his sister said. She rarely laid down decrees, preferring to run his household with a smile, albeit a fierce smile. But this was a command. "Let the woman see you as a man, not a father. No one wants to marry a father."

Hugo swore under his breath, and then shouted, "I'm not leaving until next week," as the door closed behind her.

Chapter Two

Lady Gryffyn's ball
London
One month later: November 9

*Y*ou're so fortunate that you needn't bother with another husband," Maddie Penshallow lamented. "You have the best of all worlds, Phee. Your husband was perfectly nice—and, of course, we're all sorry that Sir Peter passed away—but he left you with that darling little girl and not a care in the world!"

Ophelia winced at this blithe summary of widowhood, but her cousin didn't pause for breath as she launched into an account of her marital woes. Apparently, Maddie's husband, Lord Penshallow, was like the rest of his sex: He didn't brush his teeth enough, made impolite noises at dinner (farted, Ophelia interpreted), and—

"He has *two* mistresses?"

"Two," Maddie said, with dramatic emphasis. "One I could tolerate. In fact, I would happily encourage it. But two is an insult. Two means that everyone in London suspects that I refuse to bed him."

"Which you do," Ophelia said.

"That's private," Maddie objected.

"No, it isn't. It hasn't been since you lost your temper and threw a bowl of cherries at him last month at the Terring Hunt Ball."

"Glacé cherries," Maddie said, looking somewhat more cheerful. "When I'm particularly irritated, I bring to mind the way they bounced off his fat head like little tomatoes."

"Well, after that no one could believe that you maintain cordial relations in the bedchamber. Not when you were screaming about—"

"No need to go into the details," Maddie said hastily. "It's not as if you don't have a temper yourself."

"I'm trying to change," Ophelia said.

Her cousin snorted.

"How is your snorting different from his breaking wind?" Ophelia inquired.

"You're not listening to me, Phee!" Maddie

cried. "My point is that you are lucky because you needn't deal with a man ever again. You don't have to hear snoring, or a lecture about what asparagus does to his digestive system, or be smirked at by his mistress—who happens to be wearing diamond earrings tonight, by the way!"

"As are you," Ophelia observed.

"Exactly the same earrings," Maddie said. "I like your emeralds much better than my diamonds, which my husband apparently bought in bulk." She cocked her head. "In fact, you're more attractive than when you debuted, Phee. I expect it's motherhood. Those curves mean that your chin doesn't look as pointed as it used to."

Ophelia broke into laughter and gave her cousin a hug. "What you're saying is that my witchy chin is now topping a fat figure?"

"Voluptuous is not fat," Maddie protested, wiggling out of Ophelia's arms. "How is my goddaughter, by the way?"

"Oh, Viola's fine. She's turned two years old, so her favorite word is 'no.'"

"She's your daughter," Maddie pointed out. "What did you expect? Do tell me that you've managed to find a good nanny?"

"Not yet," Ophelia said.

"I'll find you one," her cousin promised.

Ophelia didn't want a nanny, if the truth be

known. Kind people kept recommending nannies: stern, kindly, scholarly, playful . . . So far, she'd managed to find something wrong with each of them.

Peter had died a few weeks before Viola was born, so he'd never met his daughter. In his absence, she and Viola had become as thick as thieves, as her mother put it. If Ophelia hired a nanny, that nanny would know everything about caring for a two-year-old girl. She would know better than Ophelia.

There was an excellent possibility that Ophelia was making all sorts of mistakes that a proper nanny would avoid. She had nursed Viola herself rather than hire a wet nurse, for example, which one matron had told her was certain to lead to an unhealthy relationship with her child.

She had enjoyed every moment of that mistake.

Next to her, Maddie let out a little shriek. "Oh, look! I didn't know *he* was coming. I haven't seen the duke in London for a year . . . No, well over a year." She turned to Ophelia. "Remember what I told you? There's only one man in the world who could change my mind."

"About what?" Ophelia asked absently. Perhaps she would take Viola to the park tomorrow. Her townhouse was only a block from Hyde Park, and Viola loved to visit the duck pond.

But her coachman had said he smelled a winter storm. Bisquet was a country man, and she trusted his nose, even though the only thing she could smell in London was coal smoke.

"You never remember anything I say," Maddie complained. "You're as bad as my husband, but you're my only cousin, and you ought to be more attentive."

"I'm sorry," Ophelia said. "What did you tell me?"

"That I plan never to bed a man again in the whole of my life."

Ophelia nodded. "All right."

"Aren't you going to dissuade me?" Maddie opened her pretty blue eyes very wide.

"Why would I? Childbirth is extremely dangerous."

"My husband has two mistresses," Maddie said, "so it stands to reason that I should take a lover. Or three."

"That seems excessive to me."

"There is one man in London who might change my mind—and it isn't my husband; I can promise you that."

"It would be hard to have an *affaire* with one's own husband," Ophelia pointed out.

"I would give my virtue to only one man," Maddie said, showing her fine flair for drama.

She nodded toward the other side of the chamber. "That duke."

Ophelia couldn't think of a single duke with whom she would want to share more than a minuet, but she was reconciled to her own shortcomings. The rest of the world experienced fiery passion, but she didn't. Thankfully, she and Peter had been alike in that.

"I would probably follow him to Paris after a mere nod," Maddie said dreamily.

"Which duke?" Ophelia asked, but Maddie didn't hear because she was gawking across the room like a pig herder seeing St. Paul's for the first time. Ophelia snapped shut her fan, thinking that she probably shouldn't compare a beddable duke to a cathedral. It seemed vaguely blasphemous.

Maddie blinked and came out of her desirous haze. "Are you going to the retiring room? I shall join you. I didn't see that darling bag earlier. Oh! It matches your gloves!"

Ophelia smiled. Both her gloves and bag were made of thin, butter-soft leather, sewn with small spangles. The gloves glittered above her wrists, and her bag sparkled from every angle as it moved with her. "Thank you! A gift from my mother-in-law."

"You're so lucky," Maddie began, and broke off the sentence. "He's just over there!"

"Who?" Ophelia turned her head, but all she saw was a ballroom crowded with people she'd known her entire life.

"The Duke of Lindow, of course," Maddie said triumphantly, plucking Ophelia's sleeve and nodding toward the door. "Tell me you wouldn't have an *affaire* with him."

Ophelia wrinkled her nose. "I've heard of him, but we've never met." She didn't bother to look again, because she had no interest in that particular duke, given his unsavory reputation.

Not that it was his fault that his wife ran away with a Prussian.

Maddie was on her toes, peeking over the crowd. "He's just so beautiful," she breathed. "It's cruel what happened to him."

"Darling, I'm not going to the retiring room; I'm going to leave," Ophelia said, making up her mind. "Otherwise I'll be trapped in the supper dance and I shan't return home for ages. Viola wakes up at five in the morning and—"

"You are so unnatural," her cousin interrupted, momentarily startled out of her examination of the infamous duke. "You mean to tell me that you actually rise *with* that child?"

"She comes to fetch me," Ophelia said apologetically. The truth was that she was often awake before the patter of unsteady feet came down the corridor. She lay in bed, smiling at the ceiling, waiting for Viola to burst through the door.

Viola babbled incomprehensibly all the way from the nursery, but as soon as she came through the door, she would cry, "Mama!" She knew only a few words, but "Mama" and "no" were her favorites, and she shouted them both with great enthusiasm.

"I'm going home," Ophelia said, wondering why she had come. True, she had put aside her half-mourning attire for the first time, and was wearing a lovely new gown, but that didn't mean she actually wished to join society again.

It would have been much more fun to stay home with Viola.

"I don't want to be caught in a snowstorm," she added.

"Oh, nonsense," Maddie said. "My coachman was grumbling about the same thing. If traffic snarls up, it might take a wee bit longer to get home, but we're not in the wilds of Lincolnshire! One scarcely notices snow in London."

Ophelia wouldn't have cared if Peter were still alive and traveling in the coach with her on the way home. She was more cautious now, or perhaps less adventurous.

"Oh, very well, I'll walk you to the entrance," Maddie said, taking her arm as they began to make their way through the crowd. She lowered her voice. "His Grace is standing just to the right side of it."

Ophelia sighed. If Maddie started something with a duke whose wife had fled to the Continent—divorced or not—all society would talk feverishly about it for months, or even a year. Her husband would be furious.

Lord Penshallow would not forget, even when society moved on to the next scandal. Maddie's husband might not want his wife himself, but Ophelia was certain he didn't want another man in his bed. Men weren't rational about that sort of thing.

"Maddie," she said, striving for a tactful tone, "I believe you ought to rethink the idea of an *affaire* with Lindow."

"For goodness' sake, lower your voice," her cousin whispered. "Do you see him now? He's straight in front of us."

Ophelia looked and froze, which made her stumble. It was mortifying, not helped by the fact that Maddie burst out laughing.

"Didn't I tell you so?" she demanded.

No.

Maddie hadn't "told." She hadn't said what the Duke of Lindow looked like. He had a square chin, high cheekbones, and a straight nose that somehow came together in a way that made a woman instinctively draw in a breath.

It wasn't just that he was handsome, or broad-shouldered and tall. He was indefinably *masculine* in a way few of the gentlemen in the room were. He was wearing a magnificent peruke, befitting a duke, and a rose-colored coat that by rights should look effeminate.

It didn't.

That square chin looked stubbornly male. Her husband had never been able to grow a beard, try as he might, but the duke's chin was shadowed, though his man had undoubtedly shaved him a few hours ago.

Next to her, Maddie was still giggling. "I told you so."

Rather than respond, Ophelia kept looking. His Grace was clearly bored. He was paying no attention to the two ladies chattering beside him.

Ophelia flipped open her fan. "Why is he here?" she asked Maddie from behind its shelter. "I thought he was uninterested in society, and he certainly looks it."

The last two years she'd been in mourning, but before that, she and Peter had attended virtually every ball held in London. Peter had loved to dance.

"Keep walking," Maddie hissed. "My husband is one of His Grace's acquaintances, so I shall greet him. As for why he's here, I expect he's looking for another wife. Or should I say, broodmare."

"What?"

"Phee, don't you pay attention to *anything*? The duchess, the one he divorced, left four young children behind. That's why the private act passed so quickly. Everyone knows that he needs to marry again; apparently the discussion in Parliament circled around that issue."

"Four children," she echoed, wondering how the former duchess could have left her babies behind. She could no more leave Viola than she could cut off her own arm.

"There are more children than those four, because if I remember correctly, he had four or five with his first wife as well, though they must be nearly grown. If we don't hurry, he'll move away from the door and I'll miss my chance."

"More children than four?" Ophelia kept her fan up as they arrowed through the crowd. "How old is he?"

"Not as old as you'd think. Late thirties, I believe."

They weren't the only ones heading in the Duke of Lindow's direction. There was an unmistakable drift in the room, as if the tide were coming in, and he was the shore.

"The three or four from his first wife," Maddie said over her shoulder, "are all boys."

"Slow down," Ophelia hissed, tugging back. "You're making a spectacle out of us."

They were close enough now that she could see the duke's eyes were dark green. His face was all hard planes and angles. He was standing with one leg bent in front of him, a silver-hilted sword on his left hip.

She felt heat rising in her cheeks just from glancing at his stance. His thigh was pure muscle, and anyone could tell that his calves were not enhanced by horsehair pads. His was an aggressive leg, not a graceful one. She'd put a pretty chunk of her jointure on a bet that he didn't care to dance.

That sword? It wasn't just for show.

He wasn't the sort of man who would ever interest her. "I truly must leave," she said, with sudden resolution. "You may stop and talk to His Grace, but I am going home to Viola."

"All right," her cousin said, not listening.

Ophelia thought about pointing out that a man intent on courting a mother for his children was unlikely to conduct a highly visible *affaire* with a married woman, but she dismissed it. Maddie would soon discover whether His Grace was interested or not.

Even as a child, Maddie had always bluntly demanded whatever she wanted. Ophelia wouldn't be surprised if Maddie strode right up to the man and suggested a tryst.

They were almost at the door, so Ophelia glanced at the duke again.

He was looking at her.

Not at Maddie.

At *her*.

Blood rushed into her cheeks, and she barely caught herself before she tripped again. She was a *widow*, the relict of Sir Peter Astley. A *mother*. Not the sort of woman who welcomed a man's eyes raking over her in a ballroom, as if she were no better than a streetwalker.

She narrowed her eyes.

He blinked as if he was surprised, and then a slow smile crooked one corner of his mouth.

"The duke is looking at you!" Maddie said from somewhere to her right. "Phee, that will never do." Her cousin actually sounded alarmed. "He's far too much for you. Nothing like sweet Peter."

That shook Ophelia out of a haze caused by the duke's attention. She turned her head and smiled at her cousin. "Don't be silly, Maddie. He's probably mistaken me for someone else, that's all. Will I see you tomorrow?"

"It could be that he's walking toward me," her cousin said breathlessly. "He could be glancing at you as a decoy." She gripped Ophelia's forearm hard enough to leave a bruise. "How do you think he'd respond if I lured him into a side room and tied him up?"

Ophelia ducked behind her fan and hissed, "What on earth are you talking about? You don't tie up Penshallow, do you?"

"The duke's so *large*," Maddie said, giggling madly. "Of course, I don't . . . It was just a silly thought."

"He doesn't look like the sort of a man who would wish to be tied up for any reason." Not that she knew any man who had that sort of propensity, for all the ladies whispered about it in drawing rooms over tea.

She dropped her fan just enough to steal another glance over it.

The duke's eyes were still fixed not on Maddie but on her. He was walking directly toward them, ignoring any number of women throwing themselves into his path.

"Perhaps he knew your husband," her cousin said, sounding perplexed. "He really does appear to be looking at you, Phee."

Ophelia shared her confusion. She wasn't the kind of woman whom a man lost his head over. She had a pointed nose, a temper, a pile of red hair, and an overly generous bosom, even more so after being enhanced by motherhood. The thought of Viola brought her back to herself.

"If he was friends with my husband, he can pay me a morning call, as did Peter's other friends."

"I know!" Maddie said, her face clearing. "He's been told what a wonderful mother you are. Oh, Ophelia, you could be a duchess!"

"I'm not available to mother a flock of discarded children," Ophelia said sharply. She was conscious of a sense of disappointment. Just once, she'd like a man to look at her for herself.

Peter had been shepherded in her direction by his father and her mother during her debut ball. They danced twice and sat together at supper. Pudding hadn't even been served before he said, with his disarming smile, "I say, we get along pretty well, don't we?"

They did. They had.

But Peter hadn't the faintest idea what sort of woman she was when he asked her to marry him.

"Even to be a *duchess*?"

Ophelia frowned. "I'm perfectly comfortable as I am, Maddie."

Her cousin sighed. "It's true that I can't imagine

you in such an elevated role. It would be like hearing that the baker had been knighted."

"Maddie!" Ophelia protested. "I'm hardly a baker."

"Don't worry, I'll set him straight," her cousin said. "You'd better leave unless you want to refuse him yourself; Lady Persell caught his arm, but he'll be heading this direction again in a moment."

Ophelia definitely did not want to encounter the duke. The man looked like a hunter, strolling across the ballroom in that pink coat, pretending to be a gentleman, which he wasn't.

He absolutely was not.

She didn't know why she was so sure of that, but she was. The Duke of Lindow was a nobleman, in the old-fashioned sense of the term. He probably had vassals, serfs, a county of his own, and an escutcheon.

She gave Maddie a brisk kiss and set out for the door. After a moment she sped up, practically diving toward the entrance to the ballroom. It almost seemed as if she could feel his approach like a warm wind at her back, even though that made no sense.

Just as she turned so she could squeeze between two groups of gossiping peers without her panniers bumping them, a hand closed around her elbow.

She felt the shock of his touch through her entire body.

"Yes?" she said, turning. She managed to keep her tone cool. What she saw in the Duke of Lindow's eyes made her raise an eyebrow. "You must have mistaken me for someone else," she said, her tone almost kindly.

No one had ever looked at her, at Ophelia, like that. Not even Peter.

Perhaps Lindow thought she was a girl he had loved in his youth.

"I am not mistaken," the duke replied. His eyes were a dark, dark green, the color of spruce trees when they stood vividly against the snow.

His voice startled her because it was deeper than she would have thought. Like a bear's growl. In fact, he looked like a bear emerging from a winter's sleep, she thought irrelevantly. Coming into the world and looking for a nice rabbit to eat.

She was not a rabbit for any man's consumption. She had no need of a husband, and no desire for a lover either. Still less did she want to nurture a flock of motherless children, no matter how sad that was.

Given that her own cousin thought of her as a

baker, people would know exactly why he was courting her—to turn her into a glorified governess.

"Excuse me," she said, allowing impatience to leak into her voice. Then she gently pulled her arm from his grasp and walked away.

Behind her, a moment of silence.

And then, to her horror, a shout of laughter.

Chapter Three

S he was a delight. Hugo's heart was pounding in his chest in a way it hadn't for years.

Nineteen years, to be exact.

When he had walked into a drawing room in Windsor Castle and had seen Marie being fanned by a couple of impertinent puppies babbling non-sense and making her laugh. His future wife, his first wife, had been reclining on a sofa, a perfect lady from the tips of her scarlet shoes to the top of her extravagant, pearl-bedecked hair.

Marie was the one young lady whom every bachelor in London—and most of the married men as well—wanted for his own. She was a minx who delighted in every flirtatious glance and trill of laughter.

Remembering her made Hugo feel a nostalgic

flash of love for those heady days. He had known from the moment he entered that room that he had to have her.

This lady was Marie's opposite. She didn't look as if she indulged in flirtations. No, she looked fierce, like a warrior, a curvy, beautiful warrior blessed with masses of red hair. She'd powdered it as fashion demanded, but only lightly.

He made his way over to the woman who had been accompanying the lady before she ran out the door as if the Hounds of Hell were after her. "Who is she?" he asked, without preamble.

A hint of defiance showed in the woman's eyes. "Your Grace," she said, dropping into a curtsy.

For Christ's sake. All the same, he bowed and then lifted her hand to his lips. "Good evening, my lady. I'm afraid I'm at a disadvantage. I believe we haven't met."

"You are acquainted with my husband, Lord Penshallow," she said.

A tiresome fellow with a propensity to brag about his amorous activities. Hugo felt a dart of sympathy for the lady, but that was neither here nor there. "It's a pleasure to meet you, Lady Penshallow," he said. "I wonder if you could give me the name of the woman you were accompanying a moment ago."

Her brows drew together. "You do not know who she is?"

Hugo's gut clenched. Was she married? It had never occurred to him. A raw feeling swept through his chest at the idea that she belonged to another man.

"Is she married?" he asked, knowing his voice rumbled from his chest.

"So you *don't* know who she is," Lady Penshallow said, looking confused. "No, Phee is not married."

"Excellent," Hugo said, gentling his voice. "I'm glad to hear it." That was an understatement. *Fee.* What could that possibly be short for? Fidelia? No: Phoebe! Of course. But no Phoebes came to mind.

"I thought you had heard about her," the lady continued.

He shook his head. "I have no idea who she is."

"My cousin is a respectable widow," Lady Penshallow announced. Then she lowered her voice. "She is not looking for a dalliance, and you do her no favors by singling her out in such an obvious fashion."

Few men and even fewer women dared to defy him, so Hugo smiled at her. "You are very loyal."

"She is also uninterested in a husband, so you

needn't waste your time," Lady Penshallow explained with a shrug. There was a hint of warmth at the backs of her eyes that suggested that she would have no objection if he cared to waste his time with her. "She was very fond of her husband, and only emerged from mourning in the last few months. In fact, this is her first excursion into society, and as you saw, she chose to return home early."

"Does she have children?" Lindow Castle was a huge pile of stone that could absorb another baker's dozen of youngsters, and no one would know the difference.

"She is a wonderful mother," the lady said, watching him carefully. "She left before the dinner dance so that she won't be too sleepy when my goddaughter wakes in the morning. At five a.m."

His mouth eased into a smile. She was a mother. A real mother, the kind Marie had been. The kind he had hoped to find for his boys when he married Yvette, except he had been so appallingly wrong.

"My cousin has no wish to take care of another woman's children," the lady continued. "Perhaps you will forgive my observation that you have too many of them. And as I said, she has no wish to marry again."

Over her shoulder, half the ballroom was gaping at them, fascinated. They'd missed his real intention; they thought he was flirting with this elegant young wife. Lord Penshallow was undoubtedly watching from somewhere.

He stepped backward and bowed. "I wish you good evening, Lady Penshallow. I'm afraid that, like your cousin, I must leave before the dinner dance. Perhaps you will dance with me another time." He felt a primitive desire to get out the doors before his lady managed to run away from him.

That's what she was doing.

Running.

She had taken one look at him from under those absurdly long eyelashes and headed for the ballroom door. That meant she felt something. Maybe not the same thing he did—not the same jolt of absolute certainty—but *something*.

He could work with it.

A butler, resplendent in red livery, handed him his greatcoat. The man was dignified, but given his raisin-sized eyes, not too dignified for a bribe. A moment later, Hugo had a name.

Ophelia, Lady Astley, the widow of Sir Peter Astley.

He turned it over in his head. *Ophelia.* One of Shakespeare's heroines, and a melancholy one, if he had the play right. This Ophelia wasn't melancholy. Her eyes were intelligent and fiery; he'd bet anything she had a temper that would blaze as hot as her hair.

He walked through the door and saw with satisfaction that the street was just as snarled in carriages as it had been forty minutes ago. Carriages were taking a half hour to traverse the street before the house.

When he arrived, he had jumped out and walked, telling his coachman that he would make his own way home later. Other guests remained in their carriages like a line of patient cows waiting to be milked. Likely some of them had been here then, and they were still here now.

Night had fallen. Linkboys were milling about in front of the house and running between carriages, their flaming torches held high, biting circles into the darkness. Snowflakes were falling lazily into the patches of light, as if the white fluff popped into existence when light met the dark air.

Ophelia was nowhere in sight, which meant her coachman had escorted her to her carriage—but he doubted the vehicle had gone anywhere. Traffic was at a standstill; two coachmen had descended from their perches and were shouting about a scratched side panel.

Which carriage might she be in? To his left were three commodious family carriages, the doors picked out with crests. She wouldn't be found in one of those. Sir Peter Astley had been a baronet, not a peer.

If there was an elegant barouche, it would have gone to the heir, not to the widow. His brows drew together as he realized that many a young widow, especially one who hadn't given birth to a male heir, might find herself in financial straits. Rational thought quickly asserted itself.

Ophelia had been wearing emeralds, and a dress his sister called a sack gown. It had glowed in the candlelight of the ballroom, glittering with gold thread, but more importantly, with flowers. Hand-painted flowers on French silk.

Louisa owned one gown made of hand-painted silk, the fabric imported from France. Characteristically, Louisa's was bright with poppies. Ophelia's gown had been painted all over with charming flower sprigs. It didn't call attention to itself, and yet it must have been wildly expensive.

His heart eased. His lady wasn't worried about money. In fact, she must be swimming in guineas.

Good for Sir Peter. He had died, leaving his wife and baby girl behind, but he'd made certain that they were comfortable, cared for.

There were four carriages to his right. One

of them belonged to the Dowager Duchess of Windebank. Two were hired rigs and one . . .

That was it.

It was small but exquisite, made of rich bronze-colored wood and fashioned with three windows to a side. The carriage body looked like a delicate egg trimmed in strands of twisted brass, the body painted with bluebirds.

It was absurd, and absurdly lovely. It suited her, down to its curves.

It wasn't moving and wouldn't until those coachmen stopped their squabble.

Without haste, he walked toward it, his shoes splashing into the sludge on the streets; the first layer of snowflakes had already melted. Delicate silk curtains were drawn across the windows, and a soft glow from the inside told him that Ophelia had lit the carriage lamps.

As he grew closer, he made out her silhouette. She was leaning back against the cushions, reading a book. Hugo paused for a moment, savoring his reaction to finding her.

His life had jerked to a halt with Marie's death. In the years since, he took care of the estate, went through the motions of being married to Yvette, tried to be the best father he could to the children.

But now, unexpectedly, strangely, with no more than the sight of a tantalizing woman . . .

His heart was thumping in a rhythm he'd forgotten.

Feeling the prickle of eyes on him, he looked up and discovered that her coachman was watching him closely. The man looked like a good fellow, strong and loyal, with the tenacity and skill to fight off anyone who threatened his lady's well-being.

A groom in livery was perched behind, his gaze as hard-eyed as the coachman's.

Hugo tilted his head in a silent question.

After a moment, the coachman nodded, so Hugo sprang up beside him. The conversation took longer than he would have thought and necessitated pulling his sword out of its sheath, displaying the ducal crest set into the hilt, and finally handing it over.

They had moved approximately three carriage lengths down the street before Hugo leapt down again, having made it clear to Mr. Bisquet that, if she agreed, the lady was to become a duchess.

If she rejected him, he meant her no harm.

Now he just had to persuade the lady herself.

Chapter Four

*O*phelia was humiliated to realize how long it took her breath to calm after leaving the ballroom. It was only, she assured herself, because she hadn't been in society for some time.

A man hadn't looked at her with interest in years. Peter had *never* looked at her like that.

The duke's gaze made her feel overheated. Almost feverish, which was absurd. Thinking about her dear husband steadied her.

She and Peter had approached the bedchamber the way they had their entire life together: with a frank conversation and a generous ladling of respect. Over the years of their marriage, they had come together many times, not merely because they were determined to have children—and surprised by how long it took—but because they genuinely enjoyed each other's company.

Ophelia took a deep breath and straightened her shoulders, trying to focus on the book she was reading. *The Life and Adventures of Mr. Francis Clive*. It wasn't a restful book; the poor housemaid who found herself part of Francis Clive's "adventures" was now in the family way.

Any sensible woman could have told her that he was a rake from the first few pages of the book. As opposed to Peter, for example. Once again, the remembrance of Peter's steady love and respect made Ophelia feel calmer.

Her late husband would have understood how shocking it had felt to come into contact with the duke, a man who had palpable power and erotic . . . well, erotic something.

Promise, maybe.

The duke looked at her with a promise in his eyes, and *his* promise had nothing to do with respect.

Undoubtedly, every woman encountered a man like that during her life: a bad man, her mother would have said. A rake, no doubt. One who made all sorts of promises he didn't—

No.

The Duke of Lindow's steady gaze came back

39

to her. If he made promises, he would keep them.

She had the feeling he was offering her pleasure. Possibly a different kind of pleasure than the measured joy she and Peter had shared. Something altogether more overwhelming.

The door of her carriage swung open, followed by a blast of chilly air and the clean smell of fresh snow. Ophelia frowned, reaching toward the door. She adored the little carriage that she had helped design herself, but it wasn't the sturdiest vehicle in the world. Bisquet hadn't wished to take it this evening because of the weather, but she insisted.

Broad shoulders blocked the doorway as a man climbed into her carriage.

Ophelia shrank back, suddenly aware of how alone she was. Her heart stuttered, and a scream caught in her throat as she flung her hand to the roof, intending to yank open the trapdoor between herself and her coachman.

"I apologize." His voice filled the small space like one deep note from a cello: calm, resonant, safe.

Air slipped out of Ophelia's lungs. Her hand fell back and she leaned, boneless, against the back of her carriage seat.

The Duke of Lindow closed the door behind

himself and sat down opposite her, his intense green eyes fastened on her face. There wasn't a shred of shame in his expression. There was regret for having frightened her, but the fact he'd invaded her carriage without an invitation?

No, he had all the bravado of a pirate boarding a ship and informing the captain that he had every right to be there.

She felt a welcome spark of anger at the base of her spine and sat up straight again. She was a dowager baroness. He might be far above her in England's hierarchy, but that didn't give him the right to frighten her.

To invade her carriage.

"I did not invite you to join me," she stated, adding, after a pointed pause, "Your Grace."

The duke had stuffed his gloves into his pockets, and now he shrugged out of his damp greatcoat without answering. The beautiful wool was speckled with dark spots where snowflakes had melted.

Ophelia was well aware that the person who talks most in any confrontation loses power, so she held her tongue.

He had remarkably broad shoulders. Even his neck looked powerful. He was a male animal, lithe and powerful—but one who meant her no harm. She knew that instinctively, in her bones.

His Grace was no Francis Clive, running around looking for adventures and woe betide any young woman who got in his way.

Once out of his heavy outerwear, he shrugged, apparently uncomfortable in his closely tailored, extravagant coat. But then, in one swift movement, he crouched in front of her.

Ophelia could feel her eyes rounding as she looked down. He didn't touch her, but she felt as if his gaze settled around her like a warm blanket. A sharp sense of vertigo gripped her.

Men like this, *dukes*, had nothing to do with women like her. She had been considered tremendously lucky that Peter chose her. She was rounded, short, and not particularly beautiful. That wasn't even taking account of the pointed chin Maddie had mentioned.

What's more, she wasn't seductive or flirtatious. Not that she had ever flirted with this man before.

"Your Grace," she said. "I gather that you have formed some sort of interest in me that is groundless and unrequited. I must ask you to behave like a gentleman and return from whence you came."

A smile tugged at his mouth. "From whence I came?"

"My meaning is clear," Ophelia said, scowling at him. "Go. Back to the street, if you prefer plain speaking. You are not welcome in my carriage."

She had the absurd idea that she'd hurt his feelings, but the emotion flashed by so quickly that she wasn't sure.

"I apologize," he said again. "I just saw you for the first time."

Ophelia waited, but he didn't continue, so she said, "The fact that we are unacquainted is scarcely reason for this intrusion."

"How long were you married to Sir Peter?" he asked.

This was such an odd conversation. He hadn't touched her, and she didn't know him, and yet they were looking at each other with an intimacy that—

She pushed the thought away. She probably shouldn't answer him, but she did, because what was the harm of it?

"I married in July of 1759," she replied.

"I married Yvette in May of the same year."

Clearly, that meant something to him, but nothing to her. "Is that why you're following me?" she asked, a dash of humiliation suddenly turning scalding.

She'd got it wrong; he didn't desire her. He wanted something from her. Or had she known his previous duchess? She couldn't recall anyone by that name.

His lopsided smile appeared again. "If I hadn't

decided that Yvette looked like a good mother—
a decision so misguided as to be comical—I
would have gone to a few more balls, and I might
have met you before you were betrothed to Sir
Peter."

She raised an eyebrow. "Perhaps you think that
your presence would have affected my feelings
for my late husband, whom I loved dearly? You
do yourself too much honor, Your Grace."

His smile broadened. "I deserved that."

"Yes, you did," she said tartly. "Now, please
stop hovering at my knee or whatever it is you
are doing and take your leave before I shout at
my coachman and ask him to remove you, pistol
in hand."

"Bisquet confiscated my sword," the duke said
with a grin.

With a start, Ophelia realized that the silver
hilt that had sat so easily at his hip was no longer
there. "He did?"

"You have an excellent coachman. It took me
the better part of ten minutes to persuade him to
allow me to speak to you."

Ophelia instantly made up her mind to *speak* to
Bisquet herself and quite sharply too.

"I didn't offer a bribe, and he wouldn't have
taken one," the duke said. "May I call on you in
the morning?"

"I see no reason for that," she replied.

He was too handsome, too witty, too every-thing. There was a hint of sadness at the backs of his eyes, and a ruefulness in his tone when he mentioned his wife Yvette. He was *nuanced*.

Men were so rarely nuanced.

The word reminded her that he was some-thing else as well: divorced. Any woman asso-ciated with him would become notorious, and not merely if Ophelia became his third duchess. Everyone would watch to see if she too would find him insufficient, run away, or carry on a flagrant *affaire*.

Yvette had been, presumably, as passionate in her search for adventures as Francis Clive, and as immoral as well, since she had run away with another man. Leaving not just her children but *this* man behind. Ophelia had heard about the scandal, of course, but she hadn't seen *him*.

Who could leave him?

Yvette likely had very good reason. For exam-ple, because her former husband was the type who leapt into strange women's carriages and demanded to be heard.

"Would you deny entry to me if I paid you a morning call?" he asked.

"I am too busy for calls," she said. Which was a polite way of saying: *Yes. Yes, I would.*

He looked surprised, which was good. Men of his rank were likely never refused entrance.

"I don't know you," Ophelia continued, "and I have no reason to wish to know you. You are frank, Your Grace, so I shall be the same. As far as I can remember, I had no acquaintance with either of your former duchesses." She raised an eyebrow.

"Not to the best of my knowledge."

He was looking at her, eyes intent, seeming as comfortable on one knee as he was in the ballroom.

"And certainly not with you, so what in heaven's name are you doing, kneeling on my carriage floor?"

"Asking you to marry me."

For a confused moment, Ophelia thought she'd lost her hearing. "What?"

"You're the one for me," he said, his voice deepening to a rumble.

"The one?" To her own shock, Ophelia heard herself laughing. "*One*, Your Grace? What about your other two wives?"

He rocked back on his heels and grinned up at her.

"You!" she said, rapping him on the shoulder with her closed fan, as if he were a naughty schoolboy. "Have you lost your mind? You don't know me. I am not your 'one.' Get up, if you please."

"I wish to marry you."

"I don't wish to marry you!" Ophelia said tartly. "I don't even know you. And even if I did . . ."

She would never want to be a duchess. Duchesses were forever being gawked at. Gossip columns described what they wore, and what they said, and whom they smiled at. As Sir Peter's relict, she had slipped out of that ballroom without anyone taking notice of her.

No duchess walked from a room without people tracking her movements.

He nodded, eyes on hers. "Indeed, duchesses are always in the public eye."

"How did you know what I was thinking?"

With a swift movement, he rose and sat next to her. Practically on top of her skirts.

"Watch out!" she cried.

He waited while she rearranged her skirts, taking her time because her fingers were trembling and she needed to regain control.

"Your Grace," she said at last, raising her face to his. "I am not of your world, and I don't wish to be. I do not reference your divorce," she said swiftly, when he opened his mouth. "'Tis an infamous thing, but I understand that your wife left under—she left with . . ." Tangled in words, she stopped.

"The second part of this particular private act is the only one that matters," he said. "The act dissolved our marriage and specifically enabled 'the said Duke to marry again.' I would not have petitioned for divorce if it hadn't been for our—" He caught himself. "For *my* children."

"I see," Ophelia said, feeling desperately sorry for him.

"In case you are wondering, I did not refuse to allow the children to go with their mother. I'm not sure what I would have said, had Yvette asked for them, but she did not. She left a letter explaining that our marriage was a mistake and that she felt English children should stay on English soil."

Ophelia's gaze fell to the duke's hand, clenched on the carriage seat.

"She spelled Joan's name wrong," he said.

A soft noise came from Ophelia's mouth, unbidden.

"Joan is my baby," the duke said. "She's only two." His mouth twisted. "Her mother apparently believed we had baptized her Joanna."

Before she could stop herself, Ophelia reached out and curled her fingers around his fist. "I'm sorry."

"They are better off with me, although I don't know how I will explain to them, when they are grown up, that their mother didn't want them."

"I don't know that you'll have to," Ophelia said.

"Children are very accepting, as long as someone loves them. My daughter, Viola, has no idea that a father is missing from her life. At some point she will understand that she never knew him, but I hope it won't be a grievous loss to her."

"Sir Peter didn't choose to leave his daughter," the duke said, sounding tired all of a sudden.

Ophelia withdrew her hand, clearing her throat. "I don't—"

His Grace bent toward her, his eyes even darker green in the soft light of the carriage than they had seemed in the ballroom. Ophelia froze, her heart hammering in her throat. Carefully, delicately, he cupped his hands on either side of her face, bent his head, and brushed her mouth with his.

Ophelia's mind stuttered and fell silent. The duke's eyes were fringed with thick black lashes. They didn't curl up, the way hers did. Instead she had the feeling they hid his eyes from the world—but not at the moment.

His eyes were shining with an emotion she didn't recognize.

She swallowed hard. "This is madness."

"Yes. Love is madness. I'm not in love with you yet, Ophelia, but only because I haven't had enough time."

It was that moment that Ophelia realized that

the Duke of Lindow—a man clearly used to getting exactly what he wanted, when he wanted it, a man whom the world had blessed with beauty, power, and wealth—was truly at her feet.

Metaphorically, because he was sitting beside her and kissing her again. This time, when his mouth brushed hers, her lips parted.

Her breath stopped, and her hands rose of their own volition, flattening themselves against his chest. Through layers of silk his chest felt warm and hard. In that moment when she gasped for breath, his tongue slid into her mouth and an inarticulate male sound, a growl or a rumble, came from his chest.

Ophelia shouldn't . . . She couldn't help it. Her tongue met his, curiously. She hadn't felt desire in well over two years, but it came back to her in a rush, tingling through her veins, growing hotter and hotter.

The kiss didn't end. She and Peter had kissed each other; of course they had. But not like this. Peter had never devoured her, never kissed her as if time had stopped. The duke's kiss was a decadent kiss, unhurried, hungry, sensual.

Her heart began thudding in her chest, and under her fingers, the duke's heart was thudding too. She had the sense they could kiss all night and he wouldn't complain.

This was a get-to-know-you kiss, which was such a disgraceful thought that Ophelia shook off the erotic haze that had lured her into kissing him back and started to draw away.

"Please?" he asked. His voice rumbled from his chest, soft and dark. His hands shaped her waist and slid up her back. His hands were so large that it felt as if they covered her like a blanket.

Ophelia lost her breath again. She opened her lips and fell back into their kiss, letting it melt her, letting feelings that she'd forgotten unfurl in her body, touching her here and there with fire.

Her breasts woke up, as if she were still nursing. She wrenched her mind away from that thought. It wasn't just her breasts. Her skin was prickling to life all over, her neck, her legs, her . . .

Everything.

She didn't even think about what came next, not that there was a "next," obviously. There was just this kiss, a kiss with a stranger, that was somehow ravenous and affectionate.

That thought shocked her and she pulled away again, sharply.

He let her go instantly, his hands falling away and leaving her back cool and uncaressed. She met his gaze and saw the same surprise in his eyes that she felt. But there was a faint smugness as well.

Confidence.

He thought he had her, because he was so good at kissing. As well he should be, given the number of wives he'd had.

Ophelia took a deep breath. "That was pleasant," she said, willing her cheeks to stop burning.

"I found it so," His Grace said amiably.

The smile playing on his lips made her want to scowl at him, but that would be too revealing. "If you would please take your leave—"

As the words left her mouth, she realized that her carriage was swaying back and forth, presumably on its way to her house.

"Your coachman couldn't block the street, so when I didn't leave the carriage immediately, he set out."

Ophelia did scowl. "Don't read my thoughts. I don't like it."

The duke's laugh was husky, joyful in a masculine way.

"When we reach my house, Bisquet can return you to the ball," Ophelia said, noticing that the duke had a dimple. A dimple! In that strong face it was like a private jest.

He was so much a *duke*. It was easy to imagine him bowing before the king in snowy stockings and a powdered wig. She could picture him addressing the House of Lords, or stepping

52

out of his ornate carriage, or doing other ducal things.

But a little dimple? A husky chuckle? Dukes weren't supposed to have those—nor the mischievous look in his eyes. Not that either.

They weren't supposed to kneel before plump widows of no particular status. The notion made her feel suddenly vulnerable. It was so tempting to imagine throwing away the propriety, the rules, that had governed her entire life.

No.

Viola's reputation was tied to her own. She couldn't have an *affaire* with a duke no matter how alluring his kisses, and she didn't wish to marry him. Time to get rid of him.

"It's been very nice to talk to you," she said, "but there is nowhere . . ." She stumbled to a halt. "I do not wish to know you further."

"Not at all?"

She couldn't read his eyes, but that couldn't have been a flash of vulnerability—could it?

Or was it certainty: that's what she saw most clearly. A kind of deep, knowing certainty shining from his eyes. As if he knew something about her that she didn't.

"No," she said sharply. "My life is very pleasant. I do not wish to be a duchess. I certainly do not wish to mother six more children."

"Eight."

"Eight!" She felt indignation rising up her spine. "No one should have so many children."

He cocked his head. "The world does seem too small for the number of the bawling, squalling Wildes I have dropped into it. I apologize."

"You should not marry again," she said, less severely. "What if you had even *more*?"

The lines of his face were sharp, almost fierce, and yet they softened into a smile and that dimple appeared again. "I told my twin sister as much."

Ophelia stared at him in fascination. "You have a sister?" It was hard to imagine a female version of him.

He nodded. "Louisa."

The carriage was silent except for the rising whine of wind. As if gravel was thrown at the glass, a flurry of snow hit the windows.

He pulled back a flap of her silk curtains. "That came on fast."

"Has it turned into a snowstorm?" Ophelia frowned and plucked open the curtain at her side. In the light cast by the torches attached to the sides of her carriage, snow swirled thick and glossy. The fairy tale–like fluff that she had glimpsed over the duke's shoulder when he first joined her had turned into a howling dervish. The carriage was progressing at a crawl.

"Bisquet was concerned about snow," she confessed. "I don't live far from Lady Gryffyn's house, though, just on the other side of Hyde Park."

"In my experience, coachmen generally favor staying tucked up in a warm stable feeding their horses hot mash and themselves a hot toddy." The duke dropped the curtain.

Outside, the sudden storm battered the carriage, and Ophelia knew that if he hadn't been there, she would have felt rising anxiety, if not pure terror. How would she get home to Viola? What if the carriage overturned?

Instead she felt rosy, hot, and unsure after their kisses. Her stomach clenched, wanting more— more kisses, more caresses, *more*. That unusual sensation, put together with a wave of anxiety due to the quick-rising storm, made her uncertain and off balance.

The duke looked utterly calm. It was only when she met his eyes that she saw emotion there, and the expression in his gaze had nothing to do with storms. His eyes were fiery with desire held tightly leashed.

"We're already well into Hyde Park and will arrive at your house in no time." He sounded so sensible. He couldn't be trembling, the way she was.

Then he reached out and caught one of her

hands and brought it to his lips, and she caught another flare of desire in his eyes.

The storm didn't unsettle him—but she did. That was a surprisingly satisfying thought.

"Thank you," she said, forcing herself to relax. Her breath was catching in her chest, but she wasn't sure whether it was due to the storm or his kisses.

"I might as well point out that there are advantages to having a husband," His Grace said, his dimple making an appearance.

"Are you planning to clamber out and take the reins?" She didn't take her hand away. His was comforting, a big male hand that looked capable of anything. "You have calluses on your fingers . . . from driving?"

He nodded, turning her hand over. "Whereas your hand is delicate and pink."

"A useless hand," Ophelia said, pulling it away.

But he hung on. "A hand needn't be scarred to be useful." His mouth twitched and then he said, "Marie rocked her babes every night. Her hands were not scarred, but they were not frail."

Ophelia was caught between a sense of danger—he really *was* looking for a mother for all those children—and elation that he had understood. He wouldn't scorn her if he knew she rocked Viola to sleep.

Just as that thought went through her mind, the carriage skewed across the road. The duke reached over and plucked her into his lap as easily as she might pick up Viola.

"What are you doing?" she gasped.

He braced one large foot against the side of the carriage opposite them, and the other on the opposite seat. Ophelia craned her neck sideways to frown at him just as the carriage slipped again.

This time it slid clear across the road.

"We're likely to lose a wheel," the duke said in her ear, one arm across her chest like an iron band, the other holding on to the strap.

"A wheel?" she managed, but the crack of splitting wood drowned her voice.

His Grace said one short, brutal curse, not at all dukelike.

The carriage began to list to one side slowly, as if it were a boat on the verge of capsizing. Just when it was about to fall over, it rocked back in the other direction and she heard a crunch as the axle presumably hit the ground. They were tilted, but not upside down.

The door blew open, and, with a theatrical swirl, snow rushed into the carriage.

Ophelia hardly felt it. The duke's massive body had taken the shock of the carriage rocking, and now he tucked her closer against himself, as if his arms could ward off the winter. The wind caught the door and slammed it shut again.

"We made it," the duke said, sounding very satisfied. "Your carriage driver, Ophelia, is worth every shilling you pay him."

"My—what happened?"

"We lost a wheel, but he managed to keep us from toppling on our heads," His Grace said. "Much though I love the feeling of you in my lap, I'm going to clamber from this carriage so that I can get you out. I don't like the idea that a fool might be bowling along in the dark and run straight into us before he can stop."

Ophelia was breathless, terrified, oddly exhilarated at the same time. "I must get home to Viola." She caught his sleeve as he snatched up his gloves and pulled them on. "I must go home." It came out like a command, the way no duke was addressed, let alone by an insignificant widow.

He turned, put a hand along her cheek. "I'll carry you if I have to."

Ophelia sat back, her heart pounding. There was a horrid tension between her shoulders at the idea of being separated from Viola. At the same time, there was something so sweet in the duke's eyes that she felt dizzy.

Her cloak had fallen to the floor. He tucked it

around her, passed over her gloves, threw open the door, jumped down, and was gone.

Ophelia looked around, dazed. Her pretty, feminine carriage was changed not only by losing a wheel. She felt as if he had—the duke had—invaded it with his smile and his sensuality and his certitude.

She could say his certainty came from being born to a title, but it didn't. There was a calm confidence that was the essence of the man. It was potent, like strong tea. Not like Peter, though that was a disloyal thought, and she oughtn't to think it.

Peter would have been as excited and worried as she if this had happened. Their eyes would have met, and they would have known without words that they were feeling a shared terror.

The duke hadn't felt terror, none at all. She sensed utter calm in the steely strength of his arms, and the rumbling satisfaction in his voice when he said her coachman was worth his wages.

Bisquet would be cross with her; he had protested leaving the house because the sky was lowering. But she had insisted. It was the first invitation she'd accepted since she left off mourning.

She had wanted to arrive in her sparkling,

beautiful carriage, wearing a new dress. She hadn't spared much thought for the hot, crowded ballroom.

But then she'd seen the duke.

And now . . .

There was no point in thinking about it. Instead she thought about the way he smelled, like clean man and snow. A touch of leather and spice.

He tasted good too, faintly like peppermint. The thought of his taste and his kisses lit a spark of fire in her belly again.

The wind picked up and slammed snow against the carriage, but Ophelia had made a deliberate decision not to worry. His Grace would get her home. He wouldn't let Viola wake up alone.

It might take a few hours, but she would be with her little girl again. The sound of men's voices shouting came over the sound of the wind.

She wasn't alone.

If the duke had his way, she would never be alone again. She turned that idea over in her head. Now that he wasn't in the carriage, she could think more clearly. She truly didn't want to marry again.

She had enjoyed Peter's company, but she adored being by herself, doing whatever she wished. No one made demands on her.

Peter had liked to dance and of course she

willingly accompanied him everywhere. It wasn't until he passed away that she realized how happy she was not to spend every evening in a crowded ballroom.

And the duke? She shuddered. One could scarcely imagine the burden of social engagements that he likely had to fulfill.

These days, her time was her own.

Tomorrow, she would be alone again, and happily so.

Chapter Five

$\mathcal{H}$ugo turned his head and shouted a last instruction to John Bisquet, then gently opened the carriage door and climbed inside. Snow came with him, of course, blowing over his shoulder. His wig was matted and wet, so he pulled it off and tossed it on the tilted seat.

Ophelia was tucked in the corner of the carriage, cloak pulled up to her nose, bright eyes examining him over the velvet.

"Hello," he said, feeling the earth shift again. He wasn't a smiling man, but the corners of his mouth curled up without conscious volition. He was grinning like a fourteen-year-old fool, and he didn't even care.

"Your Grace," Ophelia said, inclining her head ever so slightly.

She had dignity. He liked that. Honesty made him admit that he'd like her just as much if she was an undignified, giggling woman.

His father had once told him that Wilde men fell in love at first sight and the rule seemed likely to hold true in this case.

The carriage was securely balanced on the snapped axle, so he sat down on the slanted seat. "We're in the middle of the park, Ophelia."

"I do *not* know why you think it's appropriate to call me by my first name, when we scarcely know each other."

Dignified—and tart.

"My name is Hugo."

"That's irrelevant, Your Grace."

He laughed, watching as her eyes narrowed—thinking he was mocking her. He would never mock her. Never. The truth of that blazed through him. Not that he had ever mocked anyone.

If someone ever mocked her in his presence, he'd go off like an exploding chestnut.

Ophelia was wearing that exquisite, hand-painted gown, and they were a good walk from her house. "We need to get you home to Viola," he said.

She nodded, her eyes solemn.

"Bisquet and your groom are taking one horse back to the mews. He reckons that your lead horse can bear both of us easily, and luckily enough, the horse is very calm and won't mind riders. No saddle, but if you'll trust me, I won't let you fall off."

"All right," she said, sitting up straight. Her velvet cloak appeared to be trimmed and lined with white rabbit fur.

He choked when she picked up a fluffy round thing that was easily the size of her upper body. "What *is* that?"

"My muff!"

"Four foxes' worth?"

"Rabbits," she corrected. "Rabbits have so plagued my country house that last summer I ordered them at every meal."

He gave a bark of laughter. "Your muff is the size of a healthy child because your lawns are overrun by rabbits?"

"My muff is *enormously* fashionable," she said, but there was a gleam of humor deep in her eyes. "I don't care for waste."

Hugo tucked that fact away in his mind. It was an excellent trait for a duchess, of course. He picked up his tricorne and leaned forward, about to put it over her head so it would keep the snow from drifting onto her pile of hair.

"No need," she said. She reached back and pulled forward a wide hood, big enough that it went up and over her hair before falling down to frame her head in a border of fluffy white fur.

He cleared his throat. It wouldn't be appropriate to kiss her again, just because she looked so adorable dressed for winter. "The good news is that the wind has let up," he told her instead. "But snow is still falling."

"I'm almost ready."

He jammed the tricorne onto his head, leaving his damp wig on the coach seat. Ophelia tucked her book into an inside pocket of her cloak and tied the ribbons under her chin. He unhooked the lantern that lit the inside of the vehicle and pushed open the door.

Outside, the snow was swirling in the air, and the sounds of London had receded, muffled as if the air itself had thickened, each breath turning to a thousand flakes.

Bisquet had positioned the mounting block before the carriage door, precisely as if the vehicle wasn't listing to one side. Ophelia took Hugo's hand and stepped out of the carriage as gracefully as a cat hopping from a chair. She looked at the mound of snow surrounding the mounting block and laughed again.

"My slippers aren't suited for this weather." She held out a foot, and Hugo looked down at an impossibly small foot clad in cream silk with fashionable flaps crossed in front, and the whole embroidered with sprigs of flowers.

"I won't let you touch the ground," he promised.

They stood in a pool of light lit by the torch Bisquet had left behind, its light protected from the snow by a neat little tin hat. Hugo hooked the lantern that usually hung inside next to the torch. He hadn't let go of her hand. They both wore gloves, but he still loved curling his fingers around hers.

God, I've fallen so deep, he thought suddenly, with a moment of blinding clarity. Then he shook it off because his lady was standing in falling snow.

Laughing. She was looking about with obvious joy, and laughing.

His skin came alive with primal, raw hunger, as well as bewildered gratitude. The sensible man he'd been before he walked into the ballroom was gone.

This new Hugo pulled his lady into his arms so suddenly that her eyes flew to his in surprise. There were snowflakes caught on her eyelashes, melting on her lips. He covered her laughing mouth with his, dazzled by the flash of cold followed by heat. Her mouth was sweet and wet, and threw him instantly into a flush of sensual hunger such as he'd had—

He pushed that thought away.

No comparisons. Ever.

The world had given him so many blessings, and he had thought never to have one of this magnitude again.

She tasted like snow. Their tongues met and twisted around each other, danced an ancient measure. His heart thudded in his chest, making his breath shudder and his hands tighten around her.

Ophelia had kissed him in the carriage. But now, with the snow swirling over their heads, she was fire and ice at once. She submitted to him and owned him all at once. When she drew back, moments later, he felt remade.

As different from his usual self as the white trees, the white carriage path, the white mound that was her little carriage. The one he would beg her to give up because its perch was too fragile to carry such precious cargo.

Tomorrow, he told himself.

She was smiling up at him, still arched against him, allowing her hand to rest in the hollow of his back.

"I'm happy," he said, hearing wonder in his voice with a touch of embarrassment. "Gentlemen aren't supposed to experience an emotion so juvenile."

"Happy Hugo?" she asked, laughing.

He snorted. "My given name is reason enough for never admitting to such a foolish emotion." He let her go and turned to the horse. Bisquet had cut the lead to use as reins and thrown a blanket over the animal. A layer of snow already covered the blanket.

The coachman had also left a brass lantern hooked to the bridle. Hugo checked, but it was no more than pleasantly warm against the horse's shoulder. The gelding snorted and twitched its ears.

"I'm going to pull off that blanket and put you straight up on his back before snow settles."

At her nod, he whipped off the blanket and lifted her up, taking care to make sure that she was well-seated, her cloak tucked around her skirts. "Sidesaddle is absurd," he muttered. "Not that we have a saddle."

"I have too many skirts to sit any other way," she pointed out. "Are you going to snuff the torch and lantern?"

"No, I'll leave them burning, in case someone tools along in the snow and doesn't see the downed vehicle until it's too late."

Keeping the reins in his hand, he stepped on the mounting block and vaulted onto the horse behind her, his right arm going around Ophelia to steady her. She put a hand on his chest and smiled up at him, and he changed his mind about sidesaddle.

If she had been seated astride before him, he couldn't have seen her face.

"We merely need to make our way through Hyde Park," he told her.

"This is *so* improper," Ophelia said a moment later, as they rode out of the circle of torchlight, leaving the carriage behind them. Their lantern cast a pale light by comparison, though the snow reflected every ray with the glint of diamonds.

Hugo pulled her close and felt an indescribable satisfaction when she relaxed against him. "It's a beautiful night," he said, trying to distract himself from imagining her leaning against him naked. "All the hedges look like puffed-up pillows."

"Or large ladies huddling under rabbit-fur cloaks."

"My daughter Betsy loves fairy tales," he said, forgetting his sister's admonishment not to mention his children under any circumstances. "Last week, she told me that snowflakes are fairies in little slippers that spin over the church steeple and don't come down until they're tired."

"How old is she?"

"She is four years old, almost five. She can already read," he said proudly. "Her brothers were much slower learning to talk, and Alexander—

my youngest son, who's three—still speaks mostly in short sentences. But Betsy could instruct Parliament in its duties."

"My daughter, Viola, is two," Ophelia said. "I'm not precisely sure what she should be saying, but she's mastered a few words."

"My Joan is two as well and she doesn't say a word," Hugo told her. "Nothing to worry about."

Chapter Six

Ophelia adjusted her hood so that she could look up at the duke. He didn't appear to be trying to impress her by telling her stories about his children. Most aristocrats didn't speak of their children with easy familiarity and pride.

She had the distinct impression that this particular duke would never try to impress a lady. Perhaps no duke would bother. The title was enough to make the female half of the population simper and beg for a ring.

That thought was souring, but he was giving her a lopsided grin. "Betsy is the most talkative of my children." A guarded look went through his eyes. "Damn it, I forgot. My sister told me not to mention them."

Laughter bubbled up in her. "The children?"

He nodded. "No talk of children while courting a lady. Please forget that I said anything about Betsy."

"I haven't given you permission to court me," she pointed out. "Although I do like children."

His hand tightened around her waist. "I couldn't have imagined being so lucky as to meet you. We *are* courting, Ophelia."

Ophelia felt as if the white-topped trees of Hyde Park had drawn closer as the horse stepped forward, the sound of its shoes lost in the soft blanket that covered the path. Snow was still falling thickly into the tall trees around them, creating a chilly boudoir, a private refuge in the middle of England's largest city.

They had kissed twice: in the carriage and the snow. Those were the duke's—Hugo's—kisses. Now she curled her gloved hand around his right hand, the one that held the reins.

He pulled up, giving the horse a soft command. It came to a halt, and then even the soft clip-clop of its hooves was gone and the only sound was the gentle swish of branches bracing themselves against white blankets.

"I feel as if time has stopped," His Grace said, the words a deep rumble from his chest.

"I'm not marrying you," Ophelia said, peaceful with the decision. "I'm going to kiss you because, as you said, this is a time stolen from our ordinary lives. And you kissed me twice."

"Which means you owe me two kisses?" he prompted hopefully.

"I haven't kissed anyone since Peter died. I didn't even think about that." How could she have let the moment go without noticing, without marking it, without a silent apology to Peter?

The duke nodded, his eyes dark. "After Marie died, I thought I'd never kiss another woman."

"But you did."

A rueful look crossed his eyes. "In the second year, I got drunk one night, and found myself in the arms of a cheerful barmaid."

Ophelia couldn't help her spurt of laughter. "The barmaid and the duke!"

"Oh, she had no idea who I was. I dropped into a public house with friends. She was friendly and warm, and she coaxed a frozen man back into life."

"I'm not frozen," Ophelia said.

"We men are stupid," he said, his shoulders shifting, uncomfortable with the subject. "I couldn't bear the pain of it when Marie died. I . . ." He sighed. "I was very young and passionate. I vaguely wanted to be Romeo to her Juliet—though she hadn't taken her own life but succumbed to a chill—but I had children. And a ferocious will to live. What I did instead was turn myself to stone."

"Stone?"

Ophelia leaned against his shoulder so she could see his eyes.

"Walking about, not really alive."

"Ah."

He shook his head. "You weren't nearly as mad, were you?"

She took a deep breath and decided to tell the truth. "It sounds as if you loved Marie in a different . . . as if you had a . . . Peter and I were enormously fond of each other."

His eyelashes closed for a moment, and the sound that came from his chest sounded like— like relief? Surely not.

"I loved him, of course," she added. "He was Viola's father and he would have adored her. I see him in her every day."

"I tell myself that if Marie hadn't died, I would have been a good father to the three boys she and I had together," His Grace said thoughtfully, "but I'm not certain. I might have followed the path of least resistance, like my parents and all my friends, and just seen the boys a few times a year."

The snowy silence felt as if it compelled truth. "I might have done the same. I know that Peter would have insisted on attending social functions every night as soon as I was in full health."

"Mourning sent me into the nursery," Hugo said, nodding.

Ophelia lifted up her face and finally remembered what she meant to do when she silently asked him to stop the horse in the midst of a snowy forest. "A kiss," she whispered huskily.

His eyes lit.

"Not marriage," she reminded him. But her lips had reached his, and the slow slide of her tongue against his made her shiver, her hand closing around the chilly wool of his greatcoat.

The snow had no intent; it fell here or there without volition. But the two bodies straining together, warm mouths, clinging arms . . . There was a ferocious *intent* in them.

Ophelia felt her limbs weaken and desire riot through her until she whimpered into his mouth and moved restlessly on the horse's broad back, her legs tingling, her flesh tender and longing for caresses.

"I want you," the man kissing her growled.

Peter never growled. He wouldn't have known how. But somehow, she found herself kissing a man whose growl came naturally from his broad chest. She was in uncharted territory, Ophelia thought dimly.

If she stayed with this man, this duke, her peaceful, quiet life would never be the same. The cheerful tenor of days spent in the nursery would change.

He would want her with him, during the day. During the night.

She and Peter hadn't shared a bedchamber; the idea was inconceivable. She had the strong feeling that this duke wouldn't consider living any other way.

His mouth slanted down over hers, hunger speaking to her in the brush of his chilly cheek against hers.

"Getting cold," she murmured sometime later. It wasn't true. She felt like a torch in his arms, as if she were burning in every pore. She could tumble into the snow and it would all melt beneath her.

She didn't know what she wanted from him: but she did know one thing. In the wake of Peter's death . . . this warmth was precious.

Worth chasing, preserving, exploring.

That low sound he made?

She wanted more of that.

"Did you say you're cold?" he asked suddenly, a kiss later. His voice grated like gravel underfoot.

"Mmm," Ophelia said. He pulled back, but that

was all right. There was the enticing smooth skin of his neck, a powerful neck with a man's sinews and a man's strength under her lips.

He shifted, said something to the horse, and they were off again.

"Your hat is covered with snow," she said, giggling.

Even with only the light from the dim lantern, she could tell that his eyes were burning hot.

"It's too cold and snowy for you to go home tonight," she added.

She felt his reaction in his body, through her dress and cloak, and his shirt, waistcoat, coat, greatcoat . . .

He jolted.

"You could stay at my house if you wished," she whispered. Between them, a snowflake spiraled down twisting in the air, melting as it reached their warm breaths.

"I do wish," he stated.

Their eyes locked. She was unnerved by the invitation she had issued. Unnerved by the kisses she had given him. Unnerved by the images going through her head: the duke without clothes. Those broad shoulders bending over her as she lay on her back, quivering all over. This desire was scorching.

It was madness.

Blissful madness.

"My invitation does not mean marriage."

Silence.

Then, "In that case, I'm not certain I should stay the night, Ophelia. To my mind, bedding means marriage."

"The barmaid?" she asked, eyebrow raised.

"I didn't bed her. She sat on my lap, kissed me a few times, and ran off to take care of other tables." He lowered his head and brushed his lips past hers. "Even drunk, I managed to remember that I had a family waiting at home."

She dragged her hands down over taut muscles, thinking about men she'd seen working in fields of wheat. Men who weren't peers. Men who had brawny chests and muscled thighs.

The idea of going to bed with him was terrifying. And fabulous.

"I'll spend the night with you, Ophelia, but I won't make love to you until you promise to marry me."

She made a disappointed sound before she could stop herself.

He laughed, a joyful noise that echoed off oak trees muffled in snow.

"You're probably right," she said, straightening her back and wrinkling her nose at him. "I have never had the ambition to become a fallen woman." She couldn't stop smiling, because she had the first inklings of that ambition in the last hour, and he knew it.

They rode out of the last line of trees, into the street. A linkboy ran toward them, inadequately dressed, and fell in at the horse's head, leading the way with his torch.

Another block and they would be home. Halfway, Bisquet came trundling down the street holding another torch, followed by two grooms.

Ophelia let male voices rise around her, the sounds urgent and yet peaceful. There was nothing men liked better than a small emergency. An obstacle that was easily overcome.

When the duke leapt off and then turned, his arms open, she slid down into his embrace, knowing that Bisquet was watching. Her grooms were there too, eyes wide.

Hugo didn't care, even though he felt Ophelia's body stiffen infinitesimally. He turned and began walking toward her house with her in his arms, holding her and her skirts, and her cloak, and her huge muff.

"I can walk," she said, nestled against his chest like an extraordinarily bedraggled bird.

"I like carrying you."

"I can see a star," she breathed, a few steps later.

He tipped his head back. "I see chimneys and snow."

"It's there. The snow is stopping."

Up the stairs to an excellent townhouse: Sir Peter had left his wife more than comfortable. Hugo spared another charitable thought for the man and pushed it away.

A stout butler with anxious eyes stood with the door open. Ophelia was obviously surrounded by good servants, which said a great deal for her. Hugo smiled. "Good evening. As you can see, I have your mistress safe and sound, if wet and cold."

"Fiddle," Ophelia said, "this is the Duke of Lindow. We are going to put him up for the night."

"Yes, madam," the butler murmured, bowing low.

"Good evening, Fiddle," Hugo said. He strode into the spacious entry and put Ophelia on her feet. The next few moments were taken up by the removal of layers of damp clothing. His greatcoat had held off most of the water, but Ophelia's velvet cloak was soaked through.

A maid took her up the stairs, and he followed the butler, who was solemnly offering a bath.

"I'll send a groom to your townhouse to inform

them that you are here, Your Grace. Roberts can serve as your man," the butler said, gesturing to a young footman. "I shall have your clothing cleaned, pressed, and returned to you by morning. Would you like a light repast after your bath?"

"Yes."

Hugo had just made an unwelcome discovery.

This wasn't his house. If Ophelia wished to sleep with him, she'd have to come to him. There was nothing he could do about it.

He was not a man who liked to be at another person's mercy. But it was Ophelia, he reminded himself. He was at her mercy in more ways than one.

He took a bath and ate an excellent meal, bundled in a warm wrapper, sitting by a crackling fire. The butler withdrew, taking the footman with him, and the house fell into silence.

It had to be two in the morning. He pulled open the curtains. Below his window a streetlamp shone through the snow, another sign of Sir Peter's care for his property and his family. Streetlamps were still unusual, though he had the feeling that one day London streets would be lined with them. Snow still fell but lighter now, drifting and spinning rather than tumbling down.

He turned from the window, leaving the curtains open so that the room was lit with a soft, romantic glow, an excellent setting for a seduction, if only a lady would join him. The bed was laid out in fine linen that smelled faintly of lemons and starch. The mattress was comfortable. A warming pan had taken the chill from the sheets.

It had everything to make a guest happy—except for one thing.

Which explained why he lay awake, staring into space, hoping.

Ophelia didn't want to be a duchess, and he didn't blame her. He had too damned many children, and yet he couldn't bear the idea that even one might not have existed—and that included his orphaned ward, Parth.

He would even marry Yvette again, knowing what lay ahead, to have their children.

Just as he was deciding to close his eyes and fight for Ophelia's hand the next day, the door opened soundlessly.

He slid out of the bed faster than he'd ever done before, threw on his wrapper, and snatched her in his arms as an involuntary groan escaped his lips. "Bloody hell," he whispered into her hair, "I feel as if my blood went to a simmer hours ago, and I haven't calmed down since."

Ophelia's hair slipped through his fingers as

she tipped back her head. She'd washed out the powder, and damp strands of silk covered her shoulders.

"I want you," she whispered. "But perhaps not as a husband. I haven't decided that yet."

"Am I on probation?" He wasn't sure what to think about that. His body had no doubts. He could seduce her, bind her to him, show her the pleasures of making love, because it was possible that Sir Peter had not.

The ethical side of him didn't feel happy about seduction without marriage.

"I'm a widow, Hugo," she said, her eyes crinkling into a smile. "I can bed whomever I wish, and I choose you. Tonight."

"What if I seduce you into marriage?"

She laughed, the sound lazy and sweet. "Do your worst, Your Grace. Do your worst."

He had her on the bed in a minute and unwrapped her as carefully as if she were made of the finest china.

And when he realized that she wore nothing under her wrapper?

In strong contention for the best moment of his life.

Chapter Seven

Ophelia hadn't bothered to put on a night-gown. Why should she? Hers were all white and edged with lace, clothing that hinted at chastity and innocence. A woman bent on sin needn't pretend to virtue.

That meant she got to see Hugo's eyes darken and his jaw clench as he pulled open her dressing gown.

She followed his eyes down. She was a creamy, curvy type of woman, whose breasts had become even more lavish after nursing Viola.

The desperation in his eyes fired her blood—past a simmer, straight to a boil that made her shift on the bed, pink rising in her cheeks, her hands reaching for him.

He moved back and pulled off his wrapper. She caught a flash of hard male body, a slice of golden skin, and then his mouth crashed down on hers and his body lowered with hardly more grace.

His weight made a sob rise in her throat. There was something so comforting about being surrounded by warm strength. The feeling of a man's body on top of hers was marvelous.

He began kissing the side of her neck, so she turned her head and ran her hands over powerful shoulders.

She felt untethered, as if she were held to the bed only by the weight of his body. How could she have forgotten the delicious feeling of skin roughed by hair, hard-muscled thighs, and hard other things? Hugo rolled against her and her arms tightened as her belly clenched. A puff of air escaped her lips.

"Tell me if I'm too heavy," he murmured.

"I like it," she said. She almost stopped there, but this man wasn't her husband—and she didn't want another husband. With a lover, she could be absolutely honest. So she kept going. "I like the way our knees knocked together, and the fact your arse is extremely muscled."

His grin was pure mischief, a man's wicked fun, not a boy's.

She let her fingers dance over his bottom, making him shiver. "I would never have mentioned that word to Peter."

"Could we forget the word 'Peter' and keep 'arse' instead?" He pulled back, coming up on his knees so she could see his face. He was older than Peter had been, with traces of laughter around his eyes.

"You don't fancy comparisons?" She reached up and traced the amused arch of his lip.

"Not allowed in polite society," he stated, with all the calm authority of a duke.

"Are there any other rules I should know about extramarital congress?"

"No thinking. Thinking is as bad as mentioning former spouses."

"I can't stop *thinking*," Ophelia said. "I think all the time." A little panic slid down her spine. She pictured the way she and Peter had made love. They were invariably courteous and kind with each other. Of course they had been thinking during the act.

She had constantly thought about what Peter would like her to do next. She had the strong feeling he had done the same. That's why their marital life had been so successful.

But just as that panic rose, it dissipated. She wasn't marrying the duke. What they did in bed this evening wouldn't set a pattern for future years to come.

"I will try to make you stop thinking," Hugo said. His voice rumbled, confident and happy at the same time. "Making love is a time to be in the flesh."

Ophelia wrinkled her nose. "Is that some sort of pun on intimacy?"

"In *your* flesh?" His eyes danced with laughter when he leaned over and kissed her, and somehow joy came with his touch.

Ophelia didn't pull back until she decided that if they didn't move on to being "in the flesh," she might burst. Her insides were tightening; no, all her muscles were tight. Every time he thrust his tongue between her lips, her heart beat faster, and her hands clutched him more tightly. Her core was aching for him in a way that she didn't remember.

Because it had been so long: that was the only reason she didn't remember. Hugo would never succeed in making her stop thinking. *Thinking* was what she did best.

Another twinge of anxiety went through her. Did she even understand how to *do* a bedding that had nothing to do with marital satisfaction, or procreation? One that was for nothing more than shared pleasure?

"Are there any other rules?" she asked, surprised by the hoarse tone in her voice.

"Experience suggests that I have energetic seed, so I will do my best to protect you." Hugo leaned over and picked up something that Ophelia instantly recognized, because Maddie had told her about it. The object had the appearance of a sausage without filling, oddly adorned on one end with a pink ribbon.

She wrinkled her nose. "I surmise that is a condom."

Hugo shrugged and dropped it back on the bedside table. "We'll have no use for it unless you promise to marry me."

"What?" Ophelia's eyes caught on his chest. He had a delicious set of indentations that led right down his torso. Muscles, presumably. And he had a trail of hair that arrowed down to his . . . And her eyes stopped again, lower.

The duke was a great deal larger than Peter had been. In fact, he was of a size that she considered—though she had never considered such a thing before—to be obstructive. Perhaps impossible.

His eyes followed hers. "Yes, there's that."

"I see," she said carefully.

Hugo moved backward, and her eyes moved with him. "It's not *that* interesting," he said.

"Actually, it is."

"Same general shape as most men's, from what I've seen."

He ran his hands down her front, his fingers pausing on her nipples, sweeping on and around her sides to her back. "Let's go back to discussing arses." His hands curved under her body, around her bottom, and a hoarse sound escaped his throat. "Yours is marvelously round. Perfect, in fact."

Ophelia's mind had split in two. Part of her brain was busily informing the rest of her that this behavior was utterly inappropriate. She couldn't take her eyes off the part of him that rose proudly, bobbing in the air. The sight of him made the melting sensation in her stomach increase. Probably that was sinful. Certainly it was embarrassing.

The other part of her mind suggested she tuck her arms behind her head, so she did, causing her bosom to rise into the air. He wasn't the only one who had impressive . . . parts.

She did as well.

"Are you commanding my attention?" Hugo inquired.

"Yes," Ophelia said, breaking into a giggle. "This is so funny," she added, allowing herself to say precisely what she was thinking. "I never imagined laughing in bed."

"Huh." Hugo slid his hands to her front and then they curved around her breasts. "I don't feel like laughing," he said, voice rough. "I don't mind if you do, Ophelia. Laugh as much as you like."

Ophelia sucked in air, all impulse to giggle leaving her. His lips drifted across the curve of her right breast, lingered just long enough to make her quiver, and then closed over her nipple.

Sound rasped through her throat and her hands flew from behind her head, winding into his hair, holding him in place. Not that he showed any particular wish to move. For long minutes his mouth caressed the curve of one breast or the other, returning to her nipples.

And Ophelia just let it happen. Behind her closed eyes, the world receded until nothing existed but a hot, heady pleasure that melted into desperation. Reason and logic floated into the dark. Desire was like hot tea on a cold day: she actually felt it slip through her body, warming her in places that hadn't felt frozen.

But had been, obviously.

Gradually, she began feeling slightly anxious, nervousness thrumming alongside desire. She didn't want to orient herself to the real world. She wanted to stay in the warm darkness, her body twisting under his caresses, low moans coming through her lips.

But . . .

Peter would have stopped long ago, moving on to the next, for lack of a better word, activity. Surely Hugo would rather be doing something else. Something less one-sided. Unfortunately, she was selfish. Self-interest choked the words in her throat.

Instead she clutched his hair more tightly, embarrassing noises flying from her mouth every time he tightened his lips or curled his tongue around her nipple.

A shrill inner voice made itself heard. She and Peter had been considerate bed partners, and after hearing stories from other women as a young bride, she had redoubled her efforts to express her appreciation for his kindness.

Yet here she was, taking without giving.

She forced her eyes open. Hugo had her breasts plumped in both hands. Far from looking restless, he was suckling a nipple with an intensity that made another moan escape her lips. He looked as if he couldn't stop himself.

Thoughts were going every which way in her head. A streak of pleasure was followed by a panicked protest that she ought to do the same for him. The breath caught in her throat, because he did something—that *thing*—with his tongue, and fire streaked down her legs. She couldn't focus on his expression because she kept closing her eyes. Her toes curled and her legs shook and she almost felt as if . . . which was absurd.

Her eyes flew open again and she craned her neck. He didn't show any signs of getting bored. But he must be getting bored. And she . . . well, she was ready for what came next. A good deal readier than she sometimes was.

Hugo lifted his head, making her hands fall from his hair, and met her eyes. "Stop thinking." His tone wasn't that of a duke accustomed to obedience. It was the growl of a man in the grip of pure lust.

For *her*.

Ophelia blinked at him. "I was just . . . I don't want you to grow bored."

Hugo broke into a chuckle.

"I thought you didn't laugh in bed," she said, her mouth curving up. She reached out to run her hands down his forearms. They were powerful, muscled. The arms of a man who could protect anyone, a child, Viola . . . Her mind wandered away from thoughts of her child.

Ophelia didn't need protecting and neither did Viola.

But Ophelia *needed* more of him. Fierce, base desire roared through her body.

Hugo reared up on his knees and shook his

head. His hands settled on his hips and her eyes were drawn precisely where he, apparently, wanted her to look.

"If a man is bored, what happens to his cock?"

Ophelia managed to stop a flinch. She was a widow, not a maiden. She had to get used to bold speaking and words that were considered fit only for sinful congress. Because that's what she was engaging in: sinful congress.

He reached down and ran a hand over his private parts. Ophelia watched with utter fascination at the way his hand clenched, even twisted a little. The head emerged from his hand looking red and—

Ophelia lost her train of thought again.

"It would wilt," Hugo said, because she hadn't answered.

"I understand," Ophelia said, though she didn't. Not really.

"I was determined to find a third wife who was uninterested in bed sports," Hugo said conversationally. "Or very experienced at them."

"I haven't promised to be your wife!" She frowned at him. "I *am* experienced. I mothered a child, in case you need a reminder."

"My first two wives were both inexperienced, to say the least. They both got the idea right away, though."

93

Then he winced, because presumably he remembered just how expert his second wife turned out to be. Or how voracious. Or . . .

She ought to be solemn and sympathetic, but Ophelia found herself giggling instead. "I guess your teaching was a mite too successful the second time around. Oh! I can't believe I said that. I'm so sorry!"

Thankfully, Hugo's mouth eased into a smile. "Either that, or the golden locks of a Prussian count cast mine into the shade."

Ophelia didn't need to glance at his thick head of hair to know which she preferred. "If we're not discussing my previous spouse, oughtn't yours to be taboo as well?"

"Certainly in the bed," Hugo said. "Where was I?" He reached out, his eyes gleaming.

"You truly don't mind?"

He raised an eyebrow.

"This," she said with a wave that vaguely indicated everything above her waist. "I thought you'd want to do other things."

"Have you ever heard of the poet Robert Herrick?"

Ophelia shook her head.

Hugo curved his hands around her breasts again. "*Display thy breasts, my Julia*—well, have to change that line, won't we? *Display thy breasts, my Ophelia, there let me behold that circummortal purity."*

Ophelia giggled, looking down at his hands and her breasts. "Circum-*what*?"

"Circummortal. No idea what it means. I'd suggest 'dazzling' in your case. Perhaps 'round.'" He pushed her breasts together and they plumped up. "Because your breasts are dazzlingly round. And God, so dazzlingly delectable." He lowered his head, and whatever he said next was muffled by her skin.

Time passed. Ophelia decided to stop bothering about what he was thinking. Peter never—no. More generally, she doubted that many men thought about poetry while they were in bed.

Hugo's fingers were making their way down her sides, creeping across her stomach. But all the time his lips kept going from one breast to the other until her legs were trembling. To her shock, her whole body was damp, her hair sticking to her brow. She couldn't stop moving either, wiggling under his weight, trying to silently suggest that he direct his attention elsewhere.

"May I?" Hugo asked sometime later.

She raised her head and stared at him. His eyes gleamed at her, desirous. He didn't look like a duke any longer.

But that was all the intelligent thought she

could muster. She'd never appreciated her breasts before. No, that wasn't true. She had been inordinately proud of them for producing milk on command when Viola had needed it.

But now?

This was different. Every time he tightened his lips around one of her nipples, heat connected to far-flung parts of her body, making her shiver.

"May you what?" she asked belatedly, hoping that he meant he would take that large . . . *tool* of his and do what God had designed it to do.

But no.

"Kiss you again," he said, with such a sweet expression that her lips shaped a smile without conscious thought. In one smooth movement, he moved up so his elbows were on either side of her ribs. They fell into a kiss. A different kiss than she'd ever experienced, because she had never, ever, felt a shivery excitement that tightened her chest and made her entangle her legs with his like a wanton.

Her hips couldn't stop arching toward Hugo. His response was to kiss her more deeply, hovering over her, kissing her with the same ferocious attentiveness that he gave her breasts. As if there wasn't something better to get to.

Finally she had to ask.

She pulled back.

"Phee?" His voice rasped, and when she put her hand on his chest, it was not heaving . . . but his heart was pounding.

"Aren't you wishful to go on to the rest?" She couldn't think how else to phrase it.

"No."

"Because I haven't agreed to marry you?"

"Yes and no." He started dotting kisses on her face. "I'm enamored. I'm metaphorically at your feet. I don't want to muck this up. I want to know everything about you. I could happily do nothing but kiss your breasts for hours."

She couldn't think what to say to that.

"Except I'd probably spend in your bedsheets," he added, in the most matter-of-fact tone imaginable.

Ophelia shook her head. "I don't think—"

"You're not ready for this?"

"Is that terrible? I'm sorry." Her voice dropped to a whisper. "I'm supposed to be a merry widow, and I was feeling . . . But this is just all so *new*."

He brushed his lips over hers. "Absolutely fine. Deliciously fine. You allowed me to kiss your breasts. Bloody hell, the man who wasn't grateful for that would be dead. Why do you look so worried?"

"It's like . . . It feels as if the maid has served tea but no biscuits," she said, trying to explain.

"I don't want biscuits," Hugo said. He leaned toward her again, face intent, and kissed her precisely on the nose, on each eye. "Tea, glorious tea, is every Englishman's delight. I never touch biscuits. Wouldn't, even if you begged me."

A smile curved on Ophelia's lips despite herself. "Not even if I *begged* you?"

"Never." His expression took on the stoic heroism of a British officer facing a French battalion. "Tea is enough to sustain me forever."

"Huh." Ophelia's mind slipped away again, into a memory of her marriage—but she pushed that away. No thinking of Peter here, in bed.

Instead she pushed herself up against the headboard. She was still quivering, aware of a disturbing throbbing sensation between her legs, sweat behind her knees, a fast heartbeat. Evidence that—

Hugo shifted and moved to sit beside her. His legs were very hairy, his skin a darker color than hers. Obeying impulse, she leaned over and trailed her fingers over his knee and up his leg. She avoided the . . . avoided the *private* part of him, which was standing up in a very public fashion.

Her caress had an effect on it, and she heard a muffled sound in Hugo's throat.

"Aren't you going to put it to rest?" she asked, feeling her ears grow hot with embarrassment.

"To rest?" He turned, his face alive with pure delight. "Darling!"

"What?" she asked. "I'm sorry if I used the wrong terminology."

"I rather like the idea that I have control over my privates."

"Don't you?"

"Not around you."

Ophelia shook her head. The night was getting odder and odder, so odd that she could scarcely remember how it began. "I'm not that sort of woman."

"I do not think you are a loose woman, if that's what you're saying."

"I mean that I'm not the sort of woman a man loses his head over." She took a shuddering breath. "In fact, we should be honest with each other." She looked at him. "I don't know why you're in my bed, but it hasn't much to do with me, has it?"

He looked at her, every inch of his expression conveying a stubborn belief that it *did*, in fact, have a great deal to do with her.

"I'm not the sort of woman who drives a man to desperation," she said, trying again. "I'm short and fairly round."

His eyes shifted to her breasts, and from the corner of her eye she saw his tool jerk forward, as if it was volunteering an opinion on her round-ness.

"You seem not to mind that," she added.

"I don't."

"Well, my point is that there are many round-ish women in London."

"They aren't you."

"You don't know me."

"I'm getting to," Hugo said. "I like everything I've found so far." He grinned, just in case she missed the innuendo. "I see your point, though."

"You do?" The news wasn't entirely welcome.

"We need to get to know each other better. May I spend the day with you?"

"Here? Why would you stay here?"

"To get to know you better," he said promptly. His smile had a fiendish kind of pleasure to it, a ridiculously boyish stubbornness for a grown man.

"You're a *duke*," she said. "You have better things to do."

He paused just long enough to give a semblance of having thought it over. "Can't think of anything."

"What do you mean by 'getting to know you'?" she asked. Suspicions crowded into her head. After all, she was sitting in bed with him.

"Go riding together?"

"In the *snow*?"

"I'm trying to remember how people become friends," he said. "It's been years since I've had much to do with society, and all I remember of Marie, my first wife, was dancing, flirting, and kissing her in dark corridors."

She elbowed him. "Remember the rule?"

"No spouses in bed," he said obediently. "I won't tell you how Yvette and I got to know each other."

His voice cooled, just enough so that she noticed. She hadn't known his second duchess, but she had heard gossip, after Yvette had fled England. The interesting thing was that Hugo had apparently thought his wife had been a virgin when they married.

Fairness intervened. Rumors were no more than rumors.

"We often read aloud to each other," she said, avoiding Peter's name.

"Ah."

"Are you a reader?"

"I am reading a book of reflections," he said. "Translated from the French."

"Reflections on what?"

"Ridicule."

She glanced at him and miraculously managed not to roll her eyes. "You're jesting."

"Unfortunately not," Hugo said amiably. "I don't suppose you'd be interested."

A flare of temper went up Ophelia's spine. She hated that men made assumptions about what would and wouldn't interest a woman.

She glanced at him; he had picked up her left hand and appeared to be examining her fingers. She drew her hand away. "Why wouldn't I be interested?"

She kept her tone sweet, but Hugo's eyes shot to hers. Perhaps being married twice had taught him something about women.

"The full title is something like this: *Reflections upon Ridicule, or What It Is That Makes a Man Ridiculous, and the Means to Avoid It.*"

"Are you learning from the author's reflections?" She studiously kept her tone from implying that it was too late for whatever lessons he garnered.

Hugo sighed. "No, it's hopelessly foolish. I lost a bet and my twin sister demanded I read it, by way of punishment."

"You're so lucky to have a sister." Ophelia was aware there was a thread of wistfulness in her voice.

"Are you an only child?"

She nodded. "Much beloved and cosseted, but the only one."

"My twin sister, Louisa, Lady Knowe, does not

102

care for cities, so she resides in the country." He paused. "Are you greatly enamored of London?"

"I am not," Ophelia replied. "Peter loved the Season, though. In particular, he loved to dance."

Hugo winced. "I'm not a very good dancer. My sister says that I resemble a tree forced to bend in a high wind."

"Do you creak?" Ophelia asked, laughing.

"I clomp around the ballroom, looking faintly horrified." Hugo propped himself up on his elbow. "Do you float about like thistledown?"

Ophelia moved her shoulders uncomfortably. "I'm a good dancer." Then she added, in a rush, "I think that's why Peter asked for my hand in marriage. Besides the fact that our parents approved, I mean."

Hugo raised an eyebrow. "An odd qualifier." His eyes drifted down her body. "There are so many reasons that a man would want to marry you, Phee. Do you mind if I call you that?"

"I suppose not. How did you learn it?"

"Your cousin."

"Maddie? Oh, is that how you knew to climb into my carriage?" Ophelia would have frowned at the idea her cousin shared her name and sent the duke out of the ballroom to find her . . . except a small clear voice in the back of her head informed her that Maddie had done her a great favor.

"No," Hugo said. "Maddie refused to tell me your last name; she merely referred to you as Phee and informed me that you were not a governess, and I should not pursue you. I deduced that the beautiful, mysterious lady I was determined to meet was called Phoebe."

"Ophelia didn't occur to you?"

"A somewhat lachrymose name," Hugo pointed out. "Perhaps I shall call you Phoebe . . . such a cheerful name."

"I like Ophelia," she said.

She felt a flood of relief that she had been right to turn down the duke's offer of marriage. He was such a *dukelike* man, renaming her because he didn't like the literary connotations of her name. "I think it's unlikely that I would take my own life, the way Shakespeare's Ophelia did, based on my name. If my parents had named me after Lady Macbeth, would you expect me to turn to murder?"

"What *was* Lady Macbeth's name?"

She frowned. "I don't think anyone knows."

"Names are important," Hugo said, toying with a lock of her hair. "I'd bet you anything that her name wasn't Beth."

"Beth? Why not Beth?"

"Because Beth is a timid name."

Ophelia shook her head. "That's cracked."

"Names are important," Hugo insisted again. "I named all my children after warriors."

"Warriors? All eight of them?"

Hugo's mouth twisted. "Yes, in fact. My first three are Horatius, Roland—whom we call North—and Alaric, now at school, along with Parth, who was first my ward and became my son when his parents died. He too is named after a warrior, though I had nothing to do with that."

"Did the naming work?"

"In a manner of speaking. They're ungodly naughty. Satanic imps. Especially, I have to say, Parth. He eggs on the others to worse misdeeds. Besides the older boys, Yvette and I had Leonidas, Boadicea, Alexander, and Joan."

"You named your daughter *Boadicea*?" Ophelia shook her head. "Why did your wife allow it? Do you know how often people have commented on my unfortunate name?"

"Boadicea was a great warrior," Hugo protested.

"Insanity," Ophelia muttered. Definitely she was right not to marry him, if only on the basis of crimes of nomenclature.

"I have to admit that Boadicea has threatened to eviscerate anyone who calls her by her given name, so we call her Betsy."

"Are your second four as naughty as the first round?" Ophelia asked.

"Very naughty, especially Joan." His brows drew together. "She's the reason I came to London to find a wife, actually."

"How old is she?"

"Two years old. She likes nothing better than to throw crockery to the ground and listen to it shatter."

"Exactly the same age as my Viola!" Ophelia beamed at him. "Viola is not naughty in the least, though."

"Viola is *not* a warrior's name," the duke murmured. He leaned over and brushed a kiss on her lips.

Oddly enough, their conversation felt more intimate than their kisses, though Ophelia didn't shape that thought until she came back to herself enough to realize that Hugo was now lying partially on top of her. He'd returned to her breasts and was lavishing them with attention.

"You—you look as if you might never stop," she whispered.

"I could die here at your breasts, and I'd be happy," he said, raising his head.

"That's a very odd thing to say. A very odd thing to *think*."

"Why?"

"I wouldn't want to die anywhere if Viola wasn't near me, if I couldn't say goodbye to her."

Hugo dropped a last affectionate kiss on the curve of Ophelia's breast and moved to sit beside her again. "You are a marvelous mother."

"That's why you're here, isn't it? Why you followed me, because you want a mother for your children, for Joan in particular."

"No."

She gave him a faint smile. "All evidence, including your own statements, is against you. But I don't want to mother anyone other than Viola. I am not the wife for you."

The duke nodded, and something in Ophelia eased. He accepted her decision.

"I might have an *affaire* with you," she said. "But only if you understand that there is but one outcome, when we separate and return to our lives. Since you need to find a mother—and I agree that a two-year-old girl is a good reason—we should part now. Or at least, in the morning."

"I gather that the strongest relationship you've had in your life is with Viola?"

Ophelia pushed herself up against the headboard. "Viola means more to me than anything or anyone on earth. In general, I believe a mother's love is commonly referred to as the strongest attachment a person can feel."

He was silent a moment. "Not having been a mother, I cannot dispute your feeling. My strongest bond has been with Marie. She was mine, and I was hers."

"That's a lovely sentiment."

He shook his head. "It wasn't a sentiment. It was a rock-hard fact that was the most important thing in the world to me while she lived. In some ways, it still is."

Another good reason not to become his duchess. Ophelia barely stopped herself from patting his hand. "I'm happy that you had such a passionate bond with your wife, your first wife."

"I was very lucky. I walked into a room and saw Marie; I instantly knew that I would love her for the rest of my life."

Ophelia leaned over and kissed his cheek. "Does anyone know what a romantic spirit lurks behind the Duke of Lindow's aristocratic countenance?"

"I don't give a damn if they do." He said it simply, without shame.

Many men would have been mortified to admit to feeling so strongly. Certainly Peter would have been startled and annoyed had he been struck by such a ferocious emotion.

"I felt exactly that way when I saw Viola,"

Ophelia said, pulling up her knees and wrapping her arms around them. "She was wrinkled and her head had the oddest shape. I thought she might be deformed for life. And yet I loved her so much that my heart didn't seem to have enough space for the emotion."

"When you have another child, your heart will magically find room. Horatius is a pompous boy, and yet I cannot stop myself from adoring him. Alaric is wild and curious; North is a philosopher at heart and a devil-may-care horseman; Parth is determined to be the richest man in England. The boys tease him for his mercenary goal, but he doesn't give a damn."

"And your other children?"

"I don't know them as well yet," Hugo said. "We fathers aren't encouraged to spend time with very young children. Marie spent a great deal of time in the nursery, so I would go there to find her." He frowned. "I know the boys much better than Yvette's children, because she didn't believe in nursery visits. She thought it disrupted children's routine and might confuse them."

"A man doesn't need permission from his wife to visit his own children," Ophelia said, her tone rather tart.

Hugo leaned against the headboard. "I do visit

these days, but briefly, I'm afraid. I'm often very busy. I'm not offering that by way of excuse, but virtually every day brings some complication."

"What sort of things do you do?" Ophelia asked. "Peter—" She caught herself. "My estate is small, of course. It takes me one morning a week, at most."

"I am the judge for my county court, which encompasses three villages. Two hundred tenants work in and around the castle, and then I own a townhouse in London, and an estate in Scotland. And a few other concerns."

Ophelia nodded. "It does sound like a great deal of work."

"Not enough to make up for the fact that I don't know my four younger children as well as I should."

"That is also true." Ophelia kept her tone even, because Peter hated nothing more than disapproval from her. A spouse, he always said, was the bulwark against the world's unkindnesses and should never be critical.

Hugo just nodded. "What do you suggest I do?"

"Spend part of every day with them. Not just a visit to the nursery. Do things together."

"They are very small," Hugo objected. "Joan cries every time she sees me."

"That must make you feel terrible."

"I would like to say yes," he said. "I want you to think—well, to admire me. But to be honest, I always thought that at some point she would stop crying. Perhaps by the time she was able to carry on a conversation. As I told you, Joan's nanny reports that she doesn't speak yet."

"Joan has her own nanny?"

He nodded. "The two younger children have nannies, Mrs. Banks and Mrs. Winkle. There's a governess, Miss Trelawny, for the older children. And some nursemaids, Myrtle, Flora, and Delia."

"Viola doesn't have a nanny," Ophelia confessed. She felt even guiltier upon hearing about all the people helping the duke's children become civilized adults. "I only have a nursemaid. Of course, I ought to acquire a proper nanny."

"Not if you don't want to," Hugo said.

"I am a lady, and Viola must be a lady too. What if she thinks that one's mother is no more than a playmate?" She peeked at Hugo from under her lashes. "Sometimes we play together."

He blinked, as if he had no idea what she was talking about.

"I cut out houses from foolscap. People too. Sometimes horses, though I'm rubbish at cutting around their legs."

"She plays with paper?"

"She does crumple them," Ophelia said with a

wry smile. "But not before I tell her a story about the people who live in the house."

"I cannot tell stories," Hugo said. His tone was final.

Ophelia sighed. Peter had been given to statements like that as well. Perhaps it was a male failing.

"I could try it," Hugo said, surprising her.

"You wouldn't be embarrassed?"

Astonishment crossed his eyes but he kept his answer simple. "No."

Of course he wouldn't be. Dukes were probably never embarrassed. Why should they be? Ophelia fidgeted, thinking of the way her skin crawled with embarrassment when she thought about a nanny entering her nursery and seeing the way she played with Viola.

"If you were my duchess, you needn't be embarrassed either," Hugo said, exhibiting a nimble ability to turn the conversation to his advantage. "Duchesses set the fashion; they don't follow it."

"I have no wish to set fashion," Ophelia stated.

"Your dress last night was very elegant, and so was your carriage."

"I ordered both because I enjoyed the designs, not because I wanted them copied by others."

"You are already a duchess," Hugo murmured, leaning over to kiss her cheek. "Would you be offended if I mentioned that I haven't had a cockstand this long for years? Since I was a young man."

Cockstand? Ophelia tried out the word in her head and decided it was useful. "Is that a compliment?"

"Of a sort."

"Would you like me to return to my bedchamber? It's just next door, to be frank."

"Absolutely not. Unless you wish to go."

Ophelia thought about that for a moment. This was a night stolen out of time, in a way. She had decided not to marry the duke, and he wouldn't bed her without that promise. So they were at an impasse.

But perhaps . . .

"We could be friends," she said, blurting it out.

"What?"

"We can't be spouses, because I don't wish to marry you. We can't be lovers, because you don't want to bed me without a wedding ring."

"Oh, I *want* to," the duke growled.

Ophelia waved her hand, ignoring the fact that her body clenched at the rough desire in his voice. "You know what I mean."

"Not lovers, not spouses." His voice was mournful. "Friends? I don't want to be your friend, Ophelia."

That stung, but why would he want to be friends? She had been at risk, for just a moment, of forgetting the real reason he had singled her out: because she was a good mother. Because he had children whom he didn't know, by the sound of it.

"I understand," she said, keeping her expression absolutely even. She'd learned that trick during her marriage, because of Peter's dislike of disapproval. She'd practiced in a glass until she knew the exact arrangement of her features that portrayed benign interest without judgment.

Without the flash of real anger that she felt inside. She was good enough to kiss and fondle, good enough to marry, but not good enough to be friends with?

"I didn't say that correctly," Hugo said.

"I think your point is an excellent one," Ophelia said. "Men and women are rarely friends, as I understand it."

"I am friends with my twin sister."

"Marvelous," Ophelia said, another stab of resentment going through her.

"What are you thinking?"

"I am wondering why a man who has so much has any need of a wife. You have all those children, and a sister to boot." She colored and looked at the expression in his eyes. "Besides *that*, I mean."

"I am lucky," he offered.

"Yes."

"I think it's very interesting that you narrow my assets to my family."

Ophelia forced a smile. This had been pleasurable, and startling, but now she wanted to be alone. A bone-deep melancholy was building up in her heart: a feeling of missing Peter. That was the problem with being widowed: Grief wasn't something one got over with a year of mourning, or even two.

"I think perhaps we should sleep alone," she said.

"Most women think that the duchy of Lindow is my greatest asset," Hugo said, taking her right hand and bringing it to his lips. "Power equals money, after all. The holder of a dukedom is all-powerful in a society like ours."

Ophelia tugged her hand free. "You seem to me an excellent representative of power and money." She swung her legs over the bed, reached over, and picked up her dressing gown. She didn't mind sitting in bed without clothing, but she wasn't going to stand up naked. The light cotton brushed over her nipples, sending a thrill of feeling down her body.

"I've mucked it up, haven't I?" Hugo said, moving off his side of the bed.

"There was nothing to muck up," Ophelia replied. "I have much enjoyed our time together. I truly have." She reached out and caught his hands in hers. "This has been a pleasure."

"Ophelia," the duke said.

She shook her head. "I do not wish to be a duchess, Your Grace."

"May I stay tomorrow?"

"I think not." She kept her voice even, without a hint of what was really in her mind. There was no reason to spend time together if they couldn't even be friends.

"Please?"

"Your Grace." She struck just the right tone. Her voice was firm, reproving but not overly proud.

He shook his head. "Phee, do you know how many people say no to me?"

"If you give your two-year-old a chance, I expect she will startle you in that respect," Ophelia told him. "Good night, Your Grace."

She left before he could answer.

Chapter Eight

*H*ugo fell back onto the bed, feeling as if he'd been struck—not for the first time that evening.

She'd said no.

Ophelia meant it too.

Marie had flirted with him, but from the moment they met, she'd been as interested as he. After that, it was a matter of mating. He'd flaunted his dukedom and his body, just the way Fitzy, the young peacock at Lindow Castle, spread his tail. Marie had pretended to run away, enjoying every moment of the game.

They had been young and beautiful. He had already inherited the title, feeling no true grief for the father he had barely known. She had been the treasured eldest child of a marquess, and had excelled at everything she chose to do—including marriage.

Marie had been amazingly precious to him, partly because she was so direct, so uncomplicated. She was a child of laughter and joy who loved him, and loved their children.

Ophelia was far more complex. She had grieved and was still mourning, unless he was wrong. She had faced life alone—in more than one way. She and her husband had been partners, but not soul mates. Not the way he and Marie had been.

That thought made his heart ache for her.

But she didn't need or want his pity.

Somewhere in that conversation he'd gone badly wrong. He was banished from the house, and his chance of winning her hand had diminished.

Think as hard as he might, he couldn't put his finger on what he had said wrong.

In the morning, the young footman returned his clothing, immaculately cleaned and pressed. His sword made an appearance as well, and Hugo buckled it on without inquiring how the coachman explained possession of the duke's weapon.

Fiddle ushered him into a charming breakfast room and informed him that Her Ladyship always broke bread with her daughter in the morning. One of Lady Astley's carriages was at his disposal, and Fiddle would order it to return

His Grace to the Lindow townhouse after the meal.

Ophelia must be in the nursery. Hugo would be damned if he'd leave without saying goodbye.

He finished the meal without haste, talking to Fiddle of this and that, learning far more of the household than the butler imagined he had revealed. Ophelia's eggs were brought from her country house, as was her meat, "and as much produce as Lady Astley deems practical," the butler said, more than a hint of pride in his voice.

Fiddle was brother to Ophelia's coachman in that: Bisquet had made it clear that he was proud to serve his mistress, and he would lay down his life to protect her.

Hugo's servants were loyal too. His butler, Prism, was devoted to the duchy and his position as head butler of several estates. In fact, most of the servants were proud of being part of the duchy. They enjoyed wearing his livery.

Ophelia was not only complicated; she had built a life for herself that he would be hard-pressed to match. No one knew better than he that the life of a duke or duchess could be a tedious, even lonely one.

Everything he did was considered interesting. If he went to chapel, by the time the service ended, there would be a throng of people outside, waiting for him to throw alms, or simply gawking at his clothing.

At his carriage.

At his children.

Could he subject Ophelia to that much scrutiny? He looked around him. The breakfast room was painted pale green, and plaster arabesques covered the ceiling. Every piece of furniture was exquisite, and each spoke to Ophelia's taste.

In contrast, Lindow Castle was a hodgepodge, a huge, sprawling mélange of towers and wings, with secret passageways, suits of armor, dusty tapestries, endless staircases.

A stuffed alligator resided in the drawing room, and the family peacock screamed warnings at any time of day or night.

Marie had been raised to be a member of the peerage. She hadn't blinked an eye at miles of bookshelves, tottering retainers grown old in service to the duchy, fourteen sets of china.

But Ophelia?

She had created a *home* for her daughter: a beautiful, graceful place.

His heart settled like a stone. He couldn't do this to her. She might come to blame him, perhaps even to hate him. He had been spoiled by the fact that Marie had instantly responded to his proposal with enthusiasm—but also by the fact that she had been raised to be a duchess.

Her mother had accompanied her to the castle and lived there for the first six months of their married life, making certain that her daughter successfully took over the household. Marie had dived into everything with joy and was never happier than when she announced she was carrying a child a month after their wedding (in truth, she must have carried Horatius up the aisle, which spoke to their mutual enthusiasm about the marriage).

By contrast, Ophelia was enthusiastic about bedding, but not about him. He frowned, not sure what happened . . . Hadn't they discussed being friends? He didn't want to be friends with her.

He wanted to be her husband.

But now he had the idea that she didn't even wish to be friends.

In the end, he didn't storm the nursery. He sent his gratitude by way of her butler, accepting Fiddle's explanation that Lady Astley never received callers before noon.

He returned to his townhouse and fell blindly into the work involved in running one of the largest duchies in all England. He went to the

House of Lords. He went to court, registering that Ophelia would probably loathe such pomp and circumstance. Or would she? He hardly knew her. He went to the opera at Covent Garden, noticing how every member of the audience swiveled his or her head when he entered the Lindow box.

He put on his pink suit and went to another ball. He danced with an eligible daughter of a marquess, who giggled and told him that she loved kittens more than life itself. He translated kittens into children, bowed, and walked off without another glance.

Next he danced with the Dowager Countess of Webbel, who told him, in so many words, that she was too old for children. She cast condescending looks in all directions when he danced with her for the second time, and then made the fatal error of asking, in a sweetly poisonous tone, about the whereabouts of his sister, Lady Knowe.

His twin was part of his household; the children thought of her as their mother. He would divorce again before he wedded a woman who would drive her away.

The following day he went back to court, and Her Highness graciously introduced him to one of her ladies-in-waiting, Lady Woolhastings, a dowager marchioness. Edith had to be fifty, far older than he.

But she didn't look fifty; she might easily pass for forty in candlelight. She had kept her figure, and her bodices displayed her bosom's girlish shape.

What's more, she knew how to manage a noble household. She met his eyes with understanding of his situation; she could and would usher his daughters through the Season. Her own two daughters were happily married.

She was even nice.

She was perfect.

He wrote his sister with the news that he'd found precisely the woman whom she bade him to marry.

He escorted Edith to a concert at St. Paul's, since she was fond of orchestral music. He wasn't, but it didn't matter. He met her daughters, who were unexceptional, well-mannered young women.

She suggested that he send his daughters to an elite seminary in London. "Children," she said, "thrive in groups, and the idea that children of the nobility do best with a governess is an old-fashioned idea." He agreed, thinking that Betsy, in particular, would enjoy school.

He decided to ask her to marry him.

He couldn't have Ophelia, and the lady was nice enough.

Chapter Nine

$\mathcal{W}$hen the duke sent a note the afternoon following their snowy adventure, accompanied by a bunch of exquisite hothouse posies, Ophelia asked Fiddle to have them put in a vase in the morning room, then changed her mind and brought them to her bedchamber.

Of course, Hugo wouldn't pay her a call. It would be a waste of his time. She had refused him, roundly and without hesitation.

He needed a wife.

Still, when the snow was cleared away and Maddie appeared a few days later, full of news about the duke's exploits around London, she felt unaccountably disappointed.

It was absurd—as absurd as the fact that she still found herself lying awake at night, her light nightdress feeling like a wool blanket, her body prickling with unusual and unwelcome desire.

After three weeks had passed, it became clear that His Grace had found his next duchess.

"Lady Woolhastings," Maddie reported, wrinkling her nose. "Really, I would have thought he could do better. She's so *old*. And so . . . Well, I do think it's sad when a woman won't accept her age, don't you think? She has to be fifty-two if she's a day and she plans to marry a man at least a decade younger."

"May I give you another cup of tea?" Ophelia asked. She was horridly shaken, but determined not to show it. Hugo was nothing to her.

One night, one silly night.

Thank goodness, no one knew of it.

"Yes, please, with sugar," Maddie said. "My husband says that His Grace is making certain there won't be any more children, and God knows, *that* is a good idea. I know Lindow is rich as Croesus, but establishing all those sons, not counting the heir, and dowrying two daughters would bankrupt anyone."

"That seems mercenary, but I suppose . . ." Ophelia's voice died away. Hugo had been willing to marry her, unless he was fooling, but she didn't think he had been. Hard thinking in the middle of the night had convinced her that her initial impressions were correct: He had looked at her as no man ever had before.

But she had sent him away.

And he had stayed away.

"It's too bad," Maddie said, putting more sugar into her tea. "He was quite taken with you. If you hadn't left the ball so suddenly, you might have bewitched him and become a duchess."

"You yourself told me that he was too much for me," Ophelia pointed out.

"I changed my mind once I spoke to him," Maddie said. "One of us should have taken him, and he didn't want me."

"If he hadn't been looking for a nanny, he might well have fallen for your charms," Ophelia said, rather hollowly. And then she added, "Although your husband would *not* have been happy."

"Who cares what Penshallow thinks?" Maddie said, hunching up a shoulder. "Yesterday I received the most horrid, ill-written note that you can imagine, informing me that my husband had been making children's stockings."

"What?"

"I was confused too, but it seems that he's gotten his mistress—one of his mistresses—with child. I made him tell me all."

"Oh, Maddie." Ophelia reached out and covered

her cousin's hand with hers. "I'm so sorry. What shall you do?"

"What *can* I do?"

But Ophelia had known Maddie for all of her life, so she just waited.

"I told that ungrateful wretch that I'd raise his child," Maddie burst out. "Oh! He's so dreadful. First I accosted him with the news, and he pretended to know nothing. Then he admitted to giving the woman ten pounds so that she could bring the child to the Foundling Hospital when it was born."

"One has to pay the Foundling Hospital?" Ophelia asked. She poured more tea, because in moments of crisis, tea helped.

Maddie added a great amount of sugar. "If you want the child to be apprenticed, yes. Penshallow had the nerve to boast that he took his responsibilities seriously! And then—oh, Phee, I can barely say this aloud, and only to you, obviously . . ."

"What is it?"

Maddie took a deep breath. "Then he suggested that if the child is a boy, we take him in and pretend that he's mine. Because Penshallow needs an heir, obviously. And I don't want to bed him ever again. I *refuse.*" Her voice rose.

Marriage was a terrible coil. Hugo's unfaithful duchess came into Ophelia's mind—and she pushed the thought away.

She was practicing a strict regimen of not thinking of the duke except in the dark of night, in her own bed, where she didn't seem to be able to control herself.

"I think you should do it," she said. "The child is Penshallow's, after all, or he believes as much."

"He says it is." Maddie looked up, and Ophelia saw to her horror that her brave, plucky cousin was starting to cry. "The poor woman hadn't known a man before him."

"But he didn't . . ."

Maddie shook her head. "Apparently, she is very beautiful and wants to take another protector and put this behind her." She gave Ophelia a lopsided smile. "I think that my husband may have been roundly told off, for all he's protesting that *he* was the one to end the liaison."

"The baby exists, and it's his," Ophelia said. "Maddie, darling, I think this child may answer many problems, if it turns out to be male. If not, Viola will have a girl cousin, and you know how much I would love her to have more family."

"She could have had any number of siblings, if only you hadn't fled the ball so early," Maddie said, sniffling as she pulled out a handkerchief.

"Nonsense," Ophelia said. "How far along is, ah, your husband's friend?"

"Far enough so that I must pad my waist immediately if I'm to carry it off," Maddie said. "Thank goodness for sack gowns, for who's to say whether I'm six months along or not?"

"That many?" Ophelia asked, startled.

Her cousin nodded, and picked up her handkerchief again.

"Maddie, it will be fine," Ophelia said, after thinking it over. "I will go around with you for a few days, and make sure everyone knows that you're carrying a child. Then you can retire here for your confinement. After a week or so, we'll leave for Lindow Castle."

"That would seem very strange," Maddie objected.

"Not at all! Everyone knows you are my dearest cousin, and since your mother is no longer with us, it would be perfectly unexceptionable for you to stay with me. Oh, Maddie, we'll have so much fun! I love babies, as you know."

"I won't have *her* here," Maddie said, with sudden energy that suggested she cared more about Penshallow's infidelity than she admitted.

"Of course not," Ophelia said. "If you wish, I'll speak to Penshallow myself. The woman must be well cared for, and not allowed to drink anything, particularly gin. I've read that it can lead to terrible problems."

"I asked about her whereabouts," Maddie said, sniffling again. "That wretch didn't even bother to look ashamed. Apparently he owns a house where he's been keeping her. I bid him to question the servants and make certain that she's eating well. He'll do it, as she may be carrying his heir."

With that, she burst out sobbing, and Ophelia gathered her up and rocked her back and forth, making plans the whole while.

"Where are you bid to tonight?" she asked, once Maddie had calmed again.

"Nowhere tonight. Thursday, the theater, followed by supper at Lady Fernby's house. I shall be in Penshallow's box, though he has informed me that he is busy, likely with his *other* mistress, the one who isn't carrying a child."

"Excellent," Ophelia said. "You must write to Lady Fernby, and tell her that due to your delicate condition, you wish me to accompany you. I'm sure that she'll have no objection; we are quite friendly."

"Oh, she loves you," Maddie said. She brightened. "The Duke of Lindow will attend the supper, so you can meet again. Lady Fernby boasted that His Grace and Lady Woolhastings would join them."

Ophelia winced, but luckily her cousin didn't notice.

"Nothing's been announced between them," Maddie continued. "Perhaps you can still be a duchess, Ophelia. What shall you wear?"

"It doesn't matter what I wear," Ophelia said. "More important is what *you* wear. You can trust your maid, can't you?"

"Of course," Maddie said. "She was my nanny—" She broke off. "Oh, goodness, I suppose I'll have to find a new maid because Dottie will wish to return to the nursery, without a doubt."

"Excellent!" Ophelia said, jumping to her feet. "When I was carrying Viola, my maid fashioned a marvelous sling since my back hurt so terribly. It will hold a pillow in just the right position at your waist. I'll ask her where it is."

"And you trust her?"

"With my life," Ophelia said. "The same for all my servants."

"All right," Maddie said, getting up. "I suppose it's better to pretend to carry Penshallow's child than actually have to carry it."

"Under the circumstances, yes," Ophelia said.

"And much safer too. Just think of how many ladies have lost their lives in childbirth."

Maddie brightened a little. "It's terrible for one's figure."

"Exactly," Ophelia said. "Just look what it did for my bosom."

"I didn't mean that," Maddie protested, following her from the room. "I would love to have your curves."

Chapter Ten

The Duke of Lindow's townhouse
Mayfair

*H*ugo was meeting with one of his estate managers when a great noise rose from downstairs. He knew instantly what it was, so he stood and offered the man a smile. "It seems that I must break off our meeting, Mr. Elms. My children are apparently paying me an unexpected visit."

"I understand," Mr. Elms said, gathering up his estate book. "May I take it that you approve of the plans for new hedgerows, Your Grace?"

"Yes," Hugo said, going to the door. "If you'll forgive me." And with that, he headed downstairs. It was stupid beyond all measure, but he had missed them. All of them, even little Joan, who wailed every time she saw him.

His sister was surrounded by footmen, one holding her high-plumed bonnet, another her exquisite French muff, a third her perfumed gloves. "Surprise!" she called, waving at him.

The entry was filled with Wildes. The boys were in their Eton coats, so his sister must have picked them up from school. Alaric was pummeling North in the shoulder and Horatius was barking a lecture. Not to be left out, four-year-old Betsy looked ready to leap into the fray, but she noticed his arrival.

"Papa!" she shrieked, running toward the stairs. All heads turned, and the babble of voices rose higher.

Hugo scooped Betsy up into his arms and gave her a kiss. North, Parth, and Alaric ran to him. They stopped a foot or so away and bobbed bows, and then as he put Betsy down, all three of them hurled into his arms. Leonidas followed, grabbing one of his legs, and even Alexander struggled to be put down and trotted toward him. Only Joan buried her face in her nanny's neck and refused to look at him.

Ophelia had made him feel like an inadequate father, but he wasn't.

His heir, Horatius, advanced two steps, and swept him an exquisite bow. "Your Grace," he said.

"Horatius, you ass," he said, "come give me a hug."

His eldest submitted to an embrace, but reluctantly. Hugo made sure not to crush his cravat, as it had obviously taken a good deal of time and starch to achieve such perfect folds.

Then Hugo walked to Joan's nanny, and with a nod, took his little girl, talking before she had a chance to start crying. "I missed you, Joanie." Looking down at the smaller children, he said, "Do you all know what I saw the other day on Bond Street? Something the older boys dearly loved when they were small."

"What?" Betsy asked.

"Wooden horses!" he said, laughing as he looked down at their excited faces.

"Children's trinkets," Horatius said, in as lofty a tone as an eighteen-year-old could manage.

"There was also a shop selling Spanish daggers," Hugo said. Horatius's eyes brightened. Joan seemed to have forgotten her fear of her father; she was sucking two fingers and staring with round eyes.

"Louisa," Hugo said to his twin, raising his voice because Leonidas and Betsy were clinging to his legs, demanding horses *now*. "This is a welcome surprise."

"My dear, all my London friends have been writing with great excitement because there is to be a Frost Fair on the Thames, and there hasn't been one since 1740. Obviously, the children couldn't miss that."

"I hadn't heard," Hugo said.

"*And* I realized that we couldn't let you make such a large decision on your own," his sister said in a lower voice, handing her pelisse to one of the footmen and then kissing Hugo on both cheeks, a habit she picked up on the continent. "I fetched the boys from Eton and Horatius from Oxford and here we are!"

"I shall miss an examination in theology," Horatius announced.

"Who cares about theology?" Alaric asked. "They'll give you top marks *in absentia* for command of supercilious nonsense."

"Good show of vocabulary," Louisa said affectionately, ruffling Alaric's hair. "Horatius, my dear, you know your don promised that you may make up any examinations you wish."

After North's and Parth's raucous laughter at the idea of requesting to make up an examination settled, Hugo said, "I am happy to see all of you. I am considering taking a new duchess, children, and that will, of course, affect your lives as well."

"I told you that had to be it!" Alaric said to Horatius. "You owe me a shilling."

Hugo grinned as he watched Horatius, punctilious as he was, instantly pull a coin from his pocket and hand it over.

"Didn't think I'd marry again, did you?" he asked his heir.

"After a divorce? I hoped not," Horatius said, doing a pretty good job of looking as stern as a bishop.

Louisa slung her arm around Horatius's shoulder. At the moment they were precisely the same height, though he would likely continue growing. "You can rest in your grave, Hugo, assured that your heir will mend your ragged reputation."

Hugo laughed. "Meanwhile, Horatius, your younger siblings are in need of a mother."

Horatius looked from his father's face to Joan's bright golden hair, and Hugo saw the realization strike him. Joan was still sucking her fingers, but thankfully, she hadn't started sobbing.

"Ah," Horatius said. He bent over and picked up Betsy. "Young ladies don't sit on the floor," he told his little sister, but not unkindly.

The future duke was arrogant and conceited,

but his heart was in the right place. He loved his family, no matter how rigid he was.

"I concur with Aunt Knowe that it is advisable that we assist, to the best of our abilities, in choosing the third duchess," Horatius announced.

"I was there when Aunt Knowe interviewed the new upstairs maid," Betsy said importantly.

"I don't think that would be appropriate," Horatius told her.

Betsy scowled at him. "I can ask questions too!"

"I hope she won't be frightened off by this horde," Louisa said. "I would be, looking at these grimy children. Prism, could I ask you to stow the varmints under the eaves, and arrange for baths all around, while I have a restorative with His Grace?"

The family butler, who had accompanied her from the country, bowed and turned to their London butler. Between them and a small crowd of nursemaids, they began ushering the children upstairs. Hugo handed over Joan, rather proud of the fact that she hadn't burst out crying.

"You don't wish to retire to your chamber?" he asked his sister, rather surprised.

"We've no time to waste," Louisa said. "I want to hear *everything*. I received your letter about Lady Woolhastings."

With that, she pulled him off to his study. Where he told her everything, because she was his twin. Including the fact that Ophelia had decided not to be his duchess.

"I knew something was wrong," Louisa pronounced. "I am never mistaken in such things. I could feel it in my gut, but I had hoped it was just the bother of finding another wife."

"As I told you, I found one," Hugo said, feeling very tired. "Lady Woolhastings will make an excellent duchess."

"I've known Edith for years, Hugo."

Her tone was dangerously even. She didn't like the woman he'd chosen. Hugo's heart sank. "I can't say that I remember her," he said.

"You wouldn't," Louisa said. "You were too busy chasing Marie around the room to notice anyone else, and Edith was already a mother when you first appeared in London."

"She seems very agreeable."

"She is," his sister said. "I've shared many a recipe for skin cream with her. She's not the sort to pretend to know nothing about a new diet regime when in fact she's eaten only cucumbers for weeks; if it works, Edith tells everyone."

"Ah," Hugo said, thinking that didn't sound very interesting. But "interesting" wasn't what he was looking for. Presumably his daughters would enjoy recipes for cosmetic restoratives. And cucumbers.

"Louisa, you told me to find a woman who would be a good mother and was uninterested in bedding me," he reminded her.

"So I did. Tell me a bit more about Sir Peter Astley's widow."

"There's no point in further discussion of Phee," Hugo said. "She doesn't want me and made that quite clear."

"I shall make that determination myself," Louisa retorted.

Hugo tossed back a glass of sherry. His twin was a pain in the arse, and she would only complicate things. "Horatius will approve of Lady Woolhastings."

"Of course he will. Edith is a pleasant woman who won't be so inconsiderate as to have more children and burden the estate."

Hugo frowned at her.

"I adore Horatius," his sister said, unrepentant. "I have since the moment I laid eyes on that bawling, red-faced little monster. But he can't help himself, Hugo. It must be some sort of disease that erupts now and then in the ducal line. He thinks like a duke, and I don't mean that as a compliment."

"He's not yet a duke," Hugo said. But he felt far older than his years at the moment.

"When will you see Lady Woolhastings next?" Louisa asked, polishing off her sherry.

"Thursday for the theater, then supper with Lady Fernby," he said, dispirited. "She's a friend of Lady Woolhastings, or Edith, I should say. Though Edith has not given me permission to use her given name."

"Lady Fernby is a friend of mine," Louisa said, looking delighted. "I shall send her a message immediately and ask her to add a cover to the table. But first I shall send Edith a message and ask her to accompany us to the Frost Fair tomorrow morning."

"With the children?"

"Of course, with the children," Louisa said. "They're your children, and if you marry, they will be *hers* as well. They must meet her."

"You told me not to mention children," Hugo objected. "If she sees how many there are, and how lively they are, she might decide not to marry me."

"I know I gave you that advice, but on reflection, I decided I was wrong. The children ought to have a chance to meet the woman who would become their stepmother."

"All right," Hugo said reluctantly.

"I shall have a word with them over breakfast about minding their manners. Edith is punctilious with regard to etiquette and deportment. Her girls were delightfully well behaved from the age of two, as I recall."

"Joan seems to have calmed," Hugo said.

"When she isn't shrieking like a night bird," Louisa said briskly. "I think she's going to have a gift for drama: She is either joyful or tragic. And just so you know, she is still throwing crockery whenever she has a chance. Leonidas has been desperately naughty in the last few weeks. I think he misses you most of all, Hugo. He needs a man in the house."

"He's only six!"

"A troublesome age for boys," his sister stated. She was given to pronouncements about children, though Lord only knew where she got the authority. She read that thought in this face, because she added, "As I well know from watching your four older sons grow up, Hugo."

"I suppose that's true." He leaned forward and kissed her cheek. "I don't know what I'd do without you, Louisa. If you are not comfortable with Edith, I shan't marry her."

"Your sister's opinion is *not* a good measure by which to choose a wife," she said, rising to her feet. "I need a bath and a restorative nap before the evening meal."

"I mean it," Hugo said. "You come before Edith. I've already scrapped one possible duchess whom I thought you wouldn't like."

Louisa raised an eyebrow.

"The Dowager Countess of Webbel."

"You must be jesting!"

Her outraged shriek carried them out of the study and up the stairs, and he found himself grinning for the first time since leaving Ophelia's house.

He would always feel a pang when he thought about Phee. But he was a grown man, who was long acquainted with disappointment—not to mention grief. He had a loving family, and that was the most important thing.

The only important thing, really.

Chapter Eleven

$\mathcal{O}$phelia woke the next morning suffused with melancholy. Perhaps she felt dour because she and Viola had been trapped in the house for weeks. Ever since the snowstorm, the weather had continued to be bitterly cold, with snow flurries blurring what sunshine made it through the London coal fog.

It had to be almost morning, but frost patterns scrolled over the window.

Hitching herself up against the pillows, she tried to decide why she felt so sad, and finally put it down to a combination of two things: She missed the Duke of Lindow, which was absurd, because she scarcely knew him. And secondly, there would soon be a baby in the house, but the baby wouldn't be hers.

Maddie would be a marvelous mother; she had no doubt of that.

She sat with the second emotion for a while, surprised by it. It had never occurred to her until she sent the duke away that by not marrying again, she had consigned herself to a life with no more babies.

Viola was perfect, of course. She almost felt guilty thinking of another child. Before she met the duke, she had been completely content.

Her thoughts tangled around each other in a beastly fashion. By the time Viola came toddling down the corridor, Ophelia was desperate to leave her bedchamber and indeed, the house altogether.

"Viola and I shall go to Hyde Park today," she told her maid later, over a breakfast tray. Her daughter was tucked beside her, and she squealed with happiness to hear it, buttered toast falling out of her mouth and landing on the linen sheet.

Ophelia brushed off the crumbs and smiled down at Viola. "You'd like to go to the park, wouldn't you?"

"Go!" Viola said with great enthusiasm.

"The park is piled with snow," her maid said. "Oh, madam, I know exactly what you should do: They were just saying in the kitchen that the Frost Fair opened last night!"

"On the Thames tideway?"

"Mr. Bisquet says as how there hasn't been a Frost Fair for a quarter of a century," her maid enthused. "You must take Miss Viola, madam. It might not happen again in her lifetime. My grandmother went to one as a girl, and she said that there were shops on the ice selling everything you can imagine, and carriages went to and fro just as if the ground were under their feet."

"Excellent," Ophelia said, pushing aside a sudden thought that Viola would be happy in a pack of children running and shrieking on the ice. *Eight* children, to be precise. "Please let Fiddle know that I intend to take Viola to the Frost Fair this morning."

Her maid nodded, and hurried through the door to talk to the butler.

Viola was nestled against Ophelia's side, busily making patterns in melted butter on the silver tray. "Come on, love," Ophelia said. "I'll show you the patterns that Jack Frost made on our windows last night."

Out of bed, she propped her daughter on her hip and took her over to the window. "Aren't they beautiful ferns?" she asked. Viola touched the cold windowpane and squealed.

The duke's children would be mothered by

Lady Woolhastings, who would never show them frost on a windowpane. Or take them to a Frost Fair, for that matter. Lady Woolhastings was the sort of woman who didn't stir from her fireplace unless it was to enter her carriage and be transferred to another warm fireside.

Ophelia stared out the window while Viola used her plump fingertips to melt the ferny patterns. The duke's eight children weren't her problem.

After a while, her nursery maid, Betty, entered. "May I take Miss Viola to her bath, madam?"

Ophelia nodded. "Yes, thank you. Please put Viola in wool stockings and her warmest clothing. We are going to the Frost Fair."

Viola shrieked when she realized that Betty had arrived to take her away, but Ophelia kissed her forehead. "Let me bathe and dress, poppet, and we'll go somewhere marvelous."

"Snow?" Viola asked.

"Another word!" Ophelia broke into a huge grin and dismissed the idea that any children could be more wonderful than the one she had. "You have a new word!"

"Go, snow," Viola said obligingly, showing her few pearly teeth.

"That's a sentence!"

"She's a bright child," Betty said cheerfully.

"Now come along, dearie. You'll need your furry pelisse because it's nippy out there."

"Nip-pe!" Viola cried.

"Did she show you her new trick, madam?" Betty asked.

Ophelia shook her head, smiling.

"Hurrah!" Betty cried, clapping.

Viola began clumsily patting her hands together. "Ray! Ray!"

"That's three new words in as many moments," Ophelia said. "Not to mention the fact that you learned how to clap, Viola. Brava!"

By the time Ophelia's carriage—not the elegant one with the broken axle, but the sturdy, family-sized barouche—reached the Frost Fair, Viola had at least twenty words and counting.

"How is this possible?" Ophelia said aloud, laughing. "You went to bed with the same two words you've had for weeks: 'No' and 'Mama.' You woke up a different person. Not a different person, but with different skills."

"Pills," Viola offered, and patted Ophelia's cheek.

Ophelia was fighting off one of those urges known to widows and widowers, a moment in which one desperately wishes to talk to a person who is no longer there.

She pushed away the image of the Duke of

Lindow as an alternative to Peter. "He's getting married!" she told herself, aloud.

"Mawied," Viola said, nodding.

"And *not* to me," Ophelia told her. "He moved on directly, didn't he? I said no, and he didn't even try to change my mind. He strode into another ballroom and picked out a different woman to mother his children."

Somehow that made her more furious than the fact he was planning to marry again.

He had replaced her with Lady Woolhastings, who was not old, exactly, but she wasn't young either. Her daughters were frightfully well-behaved and rather dull.

Hugo . . . He *couldn't* be planning to bed her. Not the way he offered to make love to Ophelia. He couldn't.

But he had said that he was looking for a woman uninterested in bedding him.

The problem with having red hair was that it proverbially goes along with a temper, and in Ophelia's case, it *did* go along with that temper. To this point, she'd been feeling disconsolate about the fact that the duke had so easily thrown her aside and snatched up another available lady.

But now a flame of anger began to burn in her chest. He had said things to her and she believed them. He had implied that he was falling in love. He had refused to make love to her unless she married him.

He had made her feel special, as if bedding him was an admission ticket to a wonderful life.

But even furious as she was, she couldn't imagine that Lady Woolhastings had paid the price of admission. But then . . .

To be a duchess?

Who wouldn't sleep with a handsome, younger man in order to be a duchess? It was just so . . .

So what?

She turned him down. She had no right to decide that he was making a horrible mistake, that he was an idiot who should have come back the next day and pleaded with Ophelia. Begged her.

The fact of the matter was that he hadn't wanted her enough to do that.

She hadn't paid the price of admission, and if that made the duke a despicable person, so be it. He hadn't meant the kind things he said, so she'd had a very lucky escape.

"Lucky," Viola said, which was the moment when Ophelia realized that she was so angry that she had said the last sentence aloud, and fiercely too.

"He's made his choice," Ophelia told Viola, kissing her. "You and I will go to the Frost Fair and have a wonderful time. We'll buy gingerbread, and *his* children will be home in the nursery. Perhaps he'll greet them, if he finds time." She shook her head. "I don't want that for your father."

The thought steadied her. It wasn't just a matter of her mothering the eight orphans; the duke would become Viola's father as well.

"*She* won't take them to the Frost Fair," Ophelia said. Somehow it felt like vindication. He was choosing Lady Woolhastings because she was related to royalty, and uninterested in bedding him. But there was more to being a mother than the name alone.

By the time they reached the edge of the Frost Fair, a great frozen expanse of the Thames, the sun was out, albeit in a chilly way. Ophelia climbed out of the carriage and took a look, her coachman standing at her shoulder.

It was as if Bartholomew Fair had set up shop on the ice with drinking booths, games to play, food for sale, a bowling alley open to the sky, a skating rink. Red-cheeked Londoners were scrambling about on wooden skates or sliding in their boots, laughing and shouting. Strings of paper lanterns in bright colors were draped between the little shops, or strung between the poles marking the skating rink.

"There'll be some ruffians in the mix," Bisquet said. "I'll send a groom with you to hold your purse, madam. The carriage will be here waiting for you. I've brought along blankets for the horses and nice warm mash in case we're here more than an hour or two."

"We'll be more than an hour," Ophelia said happily. In front of her, a line of small wooden shops wove their way across the ice, creating a curvy road. Bright flags were flying from the roofs, and a lovely smell of mingled pig roast and mulled wine drifted their way.

"On this side, there's a road for carriages," Bisquet pointed out. "There are sleigh rides as well, going all the way from Temple to Southwark."

The ice was dotted everywhere with glowing bonfires constructed inside great metal burners, around which people stood warming their hands. Some burners were outfitted with elaborate spits and one even held an entire roasting pig.

"Aren't they afraid the fires will melt the ice?" Ophelia asked, turning back to the carriage to pick up a very excited Viola.

"Oh, goodness, no," Bisquet said comfortably. "I heard as the ice is twenty fathoms deep. Look over there, madam, a horse and six, just as safe as if they were going down the cobblestone of our own street."

"Where are the sleighs?"

"Beyond the ice-carving palladium," her coachman said. "There, where you see the crimson awning? Supposedly the finest ice carvers in the kingdom are at work, and the king himself will judge them on Friday . . . if the ice lasts. Yet people are saying it might last two months, just as in the cold snap of '40."

Viola was waving her red-mittened hands. "Snow!" she crowed.

Behind them, the horses were stamping their feet.

Followed by Peters, the groom, Ophelia walked down the gentle slope and stepped onto the ice. It was covered by a trampled layer of snow, so it wasn't slippery, and they set out happily for the row of stores.

They stopped at every stall, Viola clapping at the sight of hot cider, carved wooden horses, gingerbread men . . . Whatever was for sale, she applauded. Since she was an extremely pretty little girl, her sweet face encircled with a halo of white rabbit fur, even the most hard-bitten of London merchants found himself smiling at her and offering free samples.

Ophelia couldn't allow people to give away their wares for free, so she kept nodding to Peters, following her with a purse. Before long he was festooned with string bags containing everything from apples to a carved dolly and, over his shoulder, a hobbyhorse with a red ribbon.

Now and then Ophelia and Viola met people whom they knew: the vicar and his wife, cheerily walking arm-in-arm; one of her cousins somewhat-removed who told her that he'd just eaten the best roast beef of his life; one of Peter's school friends, Lord Melton.

He was a robust man with a neatly trimmed beard that turned his chin into an exclamation mark.

He greeted Ophelia with a smile and bow, while she racked her brain trying to remember whether he was married or not. She certainly didn't want to be courted by Lord Melton. All the same, her arm was beginning to ache, and when he offered to carry Viola, she gratefully agreed.

Viola cheerfully went to him, patting his cheek with her red-mittened hands by way of greeting.

They strolled over together to sample a hot chocolate drink imported from the continent, and then headed toward the ice-carving pavilion. Lord Melton was so obviously admiring that Ophelia felt her spirits, dented by Maddie's news about the Duke of Lindow, rise.

She might not have been desirable enough to ensnare the Duke of Lindow for more than one heady night, but Lord Melton was showing every sign of considering himself ensnared.

Once they reached the ice-carving pavilion, they began walking about, admiring the carvings taking shape under the busy chisels of master carvers. She rounded a six-foot lump of ice—destined to be a reproduction of St. Paul's Tower, or so the carver informed them—and ran straight into the Duke of Lindow.

Not just the duke either, but Lady Woolhastings beside him, looking remarkably elegant in a sable-lined pelisse with exquisite butter-yellow gloves with long fringes at the wrist. No one would say that Lady Woolhastings was beautiful, but anyone from the Queen to a scullery maid would have known she was a lady with impeccable bloodlines. Her long face and limpid eyes had the unmistakable stamp of the peerage.

Ophelia realized instantly that her unpowdered hair had freed itself from the braided knot her maid had fixed in the morning. Red curls were waving around her eyes. Her rabbit fur hood, while warm and certainly economical, was hardly fashionable.

Edith Woolhastings's eyes passed over it and then over Viola's little face, framed in the same fur. She didn't sneer; she was far too well-bred for that. But she looked indifferent, which was somehow even worse. "Is this your daughter, Lady Astley?" she inquired, as politeness compelled her to say something. "She has the look of your late husband, Sir Peter."

Ophelia registered that Lady Woolhastings likely considered her final remark to be a compliment. She dropped a curtsy, noticing in turn that the lady graced her with no more than a nod of the head. Well, Lady Woolhastings was a lady-in-waiting to the queen, and likely took her position very seriously. Ophelia suddenly remembered Peter describing the lady as vexed by a joke, as is often the case with someone who has no sense of humor.

How terrible to marry someone with no sense of humor.

She turned to the Duke of Lindow, but he bowed abruptly and their eyes didn't meet.

"We're on our way to a sleigh ride," Lady Woolhastings said languidly. "Lindow has arranged everything so that we will take sleighs up to the Thames to my house. Aren't you tired, holding that child?" she asked Lord Melton. "Perhaps Lady Astley's groom should return her to the carriage."

"Not a bit of it," Lord Melton said, bouncing Viola in his arms so that she crowed with delight.

"I came to show her the fair," Ophelia said

mildly. "I can hardly do that if she is tucked away in the carriage."

"So this is your daughter," Hugo said. "Viola, am I right?"

Viola gave him her cheerful grin and clapped her hands.

Ophelia met his eyes, ready to kick him in the shins if he gave Viola an indifferent look, the way Lady Woolhastings had.

But he was smiling at Viola as if she was quite marvelous. Ophelia's heart gave a thump. It was one thing to be courted—albeit briefly—by a deliciously handsome duke. It was different when that duke smiled at her best beloved, as if he recognized how wonderful she was.

Viola liked his smile too, because she held out her mittened hands and leaned toward him. When Ophelia nodded, Lord Melton gave her up, and the duke tucked Viola into his left arm as if he was used to carrying children.

"I expect that Viola would love a sleigh ride," he said. "Your groom could bring your purchases back to your carriage and then meet us at Lady Woolhastings's house."

"You have bought a great many things," Lady Woolhastings said, clearly pained. "I distinctly smell mince pies; Lady Astley, you must discard those, or send them to be consumed in the servants' hall. One never knows what a mince pie bought in a fair might contain."

Ophelia paused, not certain what to do, but Viola was happily babbling to the duke, interspersing her new words amid a language of her own. She probably *would* like a sleigh ride.

"Mince is extremely fattening," Lady Woolhastings added.

Hugo met Ophelia's eyes. "Do join us."

It was a good thing that she wasn't marrying him, because she had the feeling that it would be hard to refuse anything he asked, if he had that expression in his eyes. She actually glanced at Lady Woolhastings to see if she caught it but the lady looked quite indifferent.

In fact, that seemed to be her expression most of the time.

Once Ophelia's groom had set off for her carriage, they began walking again, Lady Woolhastings strolling beside Ophelia, and the two men just behind.

"A respectable match," Lady Woolhastings drawled, in her high, well-bred voice.

"I'm sorry?" Ophelia said. She was listening as hard as she could to Viola and the duke, who were having a lively exchange that consisted of a stream of words from Viola, all the new ones she'd learned today jumbled in any order. His Grace was laughing, and supplying a word here or there, which Viola would instantly repeat.

"Lord Melton," Lady Woolhastings prompted. "Very appropriate. A nice estate and good blood. Not of the highest degree, but then you didn't come from those ranks, did you?"

Viola stopped babbling just at the wrong moment, and Ophelia felt a prickling embarrassment in her shoulders. She didn't dare glance about, not sure whom she was more embarrassed about: Hugo or poor Lord Melton, who had accidentally encountered her and found himself virtually married off a half hour later.

Of course, the fact that he had been carrying Viola did make it seem as if they were quite familiar.

She cleared her throat. "Lord Melton is a mere acquaintance, Lady Woolhastings."

"You could do much worse," the lady remarked.

And I could do much better, Ophelia thought to herself. *I could have* done *the duke*. Which was such an improper thought that she found herself turning pink.

Lady Woolhastings glanced over and her brows drew together. "Perhaps you should return to your carriage," she said, in a warmer tone than she had used before. "This cold is inadvisable for the complexion and I see yours is responding to this chill wind. I applied four layers of protective cream this morning."

"Ah," Ophelia said. They were nearing three large sleighs, lavishly picked out with blue paint and gold leaf. A mass of children of all ages were darting between the sleighs and horses, shouting with glee and risking being kicked by an irritable mount.

Lady Woolhastings stopped and lifted her hand. "Your Grace."

"Yes, Lady Woolhastings?" Hugo strode to stand at Ophelia's right shoulder. Viola was sucking her thumb, her head nestled on his shoulder. He had tucked her inside his greatcoat, so she must be toasty warm.

Viola blinked at Ophelia and said, "Snow," before she closed her eyes.

"I ought to bring my daughter home," Ophelia said, shoving away a keen pulse of regret. She knew that Hugo had the instincts of a good father; he was shopping for a third duchess for just that reason.

The fact that Viola looked so blissfully comfortable should not make her, Ophelia, feel prickly and sad. That was absurd.

"Your groom will have already instructed the carriage to meet you further up the Thames," the duke said, his voice kind, but absolute. "More-over, you and Viola cannot traverse the fair by yourselves."

Ophelia turned to look for Lord Melton and realized that he was nowhere to be seen.

"Lord Melton remembered that he had another engagement and asked me to convey his regrets," the duke said.

Ophelia felt herself turning red again. Likely, Lord Melton heard what Lady Woolhastings had said about marrying her and fled in horror. It was hard to tell whether that was more embarrassing than the duke's quick defection.

Hugo apparently read her mind. "No," he stated.

Lady Woolhastings was frowning at the crowd of noisy children and not paying attention.

"Lord Melton had temporarily forgotten that he was betrothed," Hugo said. His eyes didn't stray from hers but his voice dropped a register. "You can do that to a man."

She flinched. Was he telling her that he had already had an understanding with Lady Woolhastings when they met?

"Hugo!"

An imposing lady was bustling toward them, followed by a stream of children. "There you are! We've been waiting for you."

She was as tall as the duke, his age, with his

angular features and marked eyebrows, albeit softened by a fashionable hat whose ribbons streamed in the wind.

She had to be the duke's twin, Lady Knowe.

"Please give me Viola," Ophelia said urgently, turning to Hugo.

He shook his head. "Your arms are aching, are they not?"

Lady Knowe and the children arrived before she could respond, milling about them and shouting, two grooms laden with parcels in the rear.

Lady Woolhastings and Lady Knowe were acquaintanced, and Ophelia watched with a rather jaundiced fascination as Lady Woolhastings dropped into a deep curtsy. Of course, Lady Knowe was to be her sister-in-law.

"Are these children all yours?" Lady Woolhastings asked a moment later. "I knew, of course, but there are so many!"

"Yes, they are," the duke answered. "Lady Knowe, may I introduce Lady Astley? I am holding her daughter, Viola. And Lady Astley, this is my twin sister, Lady Knowe."

Ophelia dropped into a curtsy.

"What a pleasure to meet you!" Lady Knowe said. She had an angular face; what was handsome in her brother looked somewhat incongruous shaped in womanly features. But when she smiled, her eyes lit up with true charm and she looked positively beautiful.

Ophelia beamed back at her. "I feel the same; your brother told me so much about you."

"He has?" Lady Woolhastings drawled. "I was under the impression that my fiancé and you were scarcely acquainted."

The word "fiancé" slid down Ophelia's back like an icicle.

"Everyone loves to talk about me," Lady Knowe said, turning to Lady Woolhastings and smiling. "Come, Edith, you know perfectly well that my brother has the habit of chatting about me in moments when he has nothing else to say. Eccentric relatives are such a gift to polite conversation."

Ophelia put on a serene expression and said, "Certainly I couldn't describe my relationship with the duke as more than casual, since we recently met for the first time, and yet I am aware that you live mostly in the country and have kindly cared for His Grace's children, Lady Knowe."

Beside her, Hugo made a sudden movement, as if he was about to refute the word "casual," but Ophelia turned her head and allowed a flicker of authority to cross her eyes. He shut his mouth, which she appreciated.

"His Grace is certainly lucky that you were there to run the household during his misfortunes," Lady Woolhastings said to Lady Knowe.

"Which reminds me that I must introduce the children!" Lady Knowe cried. "Or would you prefer the privilege, Hugo?"

"I shall take it on," the duke said. He raised the hand that wasn't holding Viola, and the children flocked to his side.

"Lady Woolhastings, and Lady Astley, my children: Horatius, North, Parth, Alaric, Leonidas, Betsy, and Alexander. The littlest, Joan, remained in the nursery today."

Ophelia flinched. She was party to the introduction of the children to their future stepmother? She opened her mouth, about to announce that they would return home. She could take a hack if she had to.

"I am very pleased to meet all of you," Lady Woolhastings said before Ophelia could intervene, her eyes ranging over the assembled children. "Which are you?" She addressed a smartly dressed young man with a somewhat forbidding expression.

"Horatius, my eldest," the duke said. The youngster bowed elegantly, first before Lady Woolhastings, and then before Ophelia. The dowager inclined her head and Ophelia followed suit, giving the lad a warm smile.

"Horatius is at Oxford, and the next three are at Eton. Alaric, followed by Parth and Roland—who prefers to be called North."

"North, as in the direction?" Lady Woolhastings clarified. Her eyes rested thoughtfully on Parth, who was clearly not a Wilde by birth. "Ah, I remember now that you have a ward."

"Parth is my adopted son, not just a ward," the duke said, an edge in his voice.

"Just so," Lady Woolhastings said.

The boys turned from her and bowed before Ophelia. She met Parth's eyes and was reassured by the gleam of steady confidence she saw there. Lady Woolhastings had engaged the duke's daughter in conversation, so Ophelia smiled at Parth.

"Is that your little girl?" he asked, nodding at Viola, who was sound asleep in the duke's arms.

"Yes, she is," Ophelia said.

"So, you're married?" He nimbly jumped to the side when North kicked him in the ankle. "I'm making polite conversation!"

"I'm widowed," Ophelia told him.

"So many males," Lady Woolhastings commented. "Five of the seven, am I correct?"

"Six of the eight," the duke corrected.

"Lady Betsy has lovely features, and I'm certain she will make an excellent marriage," Lady Woolhastings announced.

Leonidas chortled and said, "Not if the fellow gets to know her first!"

Without a word, Betsy darted over to her brother and kicked him in the ankle.

"Now, Betsy," her father admonished mildly.

His daughter kicked Leonidas once more for good measure, smiled up with angelic innocence, and tucked her hand into Ophelia's. "Are you coming wif us on the sleigh?"

"Stop lisping. No one thinks you're adorable," Leonidas said, rubbing his ankle.

Lady Woolhastings watched this with a noncommittal expression. "A stern governess is needed," she said to the duke.

"I have a governess," His Grace replied, somewhat shortly.

"I agree with you, Edith. We need someone far more fierce," Lady Knowe chimed in. "Shall we make our way to the sleighs? All three are ours for the afternoon. The older boys can ride by themselves in the middle sleigh."

The four of them took off, three boys running and Horatius pacing solemnly along behind.

"I must apologize for interrupting what is clearly a family occasion," Ophelia said.

"Not at all," Lady Woolhastings said, one of those empty phrases that mean nothing except by inflection—and Lady Woolhastings's accent was so frightfully well-bred that Ophelia had no idea how to interpret it.

"We must divide up," Hugo said.

"You and I shall travel in the first sleigh," Lady Woolhastings stated. "We'll take your daughter, Boadicea, with us. An odd name."

"She prefers Betsy," the duke responded.

"Smacks of a housemaid," his fiancée said in such a calm voice that at first Ophelia didn't think she'd heard her correctly.

"The younger boys can be in the third sleigh, with Lady Knowe and Lady Astley," Lady Woolhastings continued. "You both are accustomed to children and will be of help." Her brows flexed just the smallest amount. "You really mustn't leave the house without a full complement of nursemaids and grooms, Duke."

Ophelia could interpret this without need of parsing the lady's accent. She and Lady Knowe were substitutes for the nursemaids who were unaccountably missing.

"I suppose you might as well keep the child

you're carrying," the lady said graciously to the duke.

Hugo's face darkened, but before he could respond, Lady Knowe bawled, "Little boys with me in the last sleigh!" as loudly as any constable calling the midnight hour. Leonidas and Alexander ran toward the sleigh.

Ophelia had never allowed herself to be separated from Viola before. But all she could see was her daughter's snub nose and a white ruff of rabbit fur, like a spent dandelion, cozily sheltered in the duke's greatcoat.

"I'll take good care of her," Hugo said, his eyes steady on hers.

He was broad-shouldered and sturdy. His strong embrace when her carriage turned over flitted through her mind. If anything happened, she'd rather Viola was in his arms than hers.

Plus, she certainly didn't wish to join Lady Woolhastings in the first carriage. She'd had all the condescension she could stomach for one day.

She nodded jerkily, then turned and took a groom's hand to clamber into the sleigh.

The duke followed her and looked up. "Are you certain that you don't wish to join me in the first carriage? I promise I will keep your daughter safe."

"No, she doesn't," Lady Knowe said, pushing her brother to the side so she could climb into the sleigh after Ophelia. "You run off and sit with your fiancée, Hugo. We'll be fine here."

She sat down beside Ophelia with a grunt. "My stays are entirely too rigid for climbing. Betsy, you're supposed to travel in the first sleigh with your father. Lady Woolhastings explicitly requested your presence."

The little girl didn't bother to reply; she simply hopped up after her two brothers and crowded herself onto the seat opposite Ophelia and Lady Knowe.

"You're Betsy," Ophelia said.

She nodded.

"And you are Leonidas?" she asked a very naughty-looking boy.

"He's the plague of my life after Parth," Lady Knowe said.

"I'm Alexander," piped up the third child. He had sweet eyes and a lock of hair that fell over his eyes just as the duke's hair had done in the middle of the night.

"These three are, obviously, children of the second duchess," Lady Knowe said briskly. "Including baby Joan at home."

"Do you have three?" the duke bellowed from the second carriage.

"Yes!" roared back his sister. "We always double-check," she said to Ophelia.

"Did you ever leave a child behind?" Ophelia asked, telling herself that she was deeply happy not to be stepmother to so many children, especially Leonidas, who had clambered up on his knees and was precariously leaning over the rear of the sleigh.

"Get down, Leo!" Lady Knowe ordered.

Rather to Ophelia's surprise, he obeyed.

A groom came by to slip hot bricks under their feet. He draped heavy furs over Lady Knowe and Ophelia, and tucked a large one around the three children.

The sleighs jolted into motion, runners squeaking on the ice.

"Did we leave a child behind?" Lady Knowe laughed. "We started having trouble keeping track of them as soon as there were more than six. I hope your daughter doesn't sleep through the entire sleigh ride."

Their sleigh was following a path pounded smooth that ran along the side of the Thames, passing the pleasure gardens of palatial houses.

"It's probably best that she does," Ophelia said. "I don't care to think about her reaction if she wakes up in the arms of a stranger and I'm not there."

"Will she scream?" Betsy asked with interest. "'Cause my sister Joan screams all the time."

"Very likely," Ophelia said, liking her open face. "I suspect you screamed a great deal when you were that age as well."

"A reasonable amount," Lady Knowe said. "Leonidas, if you fall out of the sleigh, you'll have to eat dinner in bed for a week."

"But *look*!" Leonidas cried, pointing out the back.

Ophelia leaned forward. A boy had caught a rope behind their sleigh and was flying on the ice behind them, his skates throwing up plumes of shaved ice.

"I want to try!" Leonidas cried.

"That's dangerous," she said.

"But so much fun! Don't you see?" He looked at her, his little-boy face screwed up with earnestness.

"Yes, I do," Ophelia said. "We don't want him to be hurt, though, do we?"

Lady Knowe had already tapped the sleigh driver on the shoulder and he was slowing to a halt. Ophelia stood up and looked over the back of the sleigh.

"His coat isn't very nice," Betsy said. "Do you have any money?"

Ophelia thrust her hand down into the pockets that hung under her skirts and fished out a guinea. "Here you are."

"Boy!" Betsy called, leaning over the back of the coach, her ringlets blowing around her head as her hood fell back. "We think you should be in the circus. Come closer."

He obeyed, which likely had something to do with the fact that young though she was, Betsy already looked and sounded like a duchess.

"Here," she said, dropping the coin into his hands.

"Thanks!" he called up, touching his cap.

"Nicely done," Lady Knowe said to Betsy. "I applaud you for not throwing it at the boy."

"He wouldn't have liked that," Betsy said, sitting back in her seat.

When the sleigh set into motion again, Betsy leaned forward. "We have questions," she said.

Ophelia blinked at her. "What?"

"Questions," Alexander explained. "Like when Aunt Knowe interviewed the upstairs maid. So we can help Father make a very large decision."

Lady Knowe coughed and looked at the children, eyes brimming with laughter. "The questions are for Lady Woolhastings, my dears. Not for Lady Astley."

"She's not married, so we can ask her too," Betsy said. She folded her arms across her chest, and the two boys followed.

"But I'm not—"

"Please let them practice on you," Lady Knowe interrupted. "I have a strong feeling that Lady Woolhastings will not entertain any questions, and they talked all the way to London about which questions were the most important."

Ophelia looked back at the three determined faces opposite her and realized exactly what Lady Knowe *wasn't* saying. These three had never had a mother. The boys in the first carriage—except for Parth, about whose parenting she knew nothing—had had Marie, and from what the duke said, she had been a loving mother.

But these three?

Everything she knew about Yvette, the second duchess, suggested that the lady spent her time in ballrooms and not nurseries.

"You may certainly practice with me," she said, the words leaving her mouth without conscious volition. "But you must understand that your father is—your father has made a promise to wed Lady Woolhastings."

"Wed Woolhastings," Alexander said, grinning.

"How old are you?" Ophelia asked, smiling at him.

"Three," he said.

"And I'm four and Leonidas is six," Betsy said. "We have three questions, because there are three of us."

"Please ask me when you are ready," Ophelia said.

Alex leaned forward and stared at her intently. "Do you have fake teeth?" he asked. "Or a glass eye?"

Ophelia blinked. "No."

"Mrs. Purdy has an elephant tooth," he said, looking disappointed.

"From a tusk," Lady Knowe clarified. Ophelia looked at her. The edges of the lady's mouth had curved into a smile that she was trying hard to suppress.

"My uncle has a tooth made from a donkey bone in his jaw," Ophelia offered. "On the bottom."

Alex's eyes brightened. "Can he spit it out?"

"No, because it's wired from behind so it stays in line with his other teeth."

"Does your uncle live with you?"

Ophelia shook her head. "He lives in Wales, quite a long way away."

Alex wrinkled his nose. "That's a pity."

"My turn," Betsy said. She fixed Ophelia with a sharp eye and said, "Do you have children other than that baby?"

"No," Ophelia said.

"The nursery is full of children," Betsy stated. "I suppose we can fit that one in, but no more."

"I understand," Ophelia said gravely.

"Do you want more children?"

"Yes," she said, without hesitation. She hadn't known that truth until today. In fact, she had thought that perhaps there wasn't room in her heart to love a child other than Viola.

That had been foolishness, she saw now. Alexander, Betsy, and Leonidas, for example. Not that she loved them . . . but they were very lovable. They had their father's tousled hair, strong eyebrows, and angled cheekbones.

But more than that, they were intelligent, lively, and clearly loved each other, for all the kicking. With a pulse of pure greed, she realized that Viola would love a family like that.

"There aren't any empty beds in the nursery," Betsy told her, folding her arms over her chest. Clearly, Ophelia had proven a disappointment.

"My turn," Leonidas said. "Mine's important. How do you feel about rats?"

"Rats?" Ophelia repeated. She glanced at Lady Knowe to see whether help was forthcoming.

"*Pet* rats," Lady Knowe said, raising an eyebrow inquiringly.

All three children stared at Ophelia, eyes expectant. She had the odd feeling that this was the most important question.

"I don't think I like rats," she admitted. "I've never met a pet rat, but in general the species is not attractive. I dislike their tails."

Leonidas gave her a reproachful glance. "That's a great pity. A rat can be a boy's best friend. Now we're going to talk about you." And with that, he pulled the huge fur cloak up and over their three heads.

"At least they'll be warm under there," Lady Knowe said. "My nose is an icicle."

Ophelia's ears were freezing because she couldn't keep her hood on her head, but there was something incredibly exhilarating about flying along at this speed.

"I feel as if we're flying," Lady Knowe said.

"Yes, exactly!" Ophelia said, smiling at her.

With a pang she realized that she and Lady Knowe could have been friends, true friends, under different circumstances . . . those being circumstances in which the duke hadn't asked Lady Woolhastings to marry him.

Because if she were honest with herself, she probably would have reconsidered his proposal had he asked. Or had he introduced her to the children. The truth of that thumped into her stomach.

If he had asked her to stepmother—no, *mother*—the three children opposite her? With their stubborn, brave faces and the questions they'd chosen . . . even with the possibility of a pet rat looming?

Who could say no to them?

Yet the die was cast. She'd had her chance at this particular happiness, and she'd said no. Hugo had moved on, asked for another woman's hand in marriage, and that was that.

The sleighs were slowing down now, drawing to the side of the riverbank where a long stretch of lawn, withered and brown but likely beautiful in the summer, stretched all the way to a substantial townhouse.

The back of Lady Woolhastings's London estate, presumably.

"Rich as Croesus," Lady Knowe muttered beside her. "Can't imagine why she wants him."

Ophelia could think of so many reasons to *want* Hugo. The strong lines of his jaw and broad shoulders were only the first that came to mind. The way he kissed her; the way he looked at her as if he truly *saw* her; the way he talked about his children. The way he made her feel safe, even to the point of giving up her child to his arms.

His twin chuckled and then broke into open laughter as color crept up into Ophelia's cheeks.

"It's this red hair," Ophelia said, deciding to

laugh as well, because she knew perfectly well she'd turned a deep rose color. "I can't hide anything."

"I'll take it from you that my brother is still reasonably attractive," Lady Knowe said, hooting.

Just in the nick of time—for Ophelia had decided that she had no interest in visiting Lady Woolhastings's house—she heard an enraged scream.

"Your baby's as loud as Joan," Betsy said, her head popping out of the fur blanket. "Guess she's mad."

"I will have to say goodbye," Ophelia said. As the sleigh ride drew to a halt, the two boys' heads appeared too. "Betsy, Leonidas, and Alexander, it has been a true pleasure meeting you."

With a smile and nod for Lady Knowe, she hopped down from the sleigh and took her screaming child away from the duke.

Lady Woolhastings's lips were thin and pressed together. "Children should not appear in public until they can compose themselves." She gave Viola a disparaging glance. "My ears are ringing."

Ophelia decided not to respond. Viola thankfully quieted down once she was in her mother's arms, so Ophelia bobbed a curtsy in Lady Woolhastings's direction and started up the lawn toward her waiting carriage, her back very straight.

She hadn't gone more than a few steps before Lady Woolhastings said, "A casual household, from what I hear, which one might guess from her appearance." Perhaps the lady didn't realize that her aristocratic tones had such carrying power.

It was true: Ophelia had no nanny. And the wind had blown her hair into a tangled cloud around her shoulders.

"The color," Lady Woolhastings added, with a tone of disdain, if not disgust.

"I look forward to seeing you tomorrow!" Lady Knowe called.

Ophelia stopped halfway up the slope, and turned. "Excuse me?"

"The opera?" Lady Knowe was walking up the slope, a devilish smile on her face. "Lady Fernby's house for dinner."

Maddie. She'd forgotten about Maddie, and the need to make all of polite society believe that Maddie was carrying a child.

Ophelia managed to paste a smile on her face. "Of course! Until tomorrow, then." She turned and walked the remainder of the slope even faster.

She and Viola belonged together.

The three children had each other, and, of course, there were all those boys from the duke's first marriage as well. The bond between the second duchess's children would weather a disengaged third duchess.

Lady Woolhastings was more than capable of launching Betsy and Joan on the market. She'd be a perfect duchess: regal, and supremely confident of her own superiority.

Whereas Ophelia climbed into her carriage, cheeks blazing, feeling inadequate in every way. Compared to Lady Woolhastings, she was short and fat. Her child was ill-behaved, and she was a bad mother for taking her into the winter weather. Her hair was scandalous and so was her nanny-free household.

Even more egregious, she was a lustful woman. She wanted the duke—Hugo—in a way that was quite improper for a lady. Her knees trembled, walking away from him. No mother was supposed to feel this way; she was certain of that.

"Mama," Viola said, popping her thumb out of her mouth. "Cake."

"I have rusks in the carriage and they'll have to hold you until we are home," Ophelia assured her.

Thankfully, Bisquet was waiting in the street.

And even better, bundled on the carriage seat were all the lovely things they'd bought at the fair.

Ophelia promptly opened the bag containing a baker's dozen of small mince pies, still holding warmth from the oven and smelling deliciously of raisins and spice.

"I want!" Viola said, learning forward eagerly.

They each ate a mince pie.

When Ophelia thought about the disdainful way that Lady Woolhastings's eyes had rested on her hips, and the way her lip curled when she talked of food bought in an open market . . .

She ate another one.

Chapter Twelve

The Duke of Lindow's townhouse
Mayfair

$\mathcal{H}$ugo arrived home with his sister and children after a lengthy tea at Lady Woolhastings's house—the very best tea from China, but no cake, as children shouldn't eat sweets and Betsy was apparently already plump for her age. When Lady Woolhastings told Betsy not to eat another buttered toast because she must start to think about her figure, Betsy's mouth fell open in surprise.

Unfortunately, the sight of her half-chewed toast disturbed their hostess. She shuddered and said, "Your governess is obviously ineffective,

Lindow. Children should remain in the nursery until they can be counted upon to behave in a refined manner."

Neither Louisa nor he said a word in response, but Lady Woolhastings—Edith—didn't notice a lapse. She engaged in a conversation with Horatius, and as they were leaving, informed Hugo that his heir would be an excellent duke.

"He shows an admirable sense of civic responsibility, paired with just respect for the crown," she said.

Hugo bowed. And left.

The moment the Wilde family walked into their own townhouse, all seven of his offspring dispatched themselves to the upper regions of the house, and he and Louisa turned as one and headed for the brandy decanter in his library.

"You've made a wretched bumble-broth of the courting I sent you to London to do," Louisa said now.

Hugo looked at his twin, and then back at the glass of brandy he was holding. "I didn't ask her to marry me."

"What do you mean, you didn't ask her to marry you?" Louisa asked.

"I didn't." Hugo's voice was wooden, but beneath it was fury and helplessness.

And beneath that was desire for Ophelia, as fierce and hot as a lava flow that buries everything in its path.

"You *didn't* ask Lady Woolhastings to marry you, although she announced that she was your fiancée?" Louisa asked, incredulous.

He finished off his brandy. "Precisely."

His sister dropped into a chair. "She said it so calmly."

"I believe it was a simple statement of fact, as she saw it. To be fair, I have escorted her to several events. She must have decided to accept my hand; therefore, my actual proposal was irrelevant."

Louisa shook her head, dumbfounded. "What is she, one-eighth royal? Purple blood must be enough to poison the brain. You'll have to have a conversation with her, albeit a painful one, and set the record straight."

"I can't."

"Why not?"

"She was right to presume that I would propose. And she shared the information with others; she announced at the Frost Fair that we were betrothed."

"Hugo, you can't marry a woman simply because she decided to take you."

"It doesn't matter, anyway," Hugo said, getting

up and pouring himself more brandy. "I did decide to marry her, although I hadn't got around to a proposal. Ophelia won't have me, Louisa. She said no."

"Of course she said no the first time, you idiot!" his sister snapped.

"After I thought about it, I realized she was right," Hugo said. "I can't offer Ophelia what she already has. She doesn't need money or status. I bring along a sullied name, eight children, and the endless trouble that comes with the dukedom. She has no wish to be a duchess."

"*You* are the only thing that matters," his sister said. She pulled off her hat and threw it on a chair. "*You*, Hugo."

"Ophelia refused my proposal."

"Oh, for—" But she bit off the words. "Where do your children come into this? Did you pay attention as Yvette's three asked their questions to Edith over tea?"

"Louisa, couldn't you have asked what the questions were before allowing them to blurt them out? It didn't help that the older boys were roaring with laughter at the idea of false teeth."

"I had no idea what their questions would be before they asked Lady Astley."

"Lady Woolhastings was greatly offended, particularly, I think, by the question of whether she had false teeth," Hugo said. "I can't blame her for that."

"I expect that Edith is sensitive about her age. She is certainly a woman who is trying to stop the clock. I don't say this to put you off, Hugo, but did you observe her hair, or rather lack of it?"

"What hair?" Hugo was aware of a leaden misery in his stomach that he hadn't felt in years. The moment he saw Ophelia walking beside Lord Melton, he was swamped by a surge of possessiveness so acute he wanted to throttle the man.

"Edith's wig," his sister said. "Your fiancée's wig."

"What about it?" Ophelia's hair had escaped in silken curls that he longed to tame. Why hadn't he remained in her house and refused to leave in the morning? In retrospect, walking away had been the most stupid action of his life.

"Edith shaves her head, one must assume," his sister said. "Her hat was pinned to her wig, and at one point the wind blew it to the side and I caught sight of bare skull."

His stomach churned. "I planned to marry a woman whom I wouldn't bed. You agreed!"

"We were wrong," Louisa said flatly. "Your supposed fiancée may claim not to have a false tooth—though based on her rather startling rage at the question, I would bet a guinea that she has at least one. That's neither here nor there. She isn't the right person to mother your children."

"Because she doesn't like rats? No one likes rats."

"She'll make you bitter," his sister said. "Another woman who doesn't love you, and whom you cannot love? We were idiots to think that was a possibility, Hugo. Can you see her at Lindow Castle? Do you think she'll tolerate the way Fitzy screams at all hours?"

"Peacocks do scream."

"She'll gild his beak and serve him for New Year's dinner," Louisa said. "The stuffed alligator in the drawing room? Dispatched to the attics. The armor in the entry? The dust heap." She hesitated. "Me?"

"She daren't ask you to leave," Hugo stated.

"She won't ask, but I'll leave." Louisa said it easily, without bitterness. "I can't live with the woman, and I do have my own estate, if you recall."

"No!" The word felt as if it was punched from his chest.

He was at a crossroads. One way was . . . *No*. He couldn't even visualize it, which didn't say much for a happy future.

The other way held Ophelia, who had refused him, but looked at him with her eyes brimming with emotion. After Lady Woolhastings's profound rudeness, Phee walked away up the slope, her hair practically on fire with righteous indignation.

Yet his fiancée would likely be surprised to hear that she had insulted Ophelia, since all she offered—to her mind—were sound observations drawn from a thorough grounding in "polite" society.

"What am I going to do?" The words ripped from his chest. "I can't marry her, Louisa."

"True." His sister came over and kissed his cheek. "I was just waiting for you to catch up to the truth. Edith's chance of being a duchess was over when she told Betsy not to eat another piece of buttered toast."

"It's a cock-up," Hugo said.

It helped to acknowledge that truth.

No matter what happened with Ophelia, he wouldn't inflict Edith on his children. That would be as stupid a marriage as his to Yvette.

"Christ," he said bleakly, thrusting his hand through his hair. "I have balls-all luck with women."

"I'd say the opposite," his sister retorted. "Marie was a darling. Ophelia is far more interesting, perhaps because we're all of an age now. Marie never had a chance to become interesting."

"But Ophelia—"

"Don't tell me again that *you* made up your

mind for *her* that she'd be better off without you. You have moments when I think the title has addled your brains, and this is one of them. Your job is to grovel at her feet and beg her for marriage. Do you hear me?"

He rubbed his shoulder absentmindedly because her poking actually hurt. "What if she won't have me?"

"Then you change her mind. You wait until she has a good look at the better parts of you. You invite her to the castle for a visit and you don't consign her to the last carriage, but keep her at your side."

"I didn't—"

"Yes, you did," Louisa said. "You went off in the first carriage with that bald woman to whom you'd supposedly offered your hand, a few days after being refused by Ophelia . . . You could scarcely have been more offensive, Hugo. I'm not the most sensitive of beings, but even I would have trouble countenancing that insult."

"It wasn't meant as an insult."

"Your intent is unimportant. I saw her eyes and you hurt her. Now, you learn from that mistake and don't make it again."

"I'll have to talk to Lady Woolhastings."

"Tomorrow at the dinner party," his sister said briskly. "I can help, Hugo. It would be best if we could convince her that being Duchess of Lindow would diminish her countenance."

"I can't imagine how, given that she decided to be duchess without a proposal," he said.

"Don't underestimate me," she said, grinning at him.

"I never do," he promised. Then he wound an arm around her shoulder. "If Ophelia marries me, you'll stay, won't you?"

"If she wants me."

"I won't take her."

Louisa hooted. "You don't *have* her, you arrogant fool! Now I need a restorative sleep because tomorrow morning I promised we would take the children to the Tower."

"We?" Hugo asked.

His sister just rolled her eyes.

Chapter Thirteen

$\mathcal{A}$s it happened, the Penshallow box at the Theatre Royal was directly across from the Lindow box. From Ophelia's point of view, it couldn't have been more unfortunate.

She and Maddie arrived in plenty of time. Maddie had cheered up and decided to enjoy her role as a woman in a delicate condition; she fanned herself constantly and entertained her friends with whispered commentary about the trials and tribulations of carrying an heir.

As far as Ophelia could see, there was near-universal acceptance of Maddie's condition, but she knew it wasn't enough to merely display Maddie with a cotton roll at her waist.

At the play's intermission, she surveyed the ladies who crowded the Penshallow box, and selected the worst gossip of them all, Lady Arden, and adroitly drew her to the front of the box, exclaiming that she hadn't seen the lady for ages.

Once they were cozily seated, Ophelia confided that she had insisted her darling Maddie keep her condition a secret.

"I understand that for the first months," Lady Arden said, looking faintly skeptical, "but so near to confinement?"

Ophelia flipped open her fan and spoke behind it. "Surely you know that my dearest cousin's marital relations are stormy."

"To say the least!" Lady Arden's eyes brightened.

"Most of London believes that it is due to a lack of passion between herself and her husband," Ophelia whispered, "but the reverse is true. There is too much emotion between them."

"Ah," Lady Arden breathed.

"Her delicate condition makes her so sensitive," Ophelia confided. "I feared for the life of the babe."

"Lord Arden likes to tell stories of a time when I behaved in a most unladylike fashion while carrying our second child," Lady Arden said, apparently won over. "Arden insisted on roast partridge for luncheon over my express command, and I could not *abide* that odor. I vomited on his shoes. Deliberately, he says."

"I have persuaded my dearest cousin that she would do best to retire from society after this evening," Ophelia said. "I certainly don't want her to lose control of her temper as she did at the Hunt Ball, only due to the emotional storms of the first months of one's delicate condition. I trust you will pay us a call? She will be resting comfortably at my house."

"An excellent plan," Lady Arden said, clearly recalling the way glacé cherries had bounced off Maddie's husband's head. "Men simply do not understand how hard it is to manage one's feelings while carrying a child."

"Lord Penshallow will visit daily, of course," Ophelia said.

"Of course," Lady Arden echoed.

Then she asked precisely the question that Ophelia had been hoping to avoid. "Did you see that the Duke of Lindow is in attendance, accompanied by Lady Woolhastings?" She nodded at the box across from them, which was as thronged as their own with visitors. "I must say, that pairing has surprised me."

"Oh?" Ophelia asked. "I know Lady Woolhastings, of course, but she is considerably older than I am." If she felt an errant thrill at that truth, it was only natural. Or so she assured herself.

"Her eldest daughter and I were presented at

St. James in the same drawing room, so yes, she is my mother's age. Just look at them together!"

Ophelia had managed not to glance at the ducal box before the play, or during the first three acts, but now she couldn't stop herself.

Hugo wore a sober coat of dark blue, enlivened by a sumptuous apricot waistcoat. He was standing, since ladies were visiting their box. Two women remained seated: Lady Woolhastings and Lady Knowe, who was wearing a gown *à la française* that made Ophelia feel a flash of pure jealousy.

"I would never wear that gown at her age," Lady Arden said.

"You wouldn't?" Ophelia breathed. "I think the blue is exquisite."

"Oh, that," Lady Arden cried. "Not *that*. Everyone knows that Lady Knowe orders all her fabric from France. No, that sack gown that Lady Woolhastings is wearing." She shivered.

Ophelia deliberately hadn't looked closely at Lady Woolhastings, the woman whom Hugo had chosen to replace her. That sounded bitter, and she had no right to bitterness, given her refusal of his proposal.

She forced herself to look at Lady Woolhastings as if yesterday's trip to the Frost Fair had never happened, as if the lady were a stranger. She was wearing a neat, small wig that covered her head with organized rows of curls, and she had a quite pretty face.

"That's a very close wig. Do you think that she's shaved her head?" Lady Arden whispered. "Ladies of my mother's generation often do so."

Ophelia raised her shoulders in a hopeless shrug. Hugo had adored her hair. She couldn't imagine him in bed with a bald woman.

"But that dress," Lady Arden moaned. "Lady Woolhastings is going to be a duchess, and she is wearing a dress that airs her entire bosom to the theater, at her age?"

The gown in question was fashioned from silk patterned with stripes of red flowers, and horizontal ruffles across the front. Almost none of that cloth appeared above the waist: the lady was flaunting oceans of creamy skin, with only a small ruffle keeping her nipples from open view.

"Of course, His Grace doesn't care about her bosom," Lady Arden said. "He's interested in her maternal side."

Ophelia tormented herself by asking another question. "Her daughters are well married, are they not?"

"Yes, she'll be a good mother to his children," Lady Arden agreed. "Though not even she could marry off his youngest, given the child's illegitimacy."

Ophelia raised a startled eyebrow. Generally, she avoided gossip of this sort, but that was precisely why she was talking to Lady Arden, of course. If *she* believed in Maddie's confinement, then everyone would.

"I hear that the youngest is the spitting image of the Prussian whom his wife ran off with," Lady Arden whispered, her eyes alight. "Golden hair and a Prussian nose."

"I'm certain there is golden hair in the Lindow family line," Ophelia said firmly, avoiding even the faintest tone of indignation. It never did to show emotion in these situations. "I can hardly imagine a two-year-old with a Prussian nose! I expect it is as stubby and round as my own daughter's."

"You are so good-natured," Lady Arden said. "It's a pity that the duke didn't look to *you*, my dear. Everyone knows what an excellent mother you are. What's more, you wouldn't make such an obvious *faux pas*. A duchess oughtn't to expose her bosom to the world."

"I couldn't wear that dress," Ophelia said with a sigh. "No *modiste* could manage to confine my bosom with such a small amount of fabric."

"Perhaps *you* would be able to marry off the

child of the Prussian, but Lady Woolhastings will not, mark my words. She won't be a powerful duchess, if you understand what I mean."

Ophelia did understand.

She herself had married above her station when she became espoused to Peter. Luckily, she'd had a relatively smooth introduction to polite society. Peter was an excellent tutor, and she learned a great deal from observation.

Lady Woolhastings was comfortably used to being among the highest in the land. She was a lady-in-waiting to the queen, for goodness' sake. She didn't care what other women said about the inadvisability of wearing a low-cut gown at her age.

All that didn't mean she was prepared to negotiate the thicket of scandalmongers.

No gossip about Lady Woolhastings had ever circulated. Ophelia, on the other hand, had faced rancorous disapproval from some who had considered her uppish and called her a night mushroom because her father had been a mere esquire. They pronounced the marriage a misalliance, eyed her waist for signs of pregnancy, and felt free to speculate about how she might have tricked Peter into proposing.

In Ophelia's opinion, Lady Woolhastings likely had no idea how vicious "polite" society could be.

Thankfully, the end of intermission was signaled by a loud trumpet, and Lady Arden rose to return to her seat.

"I saw you talking to Lady Arden," Maddie whispered, once the play began again. "Everyone else was happy for me, but I find her a bit frightening. Did you convince her of my child?"

"Oh, yes, of course," Ophelia said.

But she was thinking.

And watching the box across the way from under her lashes.

Chapter Fourteen

$\mathcal{L}$ady Fernby's supper after the opera was a small, informal affair.

"I'm so sorry to have disrupted your numbers," Ophelia said, curtsying to their hostess.

Lady Fernby manifestly didn't mind; she was a jolly woman who rushed to meet them at the door of her drawing room, genuinely thrilled by the news of Maddie's condition.

"This shall be my last public outing," Maddie announced. "But I would be most happy if you paid me a morning call, Lady Fernby. I expect these last months will be endlessly tedious, although I will be lucky enough to have my dear cousin's company."

"Of course, you must go into confinement," Lady Fernby agreed, nodding. "You're already showing, my dear. One does not wish to leave society with an unpleasant memory of one's enlarged waist."

Personally, Ophelia thought this was absurd. If she ever carried a child again—which she would not, obviously—she would do exactly as she wished, no matter her size.

"I agree," Maddie exclaimed, smiling as proudly as if she were truly carrying a child.

"Toward the end of my first confinement, I resembled a whale," Lady Fernby said. "Have you seen images of that sea beast?"

Maddie shuddered.

Who would have thought that her cousin would be such a good actress? Ophelia followed her hostess across the drawing room, silently shoring up her resolve to treat Hugo as she might any other gentleman whom she'd met once or twice.

He rose as they walked toward him, and Ophelia was unable to look away. Wearing pink silk had had a civilizing effect. But now? In sober navy?

Without a glittering, silky veneer, Hugo was all man. He looked massive and powerful, like a man whose ancestors commanded large armies and built a country. A man who could direct a horse with his knees, the better to use his hands to wield a lance or a sword.

Did he say that he was judge for the shire? He looked like a judge.

Not his expression, though.

She shivered, despite herself. He was staring at her, just as he had in the ballroom when she first saw him. And this time, she had no trouble deciphering his emotions. Hugo was burning with need and desire. There was an unmistakable intimacy in his eyes as well.

Beside her, Maddie whispered, "Phee! Did you forget to tell me something?"

They reached the group, and sank into curtsies for a round of greetings.

"We've met," Maddie said, smiling at the Duke of Lindow mischievously. "You remember, don't you, Your Grace? It was at a ball some weeks ago. You were asking me . . ." She tapped her chin with a finger. "Now why can't I remember what it was you were inquiring about?"

"A woman's memory is often affected by carrying a child," Lady Woolhastings commented.

"May I offer my congratulations on your happy state, Lady Penshallow?" Lady Knowe asked.

"Thank you," Maddie said sweetly. "I am very excited. My husband and I have been married for some years without being blessed with fruit of our union, so this is a true joy."

Something flashed through Lady Knowe's eyes

and Ophelia realized that she knew. Somehow this lady knew that Maddie had a roll of cotton tied around her waist. But one glance at her face told Ophelia that Lady Knowe would never engage in cruel gossip or divulge such an important secret.

All the same, she had better inform the world that Maddie was confined to bed for the last weeks of her pregnancy. She could handle morning calls herself, just in case more women had the same intuitive grasp of the truth as the duke's sister.

"It is a pleasure to see you again, Lady Woolhastings," Ophelia said, dropping into another curtsy. "I hope you are well?"

"Absolutely," the lady said.

Hugo didn't say a word, just kissed Ophelia's hand. But there was something about the intensity with which he looked at her . . .

Lady Woolhastings showed no signs of feeling possessive, or even particularly happy about the fact that she and Hugo were attending the supper together. And yet they were betrothed.

Strange. If Hugo were *her* fiancé . . .

"Lady Fernby," Ophelia said, pulling her hand back from Hugo's, as he showed no sign of letting it go. "Don't you have a collection of miniatures? I would dearly love to admire it."

"Of course!" Their hostess bustled over to the

side of the room, where a glass-topped cabinet presumably held her treasures. "Lady Woolhastings, do come look at the darling miniature I have of the queen!"

Hugo watched as Ophelia walked away without a backward glance.

Her features were pleasant, whereas her cousin Maddie had the cheekbones of an aristocrat. Ophelia's figure was round, and her hair—even powdered—unfashionably red.

But . . . she was the only woman for him.

She hadn't looked at him in the theater. She had been seated opposite him, in the front of the Penshallow box, laughing and talking as if he didn't exist. It was appalling to recognize what happened to him during the five acts of the bloody play—none of which he remembered.

He had entered the theater a calm, mature man. The moment Ophelia walked into the box opposite his, arm around her pregnant cousin, not even glancing in his direction . . .

It all changed. *He* changed.

By the intermission, a raging river had taken over his blood. She was his, and he loved her, and if she didn't want him, he would wait forever.

Bloody forever.

The mere idea of Edith, Duchess of Lindow, was anathema.

"Steady," his sister said, low in his ear.

He turned to her, unable to say a word.

She smiled at him with the kind of exuberant, effortless joy with which she had warmed both their lives. "You lucky bastard," she whispered.

"I am, aren't I?"

"You still have to win her."

She walked away, going to look at the miniatures. Hugo stood stock-still, letting the truth sink into his bones.

Deep down, with a ferociousness that came from loving a woman to her core, he believed that Phee could learn to love him—and that a life with love was better than the most exquisite house in all London.

He already loved her, because that was simply the way it was for him.

In fact, he had a firm belief that it was better to be loved in a messy, huge castle than be unloved in the prettiest house in the world.

He thought he was doing a pretty good job of appearing unemotional . . . until he met the dancing eyes of Ophelia's cousin, Maddie Penshallow.

"Good evening," she said. "I collect that you have come to a conclusion, Your Grace."

"I have."

"If you don't mind the impertinence, I agree

with your sister; you are a very lucky man." Without waiting for an answer, she turned in the general direction of the rest of the guests. "Oh, no," she cried. "'Tis the fault of the child I carry, but I forgot my handkerchief in my pelisse. Ophelia, dearest, won't you fetch it for me?"

"I can send a—" Lady Fernby began.

"Never!" Maddie cut her off with a shudder. "I cannot allow a stranger to touch such an intimate possession. Please forgive me, my lady."

"I completely understand," Hugo's sister chimed in. "Duke, please accompany Lady Astley to the entry. She may lose her way."

She may lose her way?

Hugo didn't snort, but it was a near thing.

After the way Ophelia managed not to see him at the theater, he would have expected her to refuse, but instead she gave him a small smile. "I would be most grateful for your company, Your Grace."

"It isn't very far," Lady Fernby said, clearly uncertain whether the structure of her house, or possibly her household, was being insulted. "This drawing room is in the back of the house, but . . ."

"I have a terrible sense of direction," Ophelia said. "His Grace and I shall return with your handkerchief in a minute or two, Maddie."

As they walked toward the door, Hugo heard Maddie ask Lady Woolhastings if she'd met his "horde of children."

Before Lady Woolhastings could respond, she added in a horror-laden voice, "I understand there are ten or eleven of them."

"Lady Penshallow is your cousin, Phee," Hugo said, once they left the chamber. "It seems she wants you to be a duchess. In fact, it could be that my sister and your cousin will unite to warn off Lady Woolhastings."

Ophelia stopped short. "What?" She looked stupefied.

"Did you mind?" Hugo asked, catching her hands in his. "You refused me, after all."

"Of course, I mind!" she said tartly. "No lady likes to think that she can be replaced in a gentleman's affections within a matter of hours." She gave him a wry look. "It is a blow to one's self-esteem."

Ophelia's red hair gleamed through the light powder she wore. She was perfect, from her deep lower lip to her pointed chin. "Do you know what I realized at the Frost Fair?" Hugo asked. "I remembered you as so beautiful that I thought perhaps I had imagined it; you couldn't have been as lovely as I believed. But you were."

She looked up at him, utter shock on her face.

"I'm not beautiful! I'm nice enough looking. Maddie is beautiful."

Hugo shook his head. They were standing in a corridor that led to the front of the house. They couldn't stay here; the butler would appear in a moment with refreshments.

He pushed open the door directly across the corridor and discovered a small morning room, probably Lady Fernby's private refuge, given the basket of knitting and the gossip sheets lying to the side of a comfortable chair.

"My lady?" he said, walking inside and holding the door open.

Ophelia bit her lip.

He smiled at her, letting the deep joy he felt show on his face. His mind was racing. Kisses wouldn't be enough to convince Ophelia to marry him. He had to woo her. Court her, the way a future duchess deserved.

But on the other hand, he . . .

She walked inside and turned about to face him. To him, she was already a duchess: utterly composed even in moments of deep impropriety, as now.

"May I kiss you?" Hugo asked, shutting the door and putting on the latch as well.

She looked rather amused. "That wouldn't be a good idea," she observed. "You accompanied another woman to this supper, Hugo. One whom you have asked to marry you."

At least she was calling him Hugo.

"I can't marry Lady Woolhastings," he said flatly. "And by the way, I never proposed to her; she seems to have misunderstood. I considered it, and then I saw you in the theater and realized that if I can't have you, I'd rather be alone."

A soundless breath came from her mouth. "Truly?"

He nodded, his throat tight. "Truly."

"But I'm not beautiful, not that kind of beauty, the kind that would inspire a man to—to turn down marriage if he can't have me. I'm . . . I'm ordinary."

"You are not at all ordinary." He said it with the confidence of a man who had always trusted his own opinion above that of others. "I'm not the only one to think so, but in any case, I'm not in love with your beauty alone. My sister told me of your first marriage. She rarely comes to London, but she has a vast number of correspondents."

"I see," Ophelia said. She folded her hands before her. She was wearing a gown that he recognized, thanks to Louisa, as being *à la française*. His sister wore monstrous petticoats this evening, with a silk gown embroidered with birds of paradise.

Hugo found he vastly preferred a simple rose stripe, albeit decorated with silver-edged ruffles.

"Sir Peter was lucky enough to be introduced to you during your first foray into society," he said now. "He was smart enough to know what he had in front of him, and he snatched you up before another gentleman had a chance."

She shook her head. "It wasn't like that. My parents knew his parents . . ."

"Your parents' only mistake was that they underestimated your charms," Hugo said deliberately. "Sir Peter saw *you*, an intelligent, gorgeous, and sensual woman, and he knew he'd found gold. I wouldn't be surprised if he proposed to you during your second dance."

She blinked. "Over supper following our second dance."

"Had he waited until the next day, he wouldn't have been able to afford you," Hugo said. "Polite society is a ruthless marketplace. I saw you during your first entry into society after widowhood. I knew that I had no time, so I followed you into a snowstorm. Why do you suppose that was?"

A smile was easing the corners of her lips. "Could we simply agree that you and Peter were slightly mad, and leave it at that?"

He shook his head. "I don't want to win you under false pretenses. I think you could likely have any bachelor of your choice in all London, Phee."

She was laughing now. "Including the twenty-year-olds, just leaving Oxford?"

"Those too." He meant it. "London is full of women who are brittle, angry, or—like my second wife—dissatisfied. You look like a person who knows how to be happy."

"I'm no happier than the next person," she said, looking startled.

He raised an eyebrow. "Were you madly in love with Sir Peter?"

"That is private."

"Yet you never succumbed to bitterness or ennui," he said, ignoring her unhelpful response. "You built a life with him, a man whom you'd known for the space of two dances. He enjoyed London, so you accompanied him here."

"That is common for married couples," she pointed out.

He shook his head. "I've been in an unhappy marriage. My wife was unwilling to be in the country for a day more than she had to, although my responsibilities did not allow me to always live in the city. She returned to London without me."

"If you would like to marry me because I would put your desires ahead of my own," Ophelia said, "I think you should return to your former theme."

"I will put your desires above my own. You love dancing; if you wish it, we can engage a dancing master to bring me up to snuff. What I am saying is that if I was lucky enough to win your hand, you would be my partner, Phee. I know that Sir Peter would agree with me that a true marital partnership is a gift from God."

"Partnership suggests friendship," she said. "You declined to be my friend."

"I wasn't clear," he said, frowning. "I want to be so much more than merely a friend. You would be my closest friend, but also my lover. The person I wish to walk beside for the whole of my life."

"Hmm," she said. Her eyes were shining, and Hugo felt a flash of hopefulness. "Let's go back to the question of whether I am more beautiful than Maddie, which is plain absurdity."

He walked closer to her, unable to resist her smile. "To me, you have the perfect nose." He kissed it. "I adore your chin." He kissed it.

"Now I know you've lost your mind!" But she didn't move away.

"Your lips are exquisite," he whispered, and dropped a kiss on them. "Your eyes are like deep, like . . . like pools of hot chocolate."

She started giggling again.

"I'm not a poet," Hugo said. "All I can say is that I am putting my life, my title, my family at your feet, Phee." He caught her hands in his. "Everything that I am. And fair warning, I shall keep trying to convince you. Last time I saw you, you were adamant that you would have nothing to do with me. But now . . . you allowed me to escort you on this ridiculous errand. You walked into this room with me."

He held his breath, hoping.

"I don't like seeing you with another woman," Ophelia confessed, a delicate wash of pink rising in her cheeks. "I didn't like it at the Frost Fair either."

"I won't marry the lady." He stated it calmly. "There will never be another woman, if you won't have me."

"You had good reasons for courting her, I'm sure."

"Your refusal was not a good enough reason," Hugo said. "Lady Woolhastings doesn't deserve a man who is more than half in love with someone else."

"Perhaps *you* deserve more as well," Ophelia suggested. She took a step toward him. Now they were close enough so that the hem of her skirt brushed his shoe, and he caught a whiff of sweet lemon from her hair.

"I love that you don't wear a wig," he said. "Damn it, you make me feel as unbalanced as a lad of fifteen."

Watching her eyes carefully, he took the last step toward her and his arms closed around her. "If you marry me, you'll lose a part of your freedom," he said, his voice roughening. "The life of a duchess is not easy, although I will do everything in my power to provide you as much privacy as I am able. I own a large castle and the grounds are protected from the public. We can do as we wish there."

Ophelia met his eyes and then cupped his face in her hands, came up on her toes, and brushed his lips with hers. "I think I might give up my freedom for you. What would I miss?"

"Had I met you while I was married to Yvette and you were married to Sir Peter, I would have said freedom was the right to love you, body and soul. Beautiful, wanton body and proper, delightful soul," he clarified.

"I *may* choose to use my minutes learning how to love you." Her eyes twinkled. "Or I may not."

Her hands fell away and she stepped back. "Your Grace, we must return to the drawing room or our absence will be marked."

Blood was running hot in Hugo's veins. He had a cockstand that was definitely not hidden by his cutaway waistcoat, and probably wasn't going anywhere as long as Ophelia was within an arm's length.

She raised a finger. "We cannot embarrass Lady Woolhastings. You must extract yourself from your obligations, no matter how ephemeral, before you pay me so much as a morning call."

A smile burst over his face, together with a wild surge of lust. "After we marry, we shall retire to my castle and live there for a month—six months!—no society, just the two of us."

She raised an eyebrow. "And a nursery full of children?" But she looked pleased. "I shall take your request into consideration."

"May I kiss you, please, Phee?"

She shook her head. "I would not kiss a man who is nominally another woman's."

A duke always realizes the limits of his power. Hugo bowed and kissed his lady's gloved hand. His heart sang.

Chapter Fifteen

When had Ophelia decided to marry Hugo? What was the precise moment when she decided to take on eight children, a duchy, and—most importantly—a man who tempted her nearly to madness?

A man who wanted to live for the next six months in a castle in Cheshire?

The duke paced along the corridor at her shoulder, seeming as quiet and tame as a house cat. But she could feel the wild energy coursing through him. The air she breathed felt like new wine.

Hugo knew what a marriage based on that excitement was like; she didn't. But now she had a glimpse of it, a sense of it, and it was intoxicating.

Returning to the drawing room, she saw Lady

Knowe seated with Maddie and Lady Woolhastings, telling them such an engaging story that they were both leaning toward her. Lady Fernby passed them on her way to the kitchen to address a small problem.

No one paid attention as Ophelia slipped into the seat beside Maddie; her cousin just squeezed her hand and said, breathlessly, to Lady Knowe, "Then what happened?"

"They were playing at pirates," she said now. "Horatius, bless that child, has grown up to be as pompous as a sixty-year-old barrister, but as a boy he could never resist an eye patch. Now he's eighteen and far too mature to play a pirate."

Hugo seated himself beside his sister, ignoring the empty seat next to Lady Woolhastings.

Lady Woolhastings paid him no attention. Her eyes were round. "You are describing extraordinary behavior," she said, obviously choosing her words carefully.

"Not for those varmints," Lady Knowe said cheerfully. "I often have to send them to bed with only bread and butter for supper. The nursemaids keep honey in the nursery and I pretend not to notice. Am I right, dear Edith, in thinking that your two children are both female?"

Lady Woolhastings nodded.

"Boys—particularly Wildes—are a completely

different breed," Lady Knowe said. "Mothering them is a Sisyphean task. Some days I lurch from crisis to crisis."

Maddie was patting her stomach as if there truly were a child there. "Oh! I hope I am carrying a boy," she cried. "I should love to play pirates! Wouldn't you, Lady Woolhastings?"

Ophelia squeezed her hand again. Maddie's irrepressible good spirits would be such a gift to the child she didn't carry, but who would be her own.

"No, I certainly would not," the lady stated, "but I have no objection to children playing whatever games they wish in the nursery. Most nurseries are on the third floor precisely so that noise does not disturb the household."

Lady Knowe wasn't finished. "After they burned down the vicarage—an accident, I assure you, and thank goodness, no one was hurt—the vicar asked me, most earnestly, if I thought they should be exercised."

"*Exercised?*" Hugo repeated.

Ophelia glanced at him and had to look away in order to stop herself from laughing. The duke's eyes were dancing.

"Oh, whatever it is you do to evil spirits," Lady Knowe said, waving her hand.

"Exorcised. He thought they were possessed?"

Lady Woolhastings said. She looked perturbed. "I, for one, would not welcome such an impudent suggestion from a cleric."

"A metaphor, I assure you," Lady Knowe said. "Help me, Duke. Defend your children. Leonidas, for example, isn't nearly as naughty as the older boys were."

"I hate to mention it, but dead chickens come to mind when one thinks of Leonidas," her brother said cheerfully.

"That is true," Lady Knowe acknowledged.

"Isn't he merely six years of age? What did he do to the chickens?" Maddie gasped.

Apparently chicken carcasses were occasionally taken from the kitchen and made their way under the covers of dislikable guests staying at the castle, thanks to little Leonidas, who would tuck them carefully under the coverlets.

"It isn't the smell that's vile," Lady Knowe said judiciously, "as much as the feathers. They paint them red, you see, so when someone puts their feet down in the bed, they encounter a disagreeably sticky, wet object. When they remove their feet, they appear to be covered with blood. Shrieking invariably ensues."

Maddie winced.

"Naughty," Lady Woolhastings stated.

"I believe you know the Bishop of Halmarken, Lady Woolhastings?" Lady Knowe asked.

The lady's eyes narrowed. "These children behaved so disgracefully toward a man of God?" For the first time, she seemed genuinely affronted. "I should send them to bed without any supper at all."

"They also played the dead-chicken trick on a scion of the Swedish royal family," Hugo said. "I do not blame Leonidas; after all, he's only six years old. My older sons planned the trick, even if Leo was dispatched to the royal bed with the infamous chicken."

"I know what I'd do," Maddie exclaimed. She was obviously enjoying herself immensely. "I'd make those boys sleep with a dead chicken at their feet for a whole night. Perhaps a week."

Lady Knowe shook her head, her eyes twinkling. "Dearest, think of the nursemaids. They are the most valuable members of a household, as you shall soon learn. They won't tolerate odor, let alone stray feathers, and one can hardly blame them." She lowered her voice. "They have much to put up with, as it is. I am loath to admit it, but His Grace's children have been *very* slow to learn to use the privy."

"Well, *that* I will not put up with," Maddie said,

nodding her head as if she had the faintest idea how to train a child.

"Wetting the bed," Lady Knowe said with a melodramatic groan. "Day and night. During naps until the age of five. We have three more years of it ahead, given that little Joan is scarcely two." She heaved a lugubrious sigh. "But, of course, they are darling children. Edith met them yesterday and I'm certain she agreed with me."

"Indeed," the lady stated.

"I brought all eight of them to London. If you don't mind plain speaking, they are tired of my oversight. I am always having to punish them for this or that."

"The boys are at Eton," Lady Woolhastings pointed out.

"When they *are* at Eton. They're constantly being sent down for some prank. I can't decide whether Alaric or Parth is the naughtier, but on balance, I think Parth wins. We had to pay the barkeeper after that most unfortunate episode with his daughter."

"One of your sons cavorted with a barmaid?" Lady Woolhastings said, turning to Hugo. Her brow was furrowed.

"'Cavorted' is a strong word," he said.

It was clear to Ophelia that Hugo knew nothing of the barmaid, and Parth didn't either. In short, Lady Knowe had begun to embroider the truth in an elaborate effort to alarm Lady Woolhastings.

"I never share such trifles with the duke," Lady Knowe said, leaning over to pat Lady Woolhastings on the knee. "A good half of each day is spent soothing the anguished spirits of those who have fallen victim to His Grace's children. I cannot wait until he takes a third duchess. I mean to retire to an estate I have in Kent and try to recover my lost youth!"

For the first time, Lady Woolhastings looked appalled. Ophelia saw her assessing Lady Knowe's wrinkles.

"They have turned my hair white," Hugo said with a shrug.

Ophelia rolled her eyes. She'd seen Hugo's hair at close range. Perhaps there was a little silver over the ears, but only enough to make him look distinguished.

Lady Knowe smiled sympathetically at her brother. "As we have both learned, when one has children, particularly so *many* children, one must give up on life's vanities."

"I did not neglect myself while raising my daughters," Lady Woolhastings stated.

"I am hoping that I carry a boy for more than one reason," Maddie chimed in. "Nothing is crueler than the contrast between the unlined skin of a young girl in the first blossom of youth and the mother who chaperones her." She clasped her (cotton-filled) belly. "If I carry a daughter, I only hope I shall face the disparity with good grace! Humiliation is too strong a word."

"The Wilde girls are, of course, extraordinarily beautiful," Lady Knowe said innocently. "As you yourself noted yesterday, Lady Woolhastings, Betsy will certainly grow up to be a beauty, and she's nothing compared to Joan. With her golden hair and perfect features, she will cast everyone in the shade when she debuts."

Lady Woolhastings had the look of a woman who has made an important decision. She rose to her feet. Hugo stood, and Maddie jumped up, which caused her "belly" to jiggle alarmingly.

"I am feeling unwell," the lady announced.

"If you'll forgive me, you *do* look rather sallow," Maddie said. "I well remember when your daughter and I attended our first balls together, my mother often retired to bed exhausted."

"At your age, dear lady, it is always best to retire early with a restorative," Lady Knowe said sympathetically. "My own dear mother—"

Lady Woolhastings bridled. "I am not the age of *your* mother!"

"I trust you will feel much improved on the

morrow, Lady Woolhastings," Ophelia said, intervening.

After a round of courtesies, Hugo led his visibly irritated fiancée toward the door in search of their hostess.

Lady Knowe, Maddie, and Ophelia said nothing until Lady Woolhastings and the duke had left the room.

Then Lady Knowe said, with a cackle of laughter, "I thought all the naughtiness would be effectual, but you found the perfect weapon, Lady Penshallow!"

"Please, call me Maddie," she said, reaching out and taking Lady Knowe's hand. "I have a feeling that we might become much better acquainted in the near future. Phee is my dearest relative and I cannot bear to lose her to the wilds of Cheshire."

Ophelia felt herself turning pink. "I believe this conversation is uncalled for," she said. "Nothing . . . That is . . ."

"Surely my brother has thrown himself on his knees and declared his love? Because he does, you know." Lady Knowe regarded Ophelia with bright eyes. "He's in love. Simply dizzy with it."

"I don't know why," Ophelia said, glancing at the door, but their hostess had not reappeared, and neither had the duke. Presumably he was escorting Lady Woolhastings to her house.

"I'll leave the whys up to him," Lady Knowe said. "If I know my brother, he'll be able to convince you of his reasoning. All I can say is that I haven't seen him so happy since Marie died. He made a mistake with Yvette, but he had the best of intentions."

"He was trying to find a mother for his children," Maddie said, nodding. "I thought that was why he asked about Phee. But then it turned out he didn't even know that Phee is an excellent mother. He didn't know who she was at all."

"He's not in love with her for *that*," Lady Knowe said. "Mothering is the least of it. I will warn you, my dear, that my brother seems to be extraordinarily potent. Yvette complained endlessly and swore he wasn't allowed to come near her without a French letter, but to no avail."

Ophelia discovered that she didn't want to hear anything more about Yvette. Or Hugo's beloved first wife either.

Lady Knowe apparently read her expression, because she turned to Maddie without taking a breath. "So, tell me, when will your child be born?" she asked, gesturing toward Maddie's pillow.

She turned a little pink. "Three months. Or so." She cleared her throat.

"Maddie will stay with me until the child arrives," Ophelia said, giving Lady Knowe a look that told her the subject was closed.

Lady Knowe broke out laughing. "In case I didn't think that you had the gumption to be a duchess, the glance you just gave me would have proved me wrong."

Ophelia felt herself turning pink again. But there was one question she had: "Will you really be leaving the castle and moving to Kent?"

"I would not wish to be in my brother's household if it would cause the least disquiet in his marriage. It can be difficult if two women share domestic duties."

"Oh, please," Ophelia said, putting her cards on the table. "I adore my daughter. I am growing . . . fond of the duke. But I think about walking into the castle and eight children . . ." She stopped hopelessly.

"You will grow to love them, because they are vastly lovable," Lady Knowe said, smiling. "Even when they are naughty."

"I was charmed by them yesterday," Ophelia said. She turned to Maddie. "The three youngest had made up some questions to determine who would be a good mother. Unfortunately, I failed all three."

Maddie blinked. "I can't imagine a better mother than you!"

"She doesn't have any false teeth, she would like another baby, and she doesn't care for the idea of a pet rat," Lady Knowe said. "Flat failure on all counts and yet, you'll be happy to know that the nursery was unanimous in their declaration that Hugo should choose you. Horatius announced their decision at dinner last night."

Ophelia could feel herself turning pink. "That was very kind of them, given that Betsy informed me that there are no free beds in the nursery."

"I have been informed that the nursery thinks a white rat would make a perfect wedding gift," Lady Knowe said.

"I would be very grateful if you would consider making your home with us," Ophelia said to her, ignoring the prospect of a pet rodent. She hadn't yet accepted the duke's proposal, but here she was, making domestic arrangements. "I have no wish to manage a castle by myself or, truly, to manage a castle at all."

Lady Knowe's eyes searched her face.

"Far more importantly, as I see it, you *are* the children's mother," Ophelia said. "To rip you away from them would be terrible. I cannot imagine moving away from my daughter, Viola. Nor would she be happy without me."

"I will admit that I find the idea of leaving them painful."

"You were never planning to leave," Maddie said. "You just told Lady Woolhastings as much to frighten her off."

"No," Lady Knowe said. "If I felt that my brother's happiness was hanging in the balance, I would leave. They are not my children, after all."

"Ah, but they *are* your children," Ophelia said, reaching out and touching her knee. "I would as soon come between a mother and her children as—" Her mind boggled.

"Right," Lady Knowe said, her eyes looking suspiciously bright. "Our hostess seems to have gone missing. Shall we have some champagne to celebrate my brother's extraordinarily good luck?"

She looked toward the door, nodded, and a footman sprang into action. A few minutes later they were holding glasses of champagne.

"Normally I do not hold with a future mother imbibing of the grape," Lady Knowe said to Maddie. "But I feel sure it would not be harmful to your child."

"No, indeed," Maddie said, taking her champagne. "We've sent Ophelia's former nanny over there to make sure that my husband's mistress— *one* of my husband's several mistresses—doesn't engage in unhealthy habits."

"Excellent forethought," Lady Knowe said,

accepting without a flicker of an eyelash the truth about Maddie's child.

"If male, that child will be Lord Penshallow's heir," Ophelia said, just to make sure that Lady Knowe knew the consequences of mentioning the child's parentage to anyone. But she had the same feeling that Maddie obviously had: One could trust Lady Knowe with one's greatest secret.

Ophelia didn't often drink wine, other than to sip it now and then. But at the moment, more than a sip was called for. She had an exhilarating feeling that her life was changing.

Surely that called for a toast.

Chapter Sixteen

$\mathcal{W}$hen the Duke of Lindow finally returned from escorting his former almost-betrothed to her house—having been told in no uncertain terms that the lady in question declined any further consideration of matrimony—he found the entire house party quite tipsy.

A small supper had been served, after which the ladies had retired to a sitting room and continued to imbibe champagne.

"Three bottles," Lady Fernby said cheerfully. "One each."

His future wife looked at Hugo with huge brown eyes and said, "Maddie went home in my carriage, but I waited for you. I'm inclined to marry you."

"I'm very happy to hear that," he said.

He couldn't stop himself from smiling. First, Lady Woolhastings had declared that he was to marry her, and now Ophelia was doing the same. Women seemed to be taking marital matters into their own hands these days.

"We've been celebrating your . . . your fourth duchess, isn't it?" Lady Fernby asked, her words slurring into each other.

"*Third*, and last," he corrected.

"My last duchess," Ophelia said dreamily. "It sounds like a poem. I'm happy to be your last duchess, and in return, you will be my first and last duke."

Hugo's heart was thumping hard. His sister—darling, wonderful Louisa—had rid him of Lady Woolhastings. And then, it seemed, she had offered toasts until she succumbed, because when he looked about for her, he found Louisa reclining serenely on a sofa, looking as prim as if she were napping in her own bedchamber.

"She was up most of the night with Alexander, who was feverish," Ophelia said. Her tone was defensive.

Hugo dropped a kiss on her head because . . . she was defending his family. To him.

"I'm afraid that Alexander caught a chill at the fair," he said. "How is Viola?"

"Very well," Ophelia said. "We're lucky, as she's never been ill."

"That will change," Hugo said cheerfully. "When one child gets sick in the nursery, they all follow suit. All of them will likely come down with fevers tonight. Was my sister drinking champagne from that tankard?" he asked, nodding toward an empty cup on the table. "No wonder she went to sleep."

"She said that champagne tastes better from a pedestrian vessel," Ophelia said. "That's a quote. Your sister has a fascinating way of expressing herself."

"Ah."

Hugo turned to say goodbye to Lady Fernby, only to discover that she too was now peacefully slumbering.

After that, he gave the butler a guinea to ensure that Louisa got home safely. "I shall escort Lady Astley to her house," he said.

"I will send the lady home in Lady Fernby's best carriage," the man promised. "Accompanied by a groom, it hardly needs to be said."

"Best send two," Hugo advised. "My sister is as tall as I am, and unless she is completely alert, one groom will find it difficult to steer her into the house."

"Excellent," Ophelia cried, jumping from her chair. "I don't know why everyone is asleep. I don't feel tired in the least."

They no sooner entered the carriage than Ophelia launched herself at him and kissed him, more clumsily than expertly, but with more than enough passion to make up for it. The feeling when her tongue met his made Hugo start shaking all over.

Perhaps it was age, he thought dimly.

Perhaps he felt things more fiercely, because time had a different meaning for him now. He knew that loved ones could die. He knew that time was finite. Perhaps that was what made a simple kiss feel like a conflagration, like no kiss he'd ever shared before.

Even with Marie.

For her part, Ophelia wrapped her arms more and more tightly around his neck, pausing only to murmur husky words that he couldn't quite make out. His body was tight, blood thumping through his loins, head fogged by the scent and the taste of her.

By the time the carriage shuddered to a halt, his breath had become a harsh noise in his ears, his heart pounding in his chest. He had his hands inside her cloak now, running over her breasts.

"I will marry you," Ophelia said to him, as

Hugo pulled his shaking hands from her cloak and tried to straighten her hair. It was hopelessly disordered, hairpins scattered all over the carriage floor.

"Thank you," he said, shocked to hear how guttural his voice had become.

He could not take her inside and seduce her, in the drawing room, in the corridor, in the butler's pantry: anywhere with a roof.

It wouldn't be gentlemanly. Not right.

She'd had too much champagne. A whole bottle, if Lady Fernby was correct.

"You are not going to feel well tomorrow," he said, running a finger down her perfectly trim little nose. "God, we're going to have beautiful children. *If* you want children," he added hastily.

"Do you want more children?"

He shook his head. "Not in the general way, but with you? Hell, Ophelia, I would love to have a child with you. As long as your first birth wasn't difficult?"

"Extremely easy," she said, dimpling at him. "Well, Duke, I suggest we go to my bedchamber and try to make a baby. Your sister assured me that I would be carrying within the week, so that means a special license."

Hugo's eyes widened. "You discussed children— having children with me—with Louisa?"

"She brought up the subject and I thought it was a good idea." She blinked at him. "Not a good idea?"

He shook his head. And then nodded. "You can discuss whatever you wish with Louisa."

"*Louisa,*" Ophelia said. "I like her name. She has promised to stay with us. Yvette's children are really hers, you know."

"I do know," he said. "Marie's are shared with her as well. Marie would never have wanted to leave them, but I am certain she approves of how Louisa has mothered them."

"I suspect my Viola will be won over immediately," Ophelia said. "By you as well. She's never had a man in her life, although she's fond of our butler. So, will you please come into the house with me, Your Grace?" A sensual little smile played around her mouth.

"I can't."

Her brows drew together. "Because of Lady Woolhastings? I was hoping . . ."

"Did you think that I was gone for two hours because she was clarifying her disinclination to marry me? She cleared that matter up in the first five minutes. After that we shared a carriage in silence for forty-five minutes, as there was a traffic snarl around Shepherd Market. It took me equally as long to return."

"I'm sorry," Ophelia said, not looking in the least sorry. "But truly, Hugo, you would have been very unhappy with her. She was not interested in being a mother."

"I thought she would be helpful with the girls' debuts," Hugo said, and shook his head. "I was wrong, precisely the kind of mistake I made when I chose Yvette."

Ophelia leaned forward and brushed her mouth over his. "Come inside."

"I can't, because you've had too much champagne," he said. Or at least he said most of that before they started kissing again and he lost track of words.

"Champagne?" she said sometime later.

Dimly, Hugo knew that a groom had opened the carriage door and closed it immediately.

"I haven't had too much champagne!" She cupped her hands around his face and grinned at him. "I'm not used to drinking wine."

"That's precisely why I cannot take advantage of you," he said apologetically. "Because it *would* be taking advantage of you, Phee, and I won't do it."

She gave him a wicked grin, leaned forward, and ran her tongue along the seam of his mouth. "I had a glass of champagne before supper."

"Yes, well—"

"And a glass of champagne with berry tart. But to be completely frank, Your Grace, your sister imbibed the better part of two bottles, and Lady Fernby polished off the third."

Hugo searched her eyes and wondered why he hadn't seen it immediately. Of course she wasn't tipsy. Her clear eyes were sparkling with laughter and desire.

"Thank God," he breathed. He pulled her into his arms and slammed his mouth down on hers.

She opened her mouth with a silent laugh that went straight from her chest to his.

After that, it was a matter of lifting Phee from the carriage and greeting the butler, Fiddle, at which point Ophelia told him that the duke would spend the night since it was late to return to his townhouse and he hadn't a carriage.

She added matter-of-factly that she'd accepted His Grace's proposal of marriage, and Hugo found the words so moving that he waited until her butler turned away and caught her in a sudden kiss. "I love you," he said fiercely, in a low voice meant for her ears only.

But when he followed the butler up the stairs, he thought that Fiddle's smile indicated that he'd overheard.

Hugo didn't mind.

"Ophelia will wish to bring her household with

her," he told the butler, on being shown into the same elegant bedchamber as last time.

"I have no doubt," Fiddle said, bowing.

"No servants will be dismissed," Hugo said, holding out his hand.

The butler shook it. "Thank you, Your Grace. I appreciate that, and so will the household."

"You've taken care of her at a time when others might have taken advantage. I can never thank any of you enough."

"We are all very fond of Lady Astley."

"As am I," Hugo said frankly.

The butler smiled.

Chapter Seventeen

$\mathcal{H}$ugo might have thought Ophelia was tipsy, but in fact she knew exactly what she was doing, and the rightness of it hummed through her veins as she bathed and allowed her maid to put her in a nightgown.

A chaste white nightgown, because that's all she had, but the very next day she meant to sally forth and order something marvelous made of silk and lace for her wedding night, whenever that occurred.

First things first.

The deep-down connection she shared with Hugo? The way she no sooner glanced at him than she felt a flutter of desire?

That trumped everything.

When she walked into his room, it was lit just

enough to create a cozy nest. Perhaps an eagle's nest, because propped on piles of snowy white pillows was a man with piercing eyes and a powerful body who—

Wanted her.

Loved her, according to his sister.

Was *in love* with her.

Was Peter ever in love with her?

The answer was obvious. They had never walked toward each other, knowing that their hearts were beating as fast as physically possible. Knowing that desire was a thrum in the blood and the legs and the head.

Of course, Hugo had climbed from the bed to greet her, his manners bred in the bone from generations of noblemen and their nannies. She paused and let him come to her. Ophelia had never felt more than pretty: Usually she thought of her face as comely, an old-fashioned word that seemed appropriate.

But under his gaze, she felt *beautiful*.

Hugo reached out and wound his arms around her, pulled her close, and put his cheek against the top of her head.

"I'm short," she said, breathing the words into his chest. He smelled like the soap she bought for guests. It made her happy, as if she owned a small part of him. As if she had changed him.

"Just the right size," he replied. She could tell by the roughness in his voice that he meant it.

She ended up smiling against his skin like an idiot, and then because there it was—smooth and warm, roughened with hair—she started to kiss his chest, brushing her lips across ridges of muscle, kissing his flat nipple and then kissing it again, harder, when she felt the effect ripple through his body.

Like the wind in a wheat field, she thought dimly, and lost track of the thought because he had scooped her up in his arms and was carrying her to the bed.

He put her down gently on her back and lowered himself on her tentatively, but Ophelia had always been the sort of person who made up her mind and then threw herself into life with abandon. She wrapped her legs around his waist in an instinctive movement that would have likely given Peter a heart attack. Hugo groaned aloud, and the sound went down her spine.

After that, she promised herself not to let Peter have even a corner of her mind, at least not when she was in bed with Hugo.

"Phee," Hugo said, lowering his head to hers. He licked into her mouth with an impatient ownership that made her shiver even more. His kiss was possessive, as possessive as the gesture of winding her legs around his hips.

"You're mine," she told him later, when her lips were plump and tingling from an endless kiss that broke only for gasps of air that sounded like groans.

"Always," Hugo said. He moved to her side and cupped her face in his large hands. "I am always yours, Phee. To death and beyond."

They had *that* together: that knowledge that life is meant to be savored, and that time is limited.

"We have a choice in every moment of life," he said, his voice brushing her body. "I choose to spend every possible one of them with you, Phee."

"Are we never leaving this bed, then?"

He kissed her again, so fiercely that her legs felt boneless. "No," he said later, enough later that her nightgown had been tossed to the floor. He raised his head from her breast to say it.

"Please don't stop," she begged.

He glinted at her and then put his mouth over her nipple. "This?"

She arched toward him. "More."

He pursed his lips. "More?"

Words were coming from Ophelia's mouth, but they didn't answer the question. It was as if her lips refused to be silent, but her brain couldn't spare the time to shape an opinion. One of Hugo's hands made its way down her belly and slipped between her legs.

"God, you're so wet," he whispered, his voice cracking.

She wound her hands into his hair and did the one thing that Ophelia Astley had never done in her life: She commanded.

"Now, Hugo," she said. "Now, damn it."

The duke who never took direction from anyone—and that had included his young wife Marie—cracked a smile and braced himself over her. "Sure?"

"Yes." Ophelia drew her knees up and made herself vulnerable in a way that she never could have imagined: body and soul. Hugo's kisses ravished a small, unnourished part of her soul that she had never suspected existed.

And yet there it was.

Making itself known with trembling intensity and a stream of inarticulate words, some of them profane.

Hugo braced himself and thrust forward, and her body melted in a confusion of grateful pleasure that rushed through her like rivers of fire. She closed her eyes and let her hands run down his muscled back all the way to his arse, loving the way that he trembled under her fingers.

She didn't even realize that she was babbling until Hugo laughed and said, "I never would have imagined you were so vocal. And so obscene."

She blinked at him, hurt burning down her spine as fiercely as desire had, and so she *saw* the moment that he realized what he'd just said and added, "No. Oh, shite, *no*. I didn't mean it that way."

"Um," Ophelia said, suddenly incredibly aware of the fact that her legs were bound around him as if she—

She unwound herself and put her feet back on the bed. "I'm not usually . . ."

"Oh, God, Phee." There was a rasp in his voice that she liked. "Please don't take offense. I'm an idiot."

He had stopped moving, and she had stopped moving, so now they lay together awkwardly, and Ophelia, for one, felt frozen.

She cleared her throat. "I apologize for the profanity."

"Fuck that," he said, breaking the obscene still life they'd created by thrusting again.

Desperate herself, Ophelia responded with a squeak and a swallowed word.

"Give me your hands."

Bemused, she brought her arms down to the bed and bent her elbows so that their fingers could entwine. Then Hugo started kissing her so deeply that even if she had thought of words, there was no air to speak them. His body took on a rhythm that made passion quake down her legs and press tighter against him.

"Here," he said, when she'd almost lost control of herself, but not quite. He uncurled his right hand, reached back, and pulled her knee up. Her pelvis tilted and she helplessly let out a broken sound.

"Put your legs around me," he growled into her mouth.

She did, and it changed the angle so that she was breathless, suddenly mad, shaking all over. She managed to keep her mouth shut, though, until he suddenly stopped and put his lips on hers.

"Please, Phee."

"Please, what?"

Their hands had fallen apart and she was clinging to him again.

"Talk to me," he growled. "Please talk to me."

She was sweaty and shaking. She wanted to come more than she had . . . well, forever. Instead of talking she kissed him and let her hips talk, but then he began moving faster, and her head fell back.

Tension was building and building and she wasn't sure when she started talking again, but she registered the joyous glint in his eyes. Then they were both gasping for air, trembling violently, and she was pushing against him with all the strength in her body.

And then the world exploded around them with a fiery intensity that she, for one, had never experienced.

"Bloody hell," she whispered a while later.

"There's my duchess," he whispered back. "My last, wonderful, beloved, profane duchess."

"Duchesses probably don't curse."

"Mine does." He licked her cheekbone. "Sweats too. I'm so lucky, so damned lucky."

Ophelia believed him, because the look in Hugo's eyes wasn't one she'd seen before, but her soul instantly welcomed it. "I've never felt . . . said anything like that before," she said, stumbling into an explanation that she suspected he didn't need.

"Lucky me," he whispered. "I suspect you know this, but I'm in love with you, Phee. And I've never used that sentence before either. Dukes don't swear."

"In love?" she said, wonderingly. "I didn't . . ."

"I am."

"Me too," she offered. "I love you too. I'm in love with you too. I will, I do."

"I do, I will."

Chapter Eighteen

At five in the morning, Lady Astley's snug little house was silent. Hugo had the idea that he woke up simply due to the lack of noise. His townhouse was rarely silent; it was too full of children for that.

The castle was too old: It groaned and talked to itself; wind scoured across Lindow Moss, the bog that lay to the east of the castle, and then whistled through its turrets.

A moment later he realized that it wasn't silence that had woken him but the patter of small feet. The door silently pushed open and a small creature dressed in a white nightie ran directly to the bedside.

He glanced over at Ophelia. Thankfully, after the third time they made love, he had donned the nightshirt provided by the butler, and Ophelia had pulled her nightgown back on, after which they had made the short journey from the guest bedchamber to Ophelia's bedchamber next door.

For good reason, it seemed.

Viola stopped at the side of the bed and looked up at him. Soft brown curls made a halo for a sweet face, with hazel eyes and luxurious eyelashes.

You, his soul said.

You too.

It was the same feeling he had had after each newborn child was presented to him: the moment in which the world adjusted so that his heart could recognize one of his tribe. One of his beloveds.

He put a finger to his lips. "Mama is sleeping," he whispered.

Her bottom lip quivered. "Mama?"

"She's right here."

Viola nodded. "Go, snow, *cake*." She held up her arms.

Hugo wasn't certain of the etiquette of inviting small females to one's bed, albeit future family members. He turned and dropped a kiss on Ophelia's cheek.

"No," she murmured. "Later, Viola."

"Viola is here now," he observed. "I don't think she wants to wait until later." Indeed, by the time he turned back, Viola had dragged a small set of steps from under the bed, climbed up, and was crawling across the coverlet toward her mother.

"Mama!" she cried joyously.

Ophelia turned over and pushed herself up on her pillow, shoving back a curtain of tangled silken strands of hair. "Sweetie," she said sleepily.

Viola crawled onto Ophelia's lap and leaned back, examining Hugo. "Snow," she said. She turned to her side and nestled against her mother, her thumb in her mouth.

"She recognizes you," Ophelia said, beaming at him. "Yes, sweetie, he's the gentleman whom we met the other day in the snow."

"I should go," Hugo said, swinging his legs over the side of the bed. "Return to my bedchamber."

"The household doesn't rise for another half hour," Ophelia said. Viola appeared to have fallen back asleep.

"I didn't expect this," Hugo said, trying to find the words to explain what he meant.

"Viola?" Ophelia wrinkled her nose to him. "When she has a nursery with siblings, I suspect she'll wake them up instead of me."

"Joan is an early riser as well," Hugo said. He looked at Viola to make certain she was truly asleep. "I had forgotten what making love was like. I had imagined it with you—hell, the image of you in bed was present in my mind within a moment of entering your carriage."

Ophelia gave him a lopsided smile. "I was not far behind you."

"But the reality of it is so much more. You're the best lover I've ever had. Marie was sweet, but she was a girl. With you, it's all different . . . Making love to a woman is—"

"Not just any woman," Ophelia said, grinning at him.

"You *are* gorgeous," Hugo said instantly. Her lips, for instance, were perfectly shaped, and but for the presence of a small child—which acted as an instinctive dampener—he'd be rolling on top of her this moment, tucking her warm body beneath his, and nipping that generous bottom lip.

"I appreciate it, given that I must look like one of Shakespeare's witches. My hair is long past rumpled."

"A beautiful witch," Hugo said, his breath catching at the look in Ophelia's eyes. How could a woman so gorgeous have even a hint of insecurity? And yet his Ophelia wasn't certain she was beautiful.

He cleared his throat. "As I was saying, making love to you isn't so good just because you are extraordinarily beautiful. It's because you're *you*, and in case you're wondering, I know that makes me sound like a complete git."

"Git?"

"Idiot."

"You're no idiot." Bright eyes held his.

"Could we perhaps return your sleeping child to the nursery?" he asked, his voice low and rough.

She shook her head. "If I move, she'll wake up, and then she'll be fussy by eleven in the morning. Her nursemaid will come along in a half hour or so and take her away for a bath."

He groaned soundlessly.

Ophelia's eyes had a mischievous gleam. "I realized last night that I announced our marriage without giving you the chance to propose."

"You wish me to propose now?"

She nodded. "Why not?"

Hugo could think of many reasons, most of which had to do with thirsty kisses that couldn't be shared over the body of a sleeping child. But he nodded, swung his legs soundlessly over the bed, and padded over to his breeches.

When he came back, he paused for a moment, just to make certain that he wasn't in a dream. Tangled silky red hair spread around Ophelia's pillow and spilled over her shoulder. Her pretty mouth was curved in a wicked smile, one that acknowledged the fact that he was lusting for her.

"I suppose that with you as a mother, the children will never be confined to a nursery, will they?"

"At night, they will," she said. "But otherwise, no. Why have children if you don't want to spend time with them?" She looked down at Viola, peacefully sleeping, and stroked a finger down her plump cheek. "I want more children, Hugo."

"After last night, you may well have at least one," he said ruefully. "I'll send my secretary around to Doctors' Commons for a special license as soon as I get home." He put a knee on the bed as carefully as he could so that he didn't wake Viola.

"Will you marry me, Ophelia? I can promise a large amount of the world's goods, but you have no use for those. I have a title, and you don't want that either. I have too many children, and by the way, they are planning to give you a pet rat as a wedding present."

"I don't know," Ophelia said teasingly. "The pet rat might sway the balance the other way . . . unless there's something else you can offer?"

"My love," he said, meaning it. "I will love you my entire life and to my last breath. I hope I can give you the children you want; certainly, I'd love to share those that I already have. But most of all, I hope that we can have years together. I'd like to grow and change and learn from you. My life next to you will be entirely different from a life without you." He hesitated. "I don't mean to sound as if the decision is just mine. I will try to give you everything you want, Ophelia."

She smiled at him. "That would be you, Hugo." The words settled into a silence broken only by a child's peaceful breathing. "If I have you, and the children we already have, I'll be one of the happiest women on earth. So yes, yes, I will marry you."

He had to swallow hard and then he opened his hand. "My family has a tradition of giving this ring from one duchess to another," he said. "In different circumstances, my mother would have given it to you. She would have loved you so much."

The ring was made of emeralds and pearls; it was exquisite and it fit perfectly on Ophelia's finger.

"My last duchess," Hugo said. He leaned over and kissed her.

"My first and last duke," Ophelia whispered back.

Epilogue

I don't care what name you give her as long as it isn't as awful as mine," Betsy said. She was lying on her stomach on the huge bed that graced the matrimonial bedchamber at Lindow Castle.

"Your name isn't awful," Ophelia said. "Boadicea was an amazing woman, who nearly conquered the Roman legions."

"Dead men piled up at her feet like logs," Alexander said in a bloodthirsty tone.

"My name is Betsy," his sister said, turning another page in her book.

"There aren't so many warriors' names left," Hugo said. He was lying on his back, propped up against the headboard. Leonidas was tucked next to him, looking at a book.

Under Ophelia's reign, the castle had become

an extension of the nursery. Where the older Wildes were, the younger Wildes likely were not far away.

The boys started coming home from Eton even when they hadn't been sent down; Horatius made trips from Oxford merely to say hello. The five younger children—which now included the inseparable pair of Viola and Joan—divided their time between the stables and their parents, whether that meant sitting under the duke's desk as he paid the accounts, or trooping after Ophelia as she conferred with the housekeeper.

Horatius looked up from the other side of the room. Although he was far too proper to join the family on the bed, he had consented to join them in the bedchamber; he and Alaric were playing chess at a game table against the wall. "We don't have an Erik in the family," he said. "Erik the Red was an excellent pirate."

"Viking," Alaric said. "Not the same thing."

"Pirates! Let's play pirates again," Alexander cried.

"Erik for a boy," Hugo said, meeting his wife's eyes. "All right with you, darling?"

"Artemisia if she's a girl," Ophelia said, patting her very round belly. "She was a very fine warrior, who challenged the Greeks."

"We'd have to call her Artie," Betsy declared.

"You can do that," her father replied reaching down to tickle her.

Then he edged over so he could kiss his wife.

"All right?" he asked.

Ophelia smiled at him with a steady love in her eyes. "More than all right."

**Keep reading for a look at the first book
in the Wildes of Lindow Castle series**

Wilde in Love

by Eloisa James

Available now from Piatkus

Chapter One

June 25, 1778
London

There wasn't a person in all England who'd have believed the boy who grew up to be Lord Alaric Wilde would become famous.

Infamous? That was a possibility.

His own father had given him that label after Alaric was sent down from Eton at the age of eleven for regaling his classmates with stories of pirates.

Piracy wasn't the problem—the problem was the uncanny way young Alaric had depicted his small-minded Etonian instructors in the guise of drunken sailors. These days he avoided portraying self-righteous Englishmen, but the impulse to observe had never left him. He watched and summarized, whether he was in China or an African jungle.

He had always written down what he saw. His Lord Wilde books were a consequence of that impulse to record his observations, a drive that appeared as soon as he learned to write his first sentences.

Like everyone else, it had never occurred to him that those books could make him famous. And he didn't think any differently when he rolled out of his berth on the *Royal George*. All he knew in that moment was that he was finally ready to see his family, all eight siblings, not to mention the duke and duchess.

He'd stayed away for years, as if not seeing his eldest brother Horatius's grave would make his death not true.

But it was time to go home.

He wanted a cup of tea. A steaming hot bath in a real bathtub. A lungful of smoky London air.

Hell, he even missed the peaty smell that hung over Lindow Moss, the bog that stretched for miles to the east of his father's castle.

He was drawing back the curtain over the porthole when the ship's boy knocked and entered. "There's a mighty fog, milord, but we're well up the Thames, and the captain reckons we'll be at

Billingsgate Wharf any minute." His eyes shone with excitement.

Up on deck, Alaric found Captain Barsley standing in the prow of the *Royal George*, hands on his hips. Alaric started toward him and stopped, astonished. Through the fog, the dock glimmered like a child's toy: a blurry mass of pink, purple, and bright blue that separated into parts as the ship neared the pier.

Women.

The dock was crowded with women—or, more precisely, ladies, considering all the high plumes and parasols waving in the air. A grin tugged at the corners of Alaric's mouth as he joined the captain.

"What in the devil is going on?"

"I expect they're waiting for a prince or some such foolishness. Those passenger lists they print in the *Morning Chronicle* are utter rubbish. They're going to be bloody disappointed when they realize the *Royal George* hasn't a drop of royal blood aboard," the captain grumbled.

Alaric, who was related to the crown through his grandfather, gave a shout of laughter. "You have a noble nose, Barsley. Perhaps they've discovered a relation you never heard of."

Barsley just grunted. They were close enough now to discern that ladies were crowded as far back as the fish market. They appeared to be bobbing up and down like colored buoys, as they strained to see through the fog. Faint screams suggested excitement, if not hysteria.

"This is Bedlam," Barsley said with disgust. "How are we supposed to disembark in the midst of that?"

"Since we've come from Moscow, perhaps they think the Russian ambassador is onboard," Alaric said, watching a rowboat set out toward them, manned by a dockworker.

"Why in the devil's name would a flock of women come looking for a Russian?"

"Kochubey is a good-looking fellow," Alaric said, as the boat struck the side of the ship with a thump. "He complained of English ladies besieging him, calling him Adonis, and sneaking into his bedchamber at night."

But the captain wasn't listening. "What the devil are those women doing on the wharf?" Captain Barsley roared, as the dockworker clambered over the side from the rowboat. "Make way for my gangplank, or I won't be responsible for the fish having a fine meal!"

The man dropped to the deck, eyes round. "It's true! You're here!" he blurted out.

"Of course I'm here," the captain snarled.

But the man wasn't looking at Barsley.

He was looking at Alaric.

Cavendish Square
London

Miss Wilhelmina Everett Ffynche was engaged in her favorite activity: reading. She was curled up in an armchair, tearing through Pliny's eyewitness account of the eruption of Mount Vesuvius.

It was just the kind of narrative she most loved: honest and measured, allowing the reader to use her own imagination, rather than ladling on sensational detail. His description of seeing a cloud of smoke shaped like an umbrella spreading ever higher and wider was fascinating.

The door burst open. "Madame Legrand delivered my new bonnet!" her friend Lavinia cried. "What do you think?"

Willa plucked off her spectacles and looked up as Lavinia spun in a circle. "Absolutely perfect. The black plume was a stroke of genius."

"I fancy it adds *gravitas*," Lavinia said happily. "Making me look dignified, if not philosophical. Like you in your spectacles!"

"I only wish my spectacles were as charming as your plume," Willa said, laughing.

"What are you reading about now?" Lavinia asked, dropping onto the arm of Willa's chair.

"Pliny's account of the eruption that buried Pompeii. Just imagine: his uncle headed directly into the smoke, determined to rescue survivors. And he wanted Pliny to go with him."

"Lord Wilde would have gone straight to the disaster as well," Lavinia said with a look of dreamy infatuation.

Willa rolled her eyes. "Then he would have perished, just as Pliny's uncle did. I must say, Wilde sounds like just the type to run straight at danger."

"But he'd be running toward danger in order to *save* people," Lavinia pointed out. "You can't criticize that." She was used to Willa's scoffing at the explorer whom she claimed to love above all else.

Except new hats.

And Willa.

"I am so happy my bonnet came in time for the house party at Lindow Castle," she said, "which reminds me that the trunks are stowed and Mother would like to leave after luncheon."

"Of course!" Willa jumped to her feet and tucked her spectacles and book into a small traveling bag.

"I am looking forward to seeing Lord Wilde's childhood home," Lavinia said, with a happy sigh. "I mean to sneak up to the nursery as soon as I can."

"Why?" Willa inquired. "Are you planning to take a keepsake? A toy he once played with, perhaps?"

"The gardeners can't keep the flowerbeds at the castle intact," Lavinia said with a giggle. "People want to press flowers between the pages of his books."

Willa could scarcely imagine the chaos if Lord Wilde himself made an appearance, but the man hadn't been seen in England for years. If you believed the popular prints, he was too busy wrestling giant squid and fighting pirates.

Sometimes Willa felt as if a fever had swept the kingdom—or at least the female half of it—leaving her unscathed.

During the Season that just ended, young ladies had talked very little about the men whom they might well marry and spend a lifetime with, and a great deal about the author of books such as *Wilde Sargasso Sea*.

Wilde *Sargasso Sea*? Wilde *Latitudes*?

The only rational response was a snort.

Willa was fairly certain that in person, Lord

Wilde would resemble every other man: likely to belch, smell of whiskey, and ogle a woman's bosom on occasion.

She tucked her hand under Lavinia's arm and brought her to her feet. "Let's go, then. Off to Lindow Castle to burgle the nursery!"

Keep reading for Eloisa James's

Storming the Castle

In print for the first time!

One of Eloisa's delightful fairytale-inspired novellas, in which a young lady flees her boorish fiancé and becomes the nursemaid in a castle, where she encounters the rakish son of a grand duke who has vowed never to wed. He offers her everything—but not his hand in marriage.

Can this fairytale possibly have a happy ending?

Chapter One

The residence of
Phineas Damson, Esq.
Little Ha'penny, Lancashire
Late Spring

𝒩ot every fairy tale begins with a prince or a princess. Some begin with a kiss that turns a man into a frog, or a tumble on the road that turns a basket of eggs into scramble. They begin with the realization that what was once tall and handsome is now green and croaky.

My story belongs in that category, because it wasn't until Miss Philippa Damson gave her virginity to her betrothed, Rodney Durfey, the future Sir Rodney Durfey, Baronet, that she realized exactly what she wanted from life:

Never to be near Rodney again.

It was unfortunate that she realized this significant point only now, standing in the barn and readjusting her petticoats after giving Rodney her most prized possession. But sometimes it takes a clear-eyed look at a man sprawled in the straw at your feet to realize just how you feel about him. One moment of weakness, ten minutes of discomfort, and now she was a woman. She felt different.

Meaner.

"Damn, that was nice," Rodney said, making no attempt to straighten his clothing. "You're as tight as a—" His imagination apparently failed him. "A lot tighter than my hand, anyway."

Philippa wrinkled her nose. "Don't you think you should get up now?"

"I waited so long that it took all the strength out of me. It isn't every day that a man loses his virginity, you know."

"Or a woman," Philippa pointed out, using her fingers to comb bits of straw from her hair.

"My friends have been poking around from the moment they got a stand. You're not innocent anymore, so it doesn't matter if I'm blunt, I reckon. I saved myself for you. Didn't want to get a disease."

The etiquette her mother had taught her did

not foresee this particular situation, but Philippa said, "Thank you."

"If you aren't the prettiest thing with your hair shining like that in the sunlight," Rodney said, stretching. "I'm about ten times as much in love with you now, Philippa. And you know I've loved you ever since I saw you the first time, ever since—"

"Ever since you saw me in church when I was seven years old," Philippa said drearily.

"You were like a little angel, and now you're a bigger one. And your bosoms are heaven-sent, all right. Damn, but I could do that all day." He reached toward Philippa's ankle, and she moved back just in time. "Shall I climb up to your window tonight? I know you never let me before, but the banns have already been posted at St. Mary's, so it seems as if—"

"No," Philippa stated. "Absolutely not. And you should cover yourself. What if one of the stable hands returns?"

Rodney peered down at the limp pinkish thing he called his own. It was draped across his thigh in a way that made Philippa feel positively ill. "I bet I'm the biggest man you've ever seen."

Philippa rolled her eyes and started braiding her hair.

" 'Course you never saw anyone else," he added.

"I know that. You were a virgin all right. Of course you were. I had to force my way, you know."

She did know, and the recollection made her grind her teeth.

"Though I did right by you too," Rodney said, as oblivious as ever.

"You did what?"

"Didn't you notice when I tiddle-taddled you?" he asked. "Diddled you right where I was supposed to, giving you women's pleasure. I expect we'll be making love two or three times a day in the next year. I expect we won't even get out of bed in the next few weeks. Not even to eat. My daddy planted me in the very first week of his marriage, and I aim to keep to the tradition."

If Philippa hadn't already made up her mind, that would have done it.

She was not going to marry Rodney Durfey. Even though he had told the whole village at age nine that he would marry her or no one. Even though she had spent her girlhood being complimented by those who thought she was the luckiest girl in the world.

Even though she had given him her virginity, which rendered her, for all intents and purposes, unmarriageable.

Just at the moment, she had absolutely no problem with that idea.

"I'm leaving, Rodney," she said.

"Won't you kiss me good-bye?" he said, his blue eyes still hazy.

"No."

And she walked out, feeling—as her nursemaid would have said—meaner than a barnyard dog. As she walked away, she realized that it wasn't an entirely new sensation. She'd been a little angry at Rodney for a long time.

After he'd made his famous declaration in St. Mary's Church, Little Ha'penny, no boy ever looked at her twice. She was "that lucky Damson miss," destined to be the next Lady Durfey. What's more, no one ever asked her what *she* thought about Rodney, about his pale blue eyes, or his round buttocks, or the way he looked at her heaven-sent bosom.

Her mother had died the summer before, clutching Philippa's hand and repeating how glad she was that her little girl was taken care of. Her father had told her over and over that he was grateful to have been spared the expense and bother of a Bath season or—even more onerous—a trip to London to be sponsored into society by her godmother.

The Damsons and the Durfeys had always celebrated Yuletide together and walked to the front of church together at Easter. When both ladies in their respective families passed away . . . well, Sir George and Mr. Damson, Esq., simply kept trudging side by side as they had before.

Their children's marriage would place Damson land in the hands of the baronet, which everyone, including Philippa's father, agreed was a good idea.

"My land runs alongside his," he had told her once, when Philippa complained that Rodney had stolen her doll and chopped off its head. "You two will be married someday, and this is the boy's way of showing affection. You should be happy to see how that lad adores you."

Everyone had always told her just how she should feel, from the time she was seven years old: lucky, special, celebrated, and beautiful.

Now, though, she felt nauseated.

She also felt like running away. Her father would never understand if she told him that she'd changed her mind about marrying Rodney. It wasn't as if she could claim Rodney was cruel, or bestial, or even unlikable.

And the moment her father found out what had just happened in the barn—which he would, because Rodney would stop at nothing to marry her—he would deliver her to the altar no matter how fervent her protests.

No, if she wanted to escape Rodney, she would have to run away.

She took a deep breath. Why on earth couldn't she have figured this out yesterday rather than after that unpleasant episode in the barn? She'd never granted Rodney more than kisses until this afternoon. Instead, she had drifted along like a twig caught in a stream, not really visualizing her life with Rodney. The *nights* with Rodney.

But now . . . there might be a baby. She walked back to her family's trim house, so different from the garish brick monstrosity that was Durfey Manor, worrying about the possibility.

She loved babies; she always tried to steal away from tea parties and find her way to the nursery. What's more, she had spent her happiest hours with her uncle, a doctor in Cheshire, who allowed her to accompany him as he ministered to village children.

Still, it was that possible baby who posed the greatest dilemma. She wasn't sentimental about the life of servants. She couldn't condemn Rodney's child to a life of servitude, which is what her life was bound to be if she was with child but nevertheless fled her intended marriage.

Her mind was spinning like a whirligig in the wind. Finally, she made a decision: she would leave it up to fate. If there was a baby, she would resign herself. Walk down that aisle, smile, become Lady Durfey. She shuddered at the thought.

But if not . . . she'd steal freedom.

THAT VERY NIGHT, she discovered that Rodney had failed to "plant" anything, to use his repulsive terminology.

Philippa was still thinking about what it meant, and what she would do next, when she realized that Betty, the upstairs maid, was chattering on and on about a castle. Elsewhere in England, people undoubtedly talked of the great castles of Windsor and Edinburgh, but around Little Ha'penny, there was only one castle worth discussing: Pomeroy. It stood on the other side of the great forest, its turrets just tall enough to be visible on a clear day. For years, Philippa had stared out her window and dreamed of a knight in shining armor who would ride through town and fall in love with her, sweeping her onto the back of his steed and taking her away.

Away from Rodney, she now realized.

No knight in shining armor ever came; in fact, the castle had been unoccupied and neglected for years until a real prince moved there a couple of years ago. He was a foreigner, from some place in Europe.

As in a real fairy tale, the prince hadn't lived in Pomeroy Castle long before he fell in love and married a princess. Or an heiress, at the least. No one really knew for sure because Little Ha'penny was far away from the polite world. Although Rodney puffed out his chest and boasted about his father's connections, the fact was that Sir George Durfey was the sort of man who stayed very close to home. He'd even kept his son home with a tutor rather than send him off to Eton.

"It's not good for the lad to be so provincial," her father had remarked, years ago. Phineas Damson, Esq., was the only other gentleman in the area, though, and if the truth be told, he wasn't all that interested in Sir George, nor in his future son-in-law. What Papa liked was to investigate battles. He spent the better part of his days in his study, surrounded by maps of places like Spain and Egypt, painstakingly translating accounts of Greek battles.

In short, no one knew anything about the castle and its royal occupants, and in keeping with their provincial outlook, most of the goodly inhabitants of Little Ha'penny had lost interest once the Prussian prince moved in.

"I'm sorry, Betty," Philippa said, "could you tell me that again? About the princess, I mean?"

"Well," Betty said importantly, "I was just

saying what I heard from Mrs. Pickle, who heard it from the coachman of the morning mail."

"And?"

"She had a baby. The princess that is, not Mrs. Pickle."

"Oh," Philippa said. "Very nice."

"You'll be having one soon enough," Betty said comfortably. "One only has to take a look at the young master's good, strong thighs to know that he's all man, if you know what I mean. At any rate, this baby up at the castle cries all the time. Has the collywobbles, like my cousin's second. I shouldn't wonder if it will die. Some of them can't take milk, and they just fade away."

Philippa's lips tightened. "Only if people insist on giving them cow's milk as a substitute."

"Well, my point is that the child isn't doing so well," Betty said. "The coachman said that he'd dropped off a footman in Manchester who is supposed to round up nursemaids and doctors, as many as he can find."

"They must be desperate," Philippa said.

"The baby's a *prince*. 'Course they're desperate. He'll inherit the castle someday, though not if he's dead."

It was that easy. Philippa packed a small bag with her plainest clothes, and wrote a note to her papa. Then she made her way to what passed for a high street in the village and paid the old drunk, Fettle, who lay around in back of the Biscuit and Plow, to drive her to Bigger Ha'penny.

There she covered up her hair, which was distinctively silver-colored and therefore annoyingly recognizable, and bought a coach ticket to London. She hopped off in a bustling inn-yard in Lower Pomeroy, reasonably certain that with all the milling passengers, no one would notice that she didn't get back on the coach.

An hour or so later, she was standing at the foot of Pomeroy Castle.

Chapter Two

Pomeroy Castle
Lancashire

$\mathcal{M}$r. Jonas Berwick, known to his half brother Gabriel as Wick, and to the castle at large as Mr. Berwick, the majordomo to Prince Gabriel Albrecht-Frederick William von Aschenberg of Warl-Marburg-Baalsfeld, was never at a loss for an answer. Well, rarely.

"What am I going to do?" Gabriel demanded again. His hair was standing on end, and under his eyes were dark circles that looked like bruises. "The baby cries, and then *she* cries, and—" He turned away abruptly, but not before Wick saw the gleam of something that looked like tears.

"Aw, hell, Gabe," he said, reaching out and

pulling his brother into his arms. "Your son is going to make it. You named him after me, and that alone will give him the balls to push on through."

"He's suffering," Gabriel said flatly. "He pulls up his legs and he cries so desperately that it would make you ill to hear it."

Wick knew. He kept breaking off his duties to dash up the stairs, to walk past the nursery, silently begging, praying that he wouldn't hear his namesake crying in that desperate, pain-filled wail. "How is Kate?"

"Kate is Kate," Gabriel said wearily. "She holds him, and she walks, then she cries, but she keeps walking. I can't get her to sleep properly, and I'm sure it's affecting her milk. And yet she will not allow him to be nursed by anyone else, not after the time when he cried all day after we tried a wet nurse. She's convinced that because the poor woman reeked of garlic, her milk didn't agree with the baby."

"What does the new nursemaid say about it?"

"I just sent her away," Gabriel said.

Wick made a mental note. He'd have to find the woman and pay her a week's wages.

"I was decent about it," Gabriel said, wearily running a hand through his hair. "I know it's not her fault. But she kept shaking her head, and she had such a sad look about her . . . I couldn't stand it. Besides, Kate won't put Jonas down anyway, not unless she gives him to me. I should go back up there." Instead, he slumped into a chair.

"I'll go," Wick said. "I'm the boy's uncle. You'll have to force Kate to give him up. I'll walk him while the two of you nap for a couple of hours. Tell her that. I will walk up and down in the portrait gallery."

Gabriel looked up, his eyes heavy. "She'll never accept it."

Wick pulled him to his feet. "Assert yourself, Gabe. Remember, you're the master of the house, the *paterfamilias*, king of the castle, and all the rest of that rubbish. Grab your son, hand him to me, and take your poor wife off to get some proper sleep. You'd better go to your old chambers up in the tower because she won't be able to hear Jonas cry from there."

When Wick let go of his arm, Gabriel actually tottered.

"How long has it been since you slept?" Wick demanded, taking hold of his arm again and hauling him along the corridor.

"Exactly how old is Jonas? I've lost track."

"Not even a fortnight. You need to get yourself and Kate to sleep," Wick said, pushing him through the nursery door. A moment later, he was holding his nephew.

"I'll sleep for one hour, then I'll be back," his sister-in-law stated. She was a beautiful woman, but just at the moment she resembled one of those weird sisters in the Shakespeare play. Wick couldn't remember which play it was, but there were three of them in the production he'd seen, and Kate would have fit right in. Her eyes were red, her face drawn, and grief and fear vibrated in the air around her. "He just had some milk . . . at least I think he did."

"More than an hour," Gabriel said firmly, pulling her toward the door.

She managed to stop her husband in the doorway. "Don't let anyone else touch him," she told Wick in a threatening tone.

He nodded.

"And whatever you do, if that doctor comes, don't let him give the baby anything. I'm certain his dose made Jonas sicker, and he wanted to try opium. I *know* that's a bad idea."

"I already forbade him entrance to the castle," her husband said, managing to get Kate into the hallway.

As the sound of their footsteps receded, Wick looked down at the baby, and Jonas looked back at him. Then Jonas opened his mouth so wide that Wick could view his interesting lack of teeth and screamed until his face turned red.

Wick's ears hurt. But something hurt in his chest too. Jonas looked thinner now than he had when he was born. His eyes were sunken, and there seemed to be a little less fire in his cry. He looked like a wizened old man, as if he'd lived an entire life in a week or two.

Wick swore under his breath and set off down the corridor, then down a flight and into the portrait gallery. After he had walked for five minutes, Jonas settled down some. He turned his face against Wick's chest and sobbed more quietly. He curled his finger around Wick's rather than flailing it in the air.

"Just don't die," Wick found himself whispering. "Please don't die."

Jonas gave an exhausted sob.

Wick walked for another half hour or so, up the portrait gallery, out into the corridor, around the bend, back down the corridor, back into the portrait gallery . . . at last, Jonas slept.

Sometime later, footsteps sounded in the stone corridor behind him. "Mr. Berwick, oh, Mr. Berwick," panted one of the footmen, as Wick turned toward him. "My apologies, Mr. Berwick, but Mrs. Apple says that the first of the new nursemaids has arrived, and she'd like you to be there for the interview."

"How can that be?" Wick whispered. "I sent off to Manchester only yesterday."

The footman had just realized what—or rather *who*—Wick held in his arms. He started walking backwards on his toes. "Don't know," he whispered back. "Shall I tell her you're unavailable?"

Wick looked down at Jonas. The baby was turned against his chest, a fold of Wick's shirt clutched in one tiny hand. "I can't stop walking," he said. "Send the woman up here. Mrs. Apple can see her first, then I will."

Fifteen minutes later, Wick had just reached the far end of the gallery for the twentieth or perhaps fortieth time and was turning around to walk back the other way when the door opened and the nursemaid entered. His first thought was that she was too young.

He had sent a footman to Manchester with explicit instructions to find experienced nannies and doctors, at least two of each. The baby didn't need a pretty bosom to nestle against: he needed someone who could figure out what was wrong with him.

But Wick walked back across the room, maintaining the same even stride with which he'd lulled Jonas to sleep. The girl didn't meet his eyes; she was staring at the baby.

"Your name and your experience with children?" he asked briskly, thinking to get the whole thing over within two minutes. There were strands of bright hair peeking out from the girl's cap, and her eyes were moss green. Plus, she had an entirely delectable bosom . . . she would never do. She'd have the footmen at fisticuffs within the week.

She didn't seem to hear his inquiry. Instead, she came straight up to him and peered at Jonas's face. "He's wanting water, that's for certain."

"Babies don't drink water," Wick said, and never mind the fact that he'd never held a baby before this one. "Babies drink milk." Her ignorance of this obvious truth was another strike against her employment.

"If they have the collywobbles, they need water as well."

"How much experience have you had with infants?" He could see the nape of her neck as she peeked more closely at his nephew. It was delicate, pale, and translucent, like the finest porcelain. "Have you been a nursemaid for long?" Then, annoyed by the fact he was looking at her neck, he added, "You're far too young."

"I don't have much experience, but what I have is the right sort," she said, looking up at him, finally. He mentally revised his assessment of her eyes: they were not the green of moss, after all, but the green of the sea on a stormy day.

Wick felt an altogether uncomfortable warmth in the area of his groin. He'd be damned if he would line up with the footmen to ogle one of his fellow servants.

He'd accepted long ago that ladies were not for him. True, he was the son of a grand duke, albeit a grand duke in far-off Marburg. But he had been born on the wrong side of the blanket. Raised in a castle and yet a bastard—which meant that he couldn't marry anyone of respectable birth. And he was too educated to settle for a milkmaid who wouldn't mind his questionable parentage.

"What sort of experience is the *right* experience?" he asked.

But she had bent near again and was studying the baby's face. "I don't like the look of him," she said, pursing her lips. They were rose-colored, those lips.

Wick looked past her lips to Jonas. "At least he's sleeping," he said. "He cried all night."

"That's because of the pain," she said. "You'd better give him to me. We have to get some water in him, first thing, then we'll deal with the milk."

Before he knew what was happening, she slipped her hands around the baby and lifted him deftly out of Wick's arms. "Here! You can't do that," he said, alarmed at the very thought of Gabriel or, God forbid, Kate knowing that he'd allowed a stranger to take the baby.

But the girl—

"What did you say your name was?" he asked.

She finished tucking the fold of the blanket under Jonas's face before she looked at him. "I didn't," she said. "I am Philippa Damson."

"Like the jam?" Wick asked. She was sweet as jam, and that part of her name suited her. He'd like to lick—

He wrenched his mind away.

"Exactly like the jam," she said, turning toward the door. "Now come along, Mr. Berwick. This baby needs water immediately."

Wick stared after her for a moment.

At the door, she looked over her shoulder. "You have to show me to the kitchen."

"Kitchen?" he echoed, trying to figure out how to get Jonas from her arms without waking him. Gabriel would never forgive him. He didn't even want to think about how Kate would react. "Look, you must give the baby back to me. I promised His Highness that I, and I alone, would hold Jonas—that is, the young princeling."

"He needs water," Miss Damson said. "Or he will die." She looked down again. "I think there's a chance he won't live through the night, actually.

Babies die awfully quickly if they don't drink enough."

Wick walked forward and pushed the door open before her. "Straight to the end of the corridor and down two flights."

When they reached the kitchen, nine or ten heads swiveled almost in unison. The castle's kitchen was a vast space with a stone floor. Worktables were arrayed around the room, scrubbed to a fare-thee-well, and covered with copper pans of all sizes and shapes. It was full of people, as always: the cook, three kitchen maids, a dairymaid, and a couple of scullery maids working at the sink to one side.

They all snapped upright at the sight of Wick, except for Madame Troisgros the cook, who considered herself his equal, if not his better. The already complex hierarchy of castle staff was further complicated by Wick's relationship to the prince. Even had Gabriel (who showed no such inclination) wished to keep their fraternity a secret, one of his elderly aunts regularly took pleasure in shocking polite company by announcing that she preferred Wick to his brother Gabriel.

By rights, a young nursemaid would find herself quite far below the cook, though certainly above the dairymaid. And yet Philippa Damson walked into that kitchen like the lady of the house. She unerringly put her eye on the cook, a lady twice as broad and four times as fierce as anyone else in the room.

"*Qu'est-ce que c'est que ça?*" snapped Madame Troisgros.

Without pausing for breath, Miss Damson broke into charming, if urgent, French. As all could see, she had the little prince in her arms. He needed water, but it must be special water, water boiled, then cooled. And she also needed a cloth, a clean linen cloth, to be boiled in a different pot of water, then cooled.

Madame Troisgros had the eyes, Wick thought, of a rabid French weasel, if such a thing existed— small and rather crazed-looking. As she opened her mouth, undoubtedly to refuse, Miss Damson walked across the kitchen to her.

"*Regardez,*" she said, drawing back the cover that protected the prince's face.

Confronted by that tiny, exhausted face, Madame Troisgros flinched and pointed with her ladle to a chair. Miss Damson obediently sat down. A few minutes later, an immaculate piece of linen was shown to Miss Damson for her approval, then carefully placed in a pot of boiling water.

Even more servants began drifting into the kitchen, although the room remained as silent as a church as everyone strove to keep Jonas asleep. The housekeeper appeared and hovered in the background; two or three footmen had apparently deserted their posts in the front hall as they now stood quietly against the walls. The knife boy had stopped sharpening his wares and was sitting on a three-legged stool, his mouth open.

"Stop hovering!" Miss Damson ordered Wick in a low voice. "Babies don't like nervous influences."

"Gabriel might have woken; he might be searching for us in the gallery," Wick said, entirely forgetting that he generally referred to his brother as His Highness in public. Miss Damson was that sort of woman. She made a man lose his head.

"Why not send a footman to stand outside the prince's bedchamber so as to inform him of our location when he wakes? Meanwhile, you'll have to take the baby while I wash my hands," she said, and slipped Jonas back into Wick's arms with no more fuss than if she were transporting a pudding.

To Wick, Jonas looked worse than he had even an hour before. The skin around his eyes was the deep blue of a bruise. His little nose stood out from his face, as if the skin had receded around it. He was an extraordinarily unattractive baby, which did nothing to assuage the feeling of pure grief and panic Wick felt at seeing his nephew in this state.

"It's not too late, is it?" he heard himself saying. Everyone in the kitchen froze.

Miss Damson had washed her hands, and was now wringing out the cloth and dipping it in the pot of boiled, cooled water. "Absolutely not," she said firmly. "Sit down."

Wick thought a bit dazedly about the fact that he never took orders except from his own brother, but he sat. She bent over and slipped the corner of the wet cloth into the baby's mouth. He sucked reflexively, realized it wasn't milk, and let out a pained cry. Quick as she could, she dipped the cloth again, returned it to his lips. Over and over and over.

It was a messy business. Within minutes the baby was wet, Wick was wet, and Miss Damson's dress was splashed with water. But Jonas kept swallowing, and soon he was crying only between sucks.

"Do you know if he has had normal bowel movements?" Miss Damson asked.

Wick blinked. "I haven't the faintest idea."

She turned to the housekeeper. "Mrs. Apple, could you perhaps help with my question?"

"Lily's the one you want," Mrs. Apple said. With a nod, she dispatched a footman to fetch the appropriate maid.

"You can't mean that the baby merely needs water," Wick said. "One of the nursemaids who was here last week said he had sciatic gout."

"Gout? Most unlikely. I think it's colic," Miss Damson said. "Surely a doctor has seen the child?"

"Yes, but he didn't hold out much hope. He said Jonas was too ill for colic. First, he thought the baby had an intestine stone, then he suggested a quartan ague. Yesterday, he tried an emetic to clean out his guts, but it made Jonas vomit, and after that the princess ordered the doctor out of the castle."

"She was absolutely right," Miss Damson observed. "The child needs more fluids, not less."

"I sent off to Manchester for other doctors. Someone must have some medicine they can give him. The doctor planned to try Dalby Carmel next, something like that."

"Dalby's carminative," Miss Damson said with obvious disdain. "And I suppose castor oil as well."

"His mother would be able to say more precisely. I believe he also suggested opium, but Her Highness disagreed."

"No medicine will work," she announced, dipping the cloth back in the pot once more.

There was a collective gasp from the kitchen staff. "No medicine," Wick repeated, his heart speeding up. "But you said—"

"It's simple colic," Miss Damson said. "I've seen it before. There's something about his stomach that doesn't like milk at the moment. But he won't die of it, not unless he goes without water or milk too long."

At that moment, the door to the kitchen burst open and a wild-eyed apparition surged through. "How could you, Wick?" Kate cried, running to Jonas.

Miss Damson plucked Jonas from Wick's arms and turned to the princess, looking as if butter wouldn't melt in her mouth. She put the baby straight into his mother's arms. "Your son is going to be all right. You see? He's not crying."

Kate's mouth was a tight line, and she glared as if this interloper were part of an invading army. "Just who are you?" she snapped.

"She's your new nursemaid," Wick intervened. He had already decided that Miss Damson's calm command of the situation was just what they needed. "She gave Jonas water, Kate. And he drank it all up. I think he looks better already."

"He's *wet*," Kate cried, horrified. "Now he'll

catch a cold. He'll—he'll—" Clutching her baby, she darted from the room without another word.

Miss Damson looked unsurprised. Rather than running after her new mistress, she turned to Madame Troisgros and, in French, thanked her for her help. Then she switched to English and thanked everyone else in the kitchen. And, finally, she had a detailed discussion with Lily, the maid in charge of the nursery, about exactly what sort of deposits Jonas had been making in his nappies.

"Are they green?" she was asking. "And how do they smell?"

She didn't sound like someone who seemed barely old enough to have her first position. Wick couldn't stop looking at her, though: at the rose color of her lips and the way her gown, where it was wet, clung to her bosom. It was a very nice bosom.

Very nice.

Wick glanced around the room and discovered that the footmen—not to mention the gaping knife boy—had noticed the same fact. With a jerk of his head, he sent them scurrying out of the kitchen.

Miss Damson, meanwhile, was giving Lily instructions about taking boiled water to the nursery three times a day. She didn't sound like any nursemaid Wick had ever seen, not that he'd seen many.

Maybe that was what housekeepers sounded like when they were young. But that idea didn't fit either.

She was a lady, Wick thought suddenly. Quality. He was amazed he hadn't seen it immediately, but he knew why: because he wasn't English. He'd bet everything he owned that she had a lady's voice except that he wasn't quite good enough with the language to tell the difference.

But then he listened closely and he realized he *could* tell the difference. After all, he and Gabriel had gone to Oxford back when they were striplings, before Gabriel took over this castle. Wick recognized the sound of her voice, the way it sounded at once sweet and a little sassy . . . that was a lady's voice, not a nursemaid's voice.

He had a cuckoo in his kitchen.

In her agitated state, Kate hadn't noticed anything untoward, obviously. And Madame Troisgros had been far too glad to find someone who spoke French to consider the nursemaid's origins. With Lily dismissed, the cook was now regaling Miss Damson with tales of the execrable vegetables she was forced to cook with, monstrous tubers fit only for pigs, or *cochons*. And Miss Damson was nodding and sympathizing . . .

Like a lady. A lady who spoke French, who had undoubtedly been brought up to a good marriage.

Wick became aware that water was running down the inside of his calf into his shoes. There was something about Miss Damson that made even a man with wet breeches hungry. Lustful. Those emotions that good servants could have only for each other—and never, ever, for the ladies they attended. Wick certainly never allowed himself that sort of inconvenient desire.

Just like that, he decided not to say a thing to Miss Damson about the question of her birth. If she was a lady who was merely presenting herself as a nursemaid for some obscure reason—well, then she wasn't for him, not for the bastard brother of a prince.

But perhaps, if he was wrong, and she wasn't a lady . . .

Not that he was looking for a wife, of course. But during the last year he had noticed the way Gabriel liked to hold Kate's hand, the way he swept his wife into his arms, the way he kissed her when he thought no one was looking.

Back in Marburg, the king would have paired Wick off by now, given him to a third or fourth daughter of a gentleman, a woman grateful to be connected in any way to the royal family, a woman whose father would willingly overlook

Wick's ignoble birth. But here in England, he had volunteered to become his brother's majordomo. He had chosen to run the castle, and he was damned good at it.

He'd known perfectly well what that choice meant for his future. As a servant, he was a servant, no matter how high in the hierarchy of service. He would never marry a gentleman's daughter. And he'd accepted that, content with an occasional trip to London to meet cheerful women who were neither ladies nor servants but happy to share a bed for a time.

Content, at least, until his brother fell in love.

One night, before the baby was born, he was making his nightly rounds and recognized Gabriel's laughter coming from the study. Thinking to find out the joke, he had his hand on the door when he heard his sister-in-law gasp in such a husky, pleading way that, disconcertingly, he realized his brother's laughter was aroused by something rather different than a mere jest.

Needless to say, he didn't go in.

Even so, he kept trying to tell himself that he had no use for a wife, given that his wife must necessarily be a servant. Kate, after all, was the granddaughter of an earl. She was a perfect person to marry a prince. Gabriel was extraordinarily lucky to have met her.

There were few Kates in the world, and none who ended up paired with bastards.

But still . . . as he followed Miss Damson's admittedly delicious figure from the kitchen, he thought, for the first time in his life, that perhaps he *could* marry a servant after all.

If the servant was a lady.

Chapter Three

$\mathcal{P}$hilippa was feeling wildly self-conscious as she walked out of the kitchen ahead of the devilishly handsome Mr. Berwick. In fact, her skin prickled all over at the idea that he was just behind her.

Which was ridiculous. Absurd.

He was a majordomo, for goodness' sake. A *butler*. Her mother would turn in her grave at the very idea that she was noticing a butler's profile, let alone his voice.

True, he was the most handsome butler she'd ever seen. He didn't bundle his hair into a little bag the way their family butler, Quirbles, did. Instead, it was pulled back from his face in a way that emphasized his brow. His eyebrows formed peaks over his eyes.

And those eyes . . . they were fierce and proud, like an eagle. Not like a butler. Nothing like a butler.

It wasn't just she who saw it either. Back in the kitchen, they had all instinctively acted as if he were a gentleman rather than a butler. Fascinating.

Her mind returned to the baby. She was almost certain that Jonas merely had a very bad case of colic. She'd seen as much several times while accompanying her uncle on his rounds, and once in Little Ha'penny itself. But the worrisome question was whether the baby might have something called intussusception, if she remembered the name right. That was when the bowels were all going the wrong way, and no matter what anyone did, the baby died.

She started walking a little faster. There was no point in mentioning this possibility to the princess since it would terrify her for no good reason. If it was intussusception, there was nothing to be done. But she was fairly sure that her uncle had told her that intussusception was always accompanied by a very slow pulse. Jonas's pulse had seemed quite normal, and in any case, Lily had not reported seeing any blood in his stool—another telltale sign.

She started ticking off in her mind all the things

she had to do: reassure Jonas's mother, first of all. Then give Jonas a warm bath, with a little massage of his tummy. She had some balsam in her bag that she could rub on it.

Her uncle had believed that massage did no good, but at least it didn't hurt, not the way that spirits did, or copious amounts of castor oil. Her uncle always said that some baby's bowels just weren't ready to digest properly.

"Nothing to do but wait," she said aloud, remembering her uncle's brusque advice to new mothers.

"What did you say?" Mr. Berwick said from behind her.

Even his voice was bewitching, with its smoky foreign tone.

She didn't turn around but just kept marching up the stairs. "I trust I am going in the right direction for the nursery?"

"It's just above the portrait gallery where I was walking Jonas, so we have another flight to go."

Philippa's legs were starting to ache. Becoming a nursemaid at Pomeroy Castle would definitely make her stronger.

"How did you learn French?" came that voice from behind her.

Her foot hesitated on the step, then she said

quickly, "My aunt was French." That wasn't true, and Philippa quite disliked telling lies. She was from thoroughly English stock, whose only claim to exoticism was the red hair that cropped up now and again.

"Your aunt was French?"

"Yes," she said firmly.

"But your mother wasn't French?"

Philippa felt panic, but managed to keep her invention aloft. "My aunt is on my father's side, that is, she was raised in a French convent, then joined him in England sometime later."

"How unusual," Mr. Berwick said after a short pause. "I was under the impression that convents generally raised young ladies. Not that I mean to imply that your family has come down in the world, Miss Damson."

"Oh, we have," Philippa said madly. "Terribly far down. I have to find a position, you see. Because we've—because we're so far down."

"How far?" Mr. Berwick asked, with interest.

She stopped, as much to catch her breath as to glare at him. "What do you mean by that?"

"Well, you do sound a bit like a heroine in a melodrama," he pointed out, stepping in front of her to push open the door.

"You shouldn't mock our hardship. It's been

heartbreaking for my family!" she snapped, feeling a surge of virtuous anger before remembering that the family in question didn't exist.

He looked down at her, and she saw something in his eyes that made her blink. "You must feel neither fish nor fowl."

Philippa swallowed. What she felt was something no young lady should be feeling. "Precisely," she said. "Fowl, fish, who knows what I am?"

"You are Jonas's nursemaid," he said, with a lightning smile as he held open the door.

She walked through, thinking about what he had just said: she had secured a position in the castle.

And now she had a position, she wasn't a lady anymore. It felt rather peculiar. Her father never employed many servants, but of course there were some. She had grown up with Quirbles and a footman to answer the door, the kitchen staff, the upstairs maid and the downstairs maid, and a boy to do all the rest. And now she had joined their ranks. She was one of them, rather than a lady.

When they reached the nursery door, she instinctively waited for Mr. Berwick to open it for her, but instead he pushed it open and preceded her. She blinked at his broad back for a moment before realizing that the butler always preceded a nursemaid.

"Kate," he was saying, "the new nursemaid is very sensible. She knew that Jonas needed water, and she boiled it before giving it to him."

Philippa stepped out from behind him. Jonas's mother sat in a chair, the baby clasped in her arms. The princess had the same battered, terrified expression that Philippa had seen on other mothers' faces when her uncle paid his visits. Instinctively, she went over to her and knelt next to the chair. "Jonas will live," she said as forcefully as she could. "He will not die."

"Of course he will not," Her Highness said. But her eyes were haunted.

"This is Miss Damson," Mr. Berwick said. "Jonas's new nursemaid."

The princess seemed not to hear him. She looked up, and asked, "Wick, who is this person, and where did she come from?"

"This is your new nursemaid, from Manchester," Mr. Berwick said, without a second's hesitation, though he'd never asked Philippa where she lived. "Miss Damson came with the highest references from esteemed doctors. I know she looks young, but her charges have been special cases, not ordinary infants."

The princess looked sideways at Philippa, still

kneeling by her chair. "Sick babies," she breathed. "You deal with sick babies." A tear ran down her cheek. "Do you know what's the matter with my son?"

"He has colic," Philippa said. "I'm almost certain that it's just colic. I can't give him a miracle medicine, because there isn't any. And my—that is, the esteemed doctors with whom I worked in Manchester feel strongly that colic is simply something that a baby must outgrow."

The princess looked down at her son. "Are you sure? The doctor who was here said that Jonas was too hot to have colic. He does seem to get a fever now and then. And then he screams so much after nursing that it seems he can hardly breathe. If you even touch his belly after he drinks, he cries and cries."

"He has a bad case. But it's still just colic. He will outgrow it."

"And doctors are on their way from Manchester who will confirm everything she says," Mr. Berwick stated.

Philippa felt a tingle of alarm. Her uncle was rather unorthodox in his ideas, and she had the impression that Manchester doctors were likely to be far more interested in doling out medicines. Her uncle was of the firm conviction that medicines did more harm than good, no matter what the disease might be.

"But my *milk*," the princess said. Then she blinked and looked at Mr. Berwick. "Shoo." He disappeared through the door in a flash.

It was all a bit odd. Philippa was very fond of their family butler, as was her father. But she would never say *shoo* to Quirbles. It simply wouldn't be appropriate, and she might offend him.

"I'm poisoning Jonas, aren't I?" the princess said. "It's my milk that's the problem. I'm killing my own baby." Another tear rolled down her cheek.

Philippa got up; her knees had started to hurt. "No, you are not poisoning your child. He needs your milk, and in fact, you are doing an excellent thing by nursing him yourself. You have a flair for the dramatic, Your Highness."

"Actually, I don't," the princess said wearily, tipping her head to rest it against the back of her chair. "I'm very sensible, in my normal state. But it's just been so awful since he was born. Not that I mean *he* is awful," she added.

Philippa bent over and took the baby from her. "This child needs you to rest. Your milk will give out if you don't sleep."

"My milk . . . Whenever I feed him, he screams

so it breaks my heart. The sound goes through the whole castle. Moments like this, when he's just sleeping and not crying, are so precious. Besides, I'm afraid that I'll come back and—"

"As long as we give him enough water, he will not die," Philippa said firmly. "He'll be thin, but he'll survive. And it will get better."

At that very moment, Jonas's eyes popped open. He looked at her blurrily, and then let out a bellow. Despite herself, Philippa flinched.

"Is that the first time you've heard it?" the princess asked wearily, rising from her chair and holding out her arms.

"He has a fine voice," Philippa said. "No, you sit down. You feed him, then I'll show you how to massage his tummy afterwards, which might help with his pain."

Two hours later, Jonas's tummy was tight as a drum, he'd been given the gentlest of massages, he'd screamed until he was blue and breathless . . . and finally, exhausted, he had fallen asleep.

Philippa carefully put him down in his cradle, humming the last few bars of the song with which she'd sung him to sleep.

"Do you still believe he will be all right?" his mother asked, bending over to tuck the blanket just under the baby's chin.

"You saw his nappy. It was perfectly normal, with no blood. He'll be fine. He's a fighter. It hurts so much, and yet he kept on trying to tell us, so we can make the pain stop. He hasn't given up."

"That's true," the princess said, brightening a little despite her fatigue. Then she added, "I don't think I've ever been this worn-out in my life."

"You must go to bed," Philippa said. "Jonas will sleep for a few hours. And if he wakes up, I'll give him some water. He still needs more water."

There was a moment of silence. Then: "What was that you sang to him?" the princess asked.

"It's an Italian song," Philippa said. "Something about sunshine and courting and all that nonsense. Mother made me—" She stopped.

"You're no nursemaid," the princess stated. "You're a lady. You sing in Italian, your mother prepared you for a debut, and your dress is quite nice—even though I think that shade of green isn't quite right with your hair, which is beautiful, by the way."

"I *am* a nursemaid," Philippa said, feeling a pulse of desperation. "My family's come down in the world, that's all."

"If that's the case, why are you wearing a pearl pendant?"

"It was a gift from my mother," Philippa said

309

firmly. Her voice didn't wobble because *that*, at least, was the truth.

"It must be a very recent family downfall. Because your shoes are lovely and not in the least worn-out. I have some just like them, and they're made of Italian leather."

Philippa looked down at her slippers. It hadn't occurred to her that she might be betrayed by the condition of her footwear.

She looked back up to find the princess grinning at her. "You've run away, likely from a loathsome marriage. Or no—you're too young for that. A loathsome suitor. And, of course, you ran away to the castle. I'm sorry to say that the prince is already married to me, because otherwise you could have married him yourself, which would have been rather romantic."

"Yes, it would have been," Philippa said uncertainly. Then she added: "You should take a good rest now, Your Highness."

"I suppose I could return to the south tower. I left my husband sleeping." She bent over the cradle again. "Do you really believe that Jonas will get better? How on earth did you gain all this knowledge about babies? Has your family truly come down in the world?"

"I'd—well—"

"Whatever you tell me, I won't be in the least shocked," the princess said, with such a sweet smile that Philippa swallowed hard. "After my father died, my stepmother treated me abominably, so I gained all sorts of knowledge that I mightn't otherwise have."

"My uncle is a doctor," Philippa found herself explaining. "I used to visit him and my aunt for a month at a time, and I always begged him to take me along on his rounds."

"If you were a man, you'd be a doctor," she said, nodding. "Sometimes I feel that, as women, we have the short end of the stick."

"Exactly," Philippa agreed. "If I were a man, I'd be a doctor, and no one could tell me what to do. I would choose—" She broke off.

"Oh, you did flee from someone awful," the princess said, with evident delight. "Do you want to boil him in oil, or is it even worse than that?"

She was so charming that Philippa couldn't help smiling back, but just then the princess gave a huge yawn.

"You really must sleep, Your Highness," Philippa said. "Jonas is going to cry a great deal. Every time he's fed, in fact, and much of the time in between, and that might go on for months. At the least, several more weeks, given his age. We

must make certain that you eat and sleep suffi-
ciently. I can hold Jonas, but I cannot feed him."

"I'm Kate," the princess said, yawning again.

"Oh, but I couldn't—"

"Of course you can," she said. "I want to hear
all about the troll of a man you're fleeing, but I
think I will go to sleep for a bit. What did you say
your name was?"

"Miss Damson," Philippa said desperately.

"Really, Miss Damson, you and I just stood
shoulder to shoulder and examined my son's
nappy. I'm Kate, and you're—"

"Philippa," she said, defeated. "But it just
doesn't seem appropriate."

"Nonsense. We're all strange birds here in the
castle. There's Wick, of course, and I was something of a maid-of-all-work to my stepmother
for years before Gabriel came along and tried to
make me into a princess."

"Tried?" Philippa asked, just stopping herself
from inquiring what Kate meant by *There's Wick,
of course*. "By all indications, you *are* a princess,"
she pointed out.

"It didn't take," Kate said, with another huge
yawn. "Princesses swan about in satin-lined carriages. What's more, everyone knows that when
a princess has a child, it has a rosebud mouth

and sunny blue eyes. Whereas I have birthed the ugliest baby in all Christendom."

"He's not that ugly," Philippa said, feeling defensive on behalf of poor little Jonas.

"Yes, he is," his mother said, leaning back over the cradle. She put a finger on his nose. "A little potato here." His eyes. "Currants are bigger than his eyes." His mouth. "Well, his mouth isn't bad. But have you ever seen a baby open his mouth wider or make such a frightful noise?"

"Never," Phillipa said truthfully. "You return to bed, and I'll bring you the baby after your nap."

"But what about you? Shouldn't you be getting settled? Oh no, what am I thinking? You'll be sleeping right through this doorway, at least as long as you're pretending to be a nursemaid. I'm too selfish to let you stop yet."

Philippa smiled. "I'm happy to be a nursemaid, Your Highness. Truly, I love babies."

"*Kate*," Kate insisted, straightening up from the cradle. "I think it would be best if you brought Jonas to the dining room when he wakes up. We eat at eight, and I wouldn't think he'll be hungry again before then. You needn't change, by the way."

"I shan't change," Philippa said, shocked. "Nursemaids don't eat in company."

"Nursemaids don't call their mistresses Kate, so you are obviously an exception."

"What about the baby?" Philippa asked. "I wouldn't want to leave him."

"He will be with us, of course," Kate said. "I don't like to have him out of my sight." And with a last touch of Jonas's nose, she went out the door.

Chapter Four

$\mathcal{T}$hree hours later, Philippa was reconsidering her chosen profession. It seemed impossibly exhausting and boring. Jonas had woken, cried for an hour or so, taken some water, and gone back to sleep. Then he'd woken again, and cried again— but had fallen back to sleep just when she'd been trying to decide whether he was hungry.

She unpacked her tiny bag in the room next to the nursery, and, during one of Jonas's quiet spells, brushed and re-brushed her hair, thinking all the while about Mr. Berwick. *Wick*, the princess had called him. He had lovely eyes, rather brooding, as if life wasn't giving him what he wanted.

That had to be because he was a butler. He didn't seem like a butler.

Jonas whimpered from the nursery, and she hastily pinned up her hair and went back into the room to soothe him.

She thought her uncle would be quite pleased with the way the baby now looked. The pinched look was gone, which meant that he had some water in him. What he needed now was more milk. And when she didn't instantly produce it, he started crying again.

"I'm sorry, little scrap," she murmured to him. "It's going to hurt your tummy. But we just have to do it."

She wrapped him in a light blanket and wondered what to do. She hadn't the faintest idea how to find the dining room. By the time she opened the door and headed into the corridor, Jonas was wailing so vociferously that his face was purple.

A tall, yellow-haired footman with a nice open face was waiting for her. "Oh, thank goodness. What's your name?" she asked over Jonas's sobs.

"William, miss," he said. "Mr. Berwick said I was to escort you to the dining room. It's awfully easy to get lost in this castle."

"It's big, isn't it?"

"Huge," William said feelingly. "The time it takes just to bring the linens round about, well, you wouldn't countenance it."

They made their way down some stairs, through

the portrait gallery, down the main stairs. "Shouldn't we be going down by the servants' stairs?" she asked.

He glanced at her. "Not you, miss."

Philippa didn't know quite what to say to that, so she jiggled Jonas against her shoulder—which had no effect whatsoever on his wails—and followed William through the vast entrance hall to the dining room.

When she entered the room, she was very relieved to find that it wasn't a cavernous formal space but a tidy little room with a table set for six. What's more, Kate was the only person in it. She rose the moment the door opened and hurried toward them. "I wanted to come to the nursery, but my foolish husband forced me to wait for you here instead. How is he?"

"Just fine," Philippa said. "He's hungry, as you can hear, but I think he feels a little better."

Kate cocked her head. "You can hear a difference?"

"Yes," Philippa said, though in reality she wasn't at all sure. Being a nursemaid was making her into a terrible fibber. "He's saying he's hungry, but not in pain." She said it firmly, the way her father would say, *England's coast is undefended*. A fact.

Kate reached out and took her baby. "There's

my sweetheart," she cooed. "I'll just take him to my sitting room and feed him."

She left, and Philippa drew in a long breath and reached up to check her hair. She'd pinned it on the back of her head, but it felt as if it might all tumble down her back any moment.

Just then the door opened, and Mr. Berwick entered.

"William left me here," she said, feeling foolishly out of place.

"Where's Jonas?"

"The princess took him to her sitting room in order to feed him. She'll bring him back in a moment, then I'll go straight back to the nursery," she promised.

"You won't," he said, walking around the table and straightening a napkin. "You are eating with the prince and princess tonight."

"I really shouldn't—"

"A place for you has already been set," he said, cutting her off. "We'll be joined by Princess Sophonisba, the prince's great aunt, who will undoubtedly appear in an inebriated state, which is merely a hint at what will happen after she has had more to drink during supper."

Another princess? She, plain Philippa Damson, who had only rarely been out of Little Ha'penny, and never even to the city of London, was to dine with not one princess but two? "I couldn't," she said, shaking her head. "I'm just a nursemaid."

"I forgot that!" he said. His eyes laughed at her. "You're a nursemaid. I suppose you don't know how to use a knife and a fork."

Philippa drew herself upright. "You may jest, Mr. Berwick, but I certainly do know how to use proper cutlery—as does every well-trained servant."

"*Are* you well trained?" he asked cordially. "We never quite got around to that part of the interview."

"Of course!"

He walked around the far end of the table and back toward her. "Do you know that there are a thousand things I ought to be doing at this moment?"

"I quite believe you," she said. "Please feel free to attend to them."

His dark eyes met hers, and he cocked a mocking eyebrow. "I can't leave new staff alone in a room with the silver."

Philippa suppressed the impulse to give him a set-down, reminding herself that she was now a servant—*just* a servant—before saying, as haughtily as she could, "Do be sure to count the forks after I leave the room."

He came a step closer. "You would make an

enticing thief. How did you hear of our need for a nursemaid, by the way? You simply appeared out of thin air, and the footman whom I sent to Manchester hasn't even returned yet."

"I didn't come from Manchester," Philippa said. His eyes made her feel rather hot, a feeling that Rodney's gaze had never aroused. Though the very thought of Rodney was dispiriting.

"Then where did you come from?" He drifted a step nearer, and now he stood directly before her. Mr. Berwick wore beautiful claret-colored livery with frogged buttons. Somehow on him it didn't look like livery but like the uniform of the Queen's own Hussars. And, like them, he was broad-shouldered and muscled and immaculately kempt.

Philippa pulled herself together, and said, "I grew up in a village not far from here. When I heard about the baby, I thought I might be able to help."

"You did?"

Perhaps he was more like a magician than one of Her Majesty's Hussars. Something about his eyes was making her feel quivery. "And I *have* helped," she stated, confident that this, at least, was not a fib.

"You are a mystery."

"There is nothing mysterious about me. I'm a very ordinary girl."

"You can sing in Italian—"

She began to explain, but he held up his hand. "Kate told me all about it."

He was like no butler she'd ever heard about. And he knew she was thinking precisely that because he gave her a slow, naughty grin. Philippa barely stopped her mouth from falling open. No one had ever given her a smile like that, not to Miss Philippa Damson, the future bride of the future baronet.

Except . . . she wasn't a future bride anymore.

Without taking a breath, she raised one eyebrow, in just the same manner as the innkeeper's wife in Little Ha'penny—whom everyone agreed was no better than she should be. "*Kate?*" she said, purring a little. "What an odd way to refer to your mistress."

For a moment she feared she'd overdone it, but his smile only deepened, causing a shiver to go right down her back. "Ah, but Kate's not my mistress," he said. "At least, not in the most important meaning of the word."

She blinked, then frowned at him. "You shouldn't even suggest something like that!"

He threw back his head and laughed. "A very young pigeon, aren't you? A very, very young—"

"I'm not so young," she said hotly.

"How old are you, Miss Damson?"

"Twenty. Which is quite old enough for—for all manner of things."

"Too old to debut," he said. But she was wise to him now.

"I wouldn't know," she said. "After my family fortunes fell, we never considered such a thing, of course."

"Ah, the fall," he said, sighing melodramatically. "Ever since the first fall, it's just been downhill all day."

"Are you talking about my family or Eve?" Philippa inquired, barely suppressing a giggle. "Because I've always thought that poor Eve was more sinned against than sinning."

"Why so?" he asked, leaning against the wall next to her. It was scandalously casual. A butler never—but never—leaned against the wall. And yet, there he was.

"Eve wasn't responsible for the sinful entice-ment of the serpent," Philippa told him, feeling her heart speed up even further. "She merely offered the apple to her companion, which demonstrated good manners, not to mention generosity."

"I don't think that good manners are an accept-able excuse for all that trouble she caused," Mr. Berwick observed.

"It's true that she probably should have avoided that particular tree," Philippa conceded. "Still, no one ever seems to notice that Adam ate the apple as well. It's half his fault."

"I blame them both," Mr. Berwick said. "Just think, if they hadn't been so foolish, we'd all be living in Paradise." He leaned a bit closer. "Very warm, I've heard. None of this English rain."

Philippa didn't move back even though he was close enough that she could smell him. He smelled delicious, like lemon soap and something else, like the wind on the moors. "I like rain," she said, unable to command her mind to come up with anything else.

"You wouldn't," Mr. Berwick said, "if we were both wandering about in it quite naked, without even a fig leaf to our name."

That hung in the air for a good second. Or ten.

Then she heard it: down the corridor came a thin, protracted wail, an agonizing sound.

"Ah, bollocks," Mr. Berwick muttered.

It was such an English expletive—and said in such a velvety, accented voice—that Philippa couldn't help laughing.

A smile spread over his lips too. "You really aren't worried about Jonas's survival, are you?"

She shook her head. "He's crying because milk

323

doesn't agree with him. But it's not a mortal condition, and his stomach will eventually get used to it."

"Fancy yourself a doctor?"

"No, but any person with common sense can see when a baby has colic," she said. "It's always better to do nothing in such cases." She hesitated.

"What?"

So she told him, in a rush, about her fear that Jonas had intussusception. "But I'm sure that my uncle told me that there would be blood in his nappy," she finished. "And there isn't." Jonas's persistent wails were coming closer.

"It sounds to me as though you're right," Mr. Berwick said. "Still, we need your uncle to come take a look at the baby. Where is he? I'll send a carriage immediately."

"You couldn't!" Philippa gasped, horrified. "He would—*no!*"

"But he's the best doctor you know. We need him."

The door opened, and Kate reentered, carrying Jonas and followed by a man who was the prince, presumably. A tottering elderly lady clutched his arm. She wore so much face paint, topped by a fuzzy and rather shabby wig, that she resembled a Chinese dog that had gone through Little Ha'penny along with a traveling fair.

But it was the prince who caught Philippa's eye. She stood rooted to the spot and looked from Mr. Berwick's eyebrows to the prince's, at their hair, their eyes, their chins . . .

"Her Highness, Princess Sophonisba, and His Highness, Prince Gabriel Albrecht-Frederick William von Aschenberg of Warl-Marburg-Baalsfeld," Mr. Berwick announced. Turning to them, he said, "May I present Miss Damson."

"Most irregular, being introduced by the butler," the old lady said irritably. "Well, who are you, then?"

"I'm—"

"She's a friend of mine," Kate interjected. "She's come to help with Jonas." She smiled at Philippa, and Philippa realized, rather to her surprise, that it was true. Even though she'd known Kate for only a matter of hours, they were friends.

"I can't hear a word over that howling," Princess Sophonisba said. "I never heard of a lady nursing her own baby before. I'm sure that's the problem." She leveled a thin finger at Kate. "What that child needs is the milk of a hardy peasant. Yours is probably thin and blue. Though now I think on it, you're practically a peasant yourself."

Philippa's eyes met Kate's, and Philippa said hastily, "I'll just walk Jonas in the corridor until he calms, shall I?"

325

"Yes, do," the elderly princess said. "He sounds like one of the devils they like to talk about in church, the kind who have nothing to do but yowl. Wick, why aren't you offering us something to drink? Just because Rome is burning doesn't mean we needn't fiddle. This screeching is terrible for my nerves."

Philippa settled Jonas into the crook of her left arm and nodded to the footman, who opened the door for her.

In the hallway, Jonas waved his tiny clenched fists and wailed. He was pulling up his legs again, so his stomach must be aching. Philippa settled him on her shoulder and patted his back gently as she walked.

If Mr. Berwick insisted on summoning her uncle, it would all be over. Her father would arrive within hours, and she would end up back in Little Ha'penny, married to Rodney. Jonas let out a big burp.

"You have a lot of air in your tummy," Philippa said. He was still crying, but he sounded more halfhearted about it. Another big burp erupted from his stomach.

She kept walking, up and down, worrying at the problem of her uncle, her father, Rodney, Jonas, colic . . . what if she was wrong? If it was intussusception, her uncle would say there was nothing to be done. But . . . .

Finally, the door to the dining room opened, and Kate emerged. "Bless you," she said, taking the baby. The moment he came off Philippa's shoulder, he screwed up his face and cried even louder.

"Hush, sweet one," Kate crooned.

"Try your shoulder," Philippa said. "Like this." She arranged the baby so he was lying over his mother's shoulder.

"But his head is hanging down. All the blood will go to his head."

"This way feels better for his stomach. Listen." Sure enough, his crying did not cease, but the wails weren't quite so desperate.

"Go eat something," Kate said, nodding toward the door. "We've worked it out. Gabriel is coming to take a turn in half an hour, and then Wick will take a turn."

Philippa nodded. "And then Princess Sophonisba, I expect?"

Kate blinked. "Well—" She caught Philippa's smirk and grinned. "Go eat!"

Philippa returned to the dining room to find the prince seated at the head of the table, and Wick at its foot. She hesitated for a moment, uncertain where to sit.

A footman stepped forward. "Miss Damson," he murmured, pulling out the chair next to Wick.

Two slender silver candelabra threw light on the silk damask covering, the gold-plated dishes, and a greater assortment of cutlery than she knew existed. For a moment, Philippa felt dizzy. Was it really only yesterday that she had been lying in the straw under Rodney?

Could it really be her, sitting in a castle, eating with royalty? She didn't dare look to her right, at Wick, or even more terrifying, to her left, at the prince himself.

Across from her, Princess Sophonisba sucked vigorously at the chicken bone she clutched. "You're pretty enough, but you look like a bit of a goose," the old lady said. "Haven't you ever been in a castle before?"

"No, I haven't, Your Highness," she said, picking up her napkin and spreading it in her lap.

"Most people in this one are dim as a snuffed candle," Sophonisba said. "In fact, one castle is the same as another. The lot of them sit around buggering each other, if not the sheep."

The prince cleared his throat and leaned forward, giving Philippa a charming smile. A smile she recognized from his—

Brother? They looked almost identical, which couldn't be accidental.

"You seem to have performed miracles already with Jonas," he said. "I don't know how we'll be able to thank you."

"Give her a gold chastity belt, I'd think," Princess Sophonisba said. "The way your brother's looking at her, she'll be dropping a bastard in a matter of nine months."

So Wick *was* the prince's brother. No wonder they looked so much alike.

The prince closed his eyes for a moment. "I apologize—"

The princess talked right over His Highness. "Actually, that's just what we need around here: More bastards. Look at Berwick, here."

Philippa didn't dare look. She could *feel* him sitting next to her, could feel his large body, his eyes resting on her.

"Look at him!" the princess ordered.

Philippa looked.

To her relief, he was grinning, his eyes alight with a deep pleasure that sent little shocks down her spine.

"A bastard," the princess said with satisfaction, licking her fingers. "And yet he's the best of the lot. My favorite, and I'm a judge of men. Always have been, ever since I dumped my barking-mad betrothed and decided never to marry."

Philippa felt a smile playing on her lips as well.

"You may be in a castle, among royalty of sorts," Prince Gabriel remarked from the other end of the table, "but I'm afraid you'll find, Miss Damson, that we descend to the lowest type of behavior while in private."

"Speak for yourself," the irrepressible princess retorted. "I've no wish to know what sort of roguery you get up to in private. Ain't a fit subject for the dinner table. Watch your manners!" And with that, she poked him in the chest with the chicken leg.

Philippa felt giggles rising in her throat. A footman leaned down beside her and gave her a portion of roast beef.

"If you want your own drumstick, I can request one," Wick said. His voice was deep and husky, as different from Rodney's as wine from water. And there was that enchanting accent, the one that made her a little breathless.

"No, thank you," she said, pulling herself together. To her relief, the prince had engaged his aunt in a discussion of Emperor Napoleon's height.

"Small as a flea," the princess said scornfully. "And his eyebrows jut out like the casements of a shop window."

"I suppose you will have gathered by now that my birth was not sanctified by matrimony," Wick said to Philippa.

Philippa nearly choked on her bite of roast beef. "I—"

"Does it appall you to hear of it?" he inquired, putting on an innocent expression. "I'm afraid that we're used to the circumstance around here since it's been the case since birth. My birth, that is," he added.

Philippa finally managed to swallow her beef. "Not at all," she said weakly.

"Give that girl some chicken," Princess Sophonisba bellowed across the table. "She's got a lung weakness, likely won't last the week."

Prince Gabriel rolled his eyes and nimbly reeled his aunt back into another topic of conversation.

"My aunt drinks too much," Wick observed.

Philippa put down her fork. She very much hoped it was the right fork; with three to choose from, she had chosen at random. "I have noticed that inebriates tend to have few teeth. However, the Princess Sophonisba seems remarkably endowed, in that respect."

"Yes, she's gnawing that bone like a champion bulldog," Wick said. "Well, then. Have you decided to tell me where to find your uncle?"

"I can't," she said. "Please don't ask me." Wick had a beautiful mouth. She jerked her eyes away and hoped he hadn't noticed she was gaping at him.

"How long does it take to ride to his house?"

"Please don't—"

"If Jonas continues to improve, I won't summon him. But if Jonas grows more ill, even suddenly, how long would it take to fetch him?"

"A day," she said relieved. "He would be back here the next morning if I sent a note along. Especially . . ." Her voice trailed off.

"Especially because said uncle is probably looking desperately for you under every hedge and hillock," Wick stated.

There was a moment of silence between them.

Philippa decided that she'd rather not answer. She'd read somewhere that prisoners couldn't be forced to incriminate themselves. So she took another bite of roast beef.

"You'll rue the day you were caught in the parson's mousetrap," Princess Sophonisba said to Prince Gabriel. "Children are women's work. Your father would be ashamed of you."

"Ah, but the cheese in that mousetrap was irresistible," the prince said politely. "If you'll excuse me, dear aunt. Miss Damson, Wick. I believe my turn has come." With that, he left.

"You'd better stop looking at that wiggle-eyed gal," Princess Sophonisba said, waving another chicken bone at Wick. She didn't seem to expect an answer because she turned about and started haranguing a footman.

"*Wiggle-eyed?*" Philippa asked.

"She means velvet," Wick said. His smile was—well—it should be outlawed. It made her insides feel hot and yielding.

"Velvet eyes?" Philippa said, pulling herself together. "I think I prefer wiggle."

"Smoky," he offered.

She wrinkled her nose. "I sound like a brothel, all velvet and smoke."

"And what do you know of brothels?" he asked. His smile made her heart pound.

"Nothing," she admitted.

"Well, I can tell you this," he said, leaning toward her. "There are no doxies with smoky sea-green eyes nor hair the color of pearls."

"Not bad," Sophonisba barked from across the table.

Philippa jumped. Caught by the sultry tone in Wick's voice, she'd forgotten all about the princess.

"You'd better look out," Sophonisba said to her, using a half-eaten chicken leg as a pointer. "The man's a devil, of course. His brother was the same. Do you think the princess had a chance once

333

Gabriel had her in his sights? Not a chance!" She snorted. "I almost had to give up my brandy, but he ended up marrying her."

"Brandy?" Philippa repeated, completely bewildered.

"Don't ask," Wick murmured.

Sophonisba had apparently reminded herself of the drink; she was now demanding some to accompany her chicken.

"You seem remarkably unscandalized by the knowledge of the unseemly circumstances of my birth," Wick said. "I'm still waiting for you to shudder and avert your eyes."

"Have people shuddered in the past?" she inquired.

"Ladies have." There was something uncompromising in his voice. A little bleak.

"I am no longer a lady," she said, shrugging. "Though of course, one must distinguish among bastards."

"*Must* one?" Wick asked.

"Absolutely," she said firmly. "There are those who earn the appellation, by their behavior, and those who are merely given it by circumstance. Besides, I've been thinking a great deal about what it means to be a lady."

"I suppose your altered circumstances led to such philosophical thoughts," he asked, his eyes laughing again. "Because true ladies never con-template the question. So what qualities did you conclude were necessary? Elegance, culture, dis-cernment? Or perhaps the ability to live in luxury is enough?"

"Sacrifice," she said flatly. "And sometimes, it just isn't worth it."

She thought his eyes . . . what she saw in his eyes couldn't be respectable, or true, so she devoted herself to her roast beef.

Chapter Five

$\mathcal{I}$n the next weeks, Philippa's life took on a rhythm. Every time Kate nursed Jonas, he would cry bitterly for hours. Philippa and Kate took turns walking him, rocking him, massaging him . . . none of it really seemed to help his aching stomach.

But, as Philippa pointed out with somewhat immodest pride, he was growing plumper, without the castor oil and emetics the doctor had prescribed. In fact, when she reached the end of her second week in the castle, Jonas's improvement was undeniable. "There's nothing wrong with you," Philippa crooned to him in the middle of the night after Kate had fed the baby and handed him over to her now-indispensable nursemaid. Jonas blinked up at her. His eyes fluttered, and he almost, almost went to sleep, but then another pang must have caught him because his face twisted in anguish, and he pulled up his legs and cried out.

"Poor baby," Philippa said, kissing his cheek. then popping him up on and over her shoulder in his favorite position. It meant that he hung gracelessly down her back, rather like a sack of beans, but it worked. Unless she stopped walking, of course.

She decided to take him to the portrait gallery because she had walked around and around the nursery earlier in the evening, and she felt that one more turn around that well-worn path would drive her mad.

The castle was warm and dark. She descended a level and made her way to the portrait gallery to find that moonlight was streaming in the windows there, its color as pale and chilly as the white gooseberries she used to gather as a child. She didn't stop for long before the portraits, just paused to examine how moonlight made the be-ruffed gallants look like faded copies of their daily selves.

She knew the moment Mr. Berwick—or Wick, as he'd insisted she call him—entered the room. It was as though the air changed somehow. He always found her in the middle of the night. He'd look for her in the nursery, or the gallery, and walk with her. When they encountered each other during the day, usually at dinner, they talked courteously enough of Jonas, of the castle, of whatever . . . but never of their nocturnal rendezvous.

All of that polite daylight conversation and observance of convention melted away in the soft glimmer of moon and candle. It was as though the obscurity of the night gave them sanction to be their true selves. The way he looked at her was nothing like the way Rodney used to look at her. Oh, Wick desired her. She could see a demand in his eyes, a hunger that he couldn't mask.

But more than that . . . he *liked* her. He thought she was funny. He actually enjoyed listening to her. It was intoxicating, it was bewitching, it was everything Rodney had never demonstrated and never could.

Philippa turned around to see Wick walking toward her, his step unhurried. He was smiling, that lopsided grin that made her feel warm all over.

"How do you manage to always look so impeccable?" she asked, when he was near. "Do you never sleep?" She wore a nightdress and a wrapper, and her hair tumbled down her back every which way. After the first night or two, when the baby had cried all night long, she'd stopped worrying about what she looked like at night.

"I don't sleep in my livery, if that's what you mean," Wick said. "How is our princeling to-night?" He peered at the baby's little head. Seeing that he had a new audience, Jonas let out a howl but quieted again.

"I think he's better," Philippa said, rubbing the baby's back. "He won't let me sit down, though, or even stop walking."

In the last nights, they had talked about every-thing from Shakespeare (she liked *Romeo and Juliet*; he thought Romeo was a tiresome melan-cholic) to lawyers (she thought they ought to donate their time to poor widows; he thought that was unlikely) to dissections (she found the idea disturbing; he was of the opinion that it was the only way to really identify the kind of illness a patient had suffered from).

Now he picked up their conversation directly where they'd left it the night before.

"I thought of another reason that dissection is important. How else are we to learn of the body's systems if we don't investigate them thoroughly?"

"I wouldn't want to learn about the body if it required cutting one open," she said with a shudder.

"Why not? I think it would be fascinating. I wouldn't want to be a surgeon; I don't like causing pain. But if the person has already left his body, why not try to find out how he died, and why?"

"All those blood and guts," she said. "*Obviously.*"

"Entrails," he said, almost dreamily. "Back when I was at university, I read that there are enough entrails in the human body to stretch all the way down an average street. I can't imagine."

"Don't listen to him," Philippa told Jonas, who had woken. "You'll feel queasy and start crying again."

Jonas burped and closed his eyes once more.

"I'm going to stop walking and sit down, Jonas," she told him. "Just for a little while." Then she sank carefully into the sofa that Wick had ordered placed in the portrait gallery after it became clear it was prime walking-Jonas territory.

"Why don't you go and dissect some dead bodies, then?" she asked, trying to ignore the fact—and utterly failing to do so—that Wick had sat down beside her. Her pulse instantly quickened. For one thing, his leg was touching hers. For another, as soon as they sat down, it felt as if the world drew in and became as small as the three of them. As if she and Wick and sleeping Jonas were utterly alone in the whole castle.

"Me?" He seemed startled for a moment. "Nonsense."

"Why nonsense? My uncle told me that there's a terrible shortage of doctors in England. You told me the other night that you'd been at Oxford; did you take a degree?"

"Of course."

"A good degree?" she persisted.

"A double first. Is that good enough for you?"

"Goodness. Well, then, all you have to do is attend the university in Edinburgh for a year," she said. "I suppose it would be better to go a little longer, but my uncle told me that many doctors attend for only a year."

"I couldn't do that."

"Why?"

"Well, because Gabriel and I—because I'm here."

"I can see that it's quite nice for your brother to have you as his majordomo," she acknowledged, "but if you wish to heal people, I think every sick person would feel that you should forfeit the butler's pantry." She heard her own voice and winced with embarrassment. It was something about him. He made her feel joyful and slightly cracked.

"My father—"

"Your father isn't here," she said, cutting him off. "I know you're a grand duke's son, Wick, but it doesn't seem to have done you much good. Why not just forget about that and do what you wish?"

"As I wish . . ." There was a tinge of wistfulness in his voice. "I would wish that my father had never seduced my mother although that would have had unfortunate consequences for myself."

"I meant realistic wishes," Philippa said, sitting up straighter so she could rock back and forth in her place, in hopes of keeping Jonas asleep.

His reply came with a rueful smile. "I cannot believe that it would surprise you to know how many doors are closed to bastards." Philippa met his eyes, and the pain in them was unmistakable.

"Those doors hold only *fools*," she said softly but fiercely. "You should be judged for the man you've become, not by the circumstances of your birth."

He was silent for a moment, his eyes still on hers. The expression in them changed somehow, and suddenly her heart was beating in her throat.

"At any rate," she said quickly, taking refuge in words, "no one here in England would have the faintest idea whether your birth was irregular or not."

"I have a responsibility to my brother," Wick said. But that expression was still there. It was almost . . . tender.

Philippa started rubbing Jonas's back again. "If

I understood the conversation at dinner last night properly, Gabriel assumed responsibility for this castle along with some members of his brother's court even though he would have preferred to be an archaeologist off somewhere . . . Tunis, was it? Looking for a city called Carthage? That seems to suggest that a sense of familial responsibility does not reside only in the lower echelons."

Wick laughed at that. "I did my best to persuade him to go to Tunis, but he refused, thinking that he had to provide an income for the castle. Then he wrote a book—not to mention married an heiress—and now he is free to go where he wishes."

"I expect you tried *very* hard to convince him. I can tell that you are extremely close."

"He was so miserable before meeting Kate," Wick explained.

"Yet he can't manage without you? Would he not wish the same happiness for you?"

There was another moment of silence. Then he smiled down at her. Philippa suddenly thought she would love to kiss him. She would give him a scandalous kiss, the kind that Rodney had demanded and she hadn't allowed.

As if he'd read her mind, he said, "I want to hear more about Rodney." She should never— *never*—have told Wick about Rodney. Somehow, during these nocturnal tête-à-têtes, it was hard to keep secrets, and Wick had already guessed she was running from someone.

"Well . . . he has a tendency to start braying when he's nervous," she offered, feeling a wicked delight in betraying her former betrothed.

Wick nodded. "I know the type. I think it goes along with the English ancestry. I expect he hunts, and delights in shouting absurdities like *tallyho*."

"I expect so," she said. She could not help but conjure a mental picture of Rodney sitting on his horse in that red hunting coat that made his buttocks look four times wider than they actually were. Involuntarily, her eyes dropped to Wick's legs.

They were all muscle, as different from Rodney's as night from day.

"Are you comparing us?" His voice had gone low and husky.

Her nerves jolted again, but she nodded. She couldn't lie to Wick any longer, now they were so close. Friends, or perhaps even something more. "You are very different."

"Perhaps because he's a baronet's son." He didn't say it bitterly.

"He's always had everything he wanted, but that doesn't excuse his fat bottom," she observed.

"Was he really seven when he fell in love with you?"

"He was nine. I was seven."

"Astounding," Wick said, staring at her as if she were some sort of exhibit in a traveling show.

Philippa caught back a smile and tossed her head. "Are you saying, Mr. Berwick, that I was not desirable at age seven?"

"You are as pretty as a fairy-tale princess," he said, his voice suddenly husky. "I'm quite certain that you were just as enchanting at age seven."

"I actually used to dream of being in a fairy story," she admitted.

"Vanity, thy name is woman!" Wick said, pulling a strand of her hair.

"Not from vanity. I always pictured a prince who would ride up on a white horse. I'd be there, in the village square, and he would sweep across and wrap his arm around me and pull me before him in the saddle."

Wick's eyebrow was up. "That would take quite a bit of skill. The story would be so disappointing if you took a hoof to the head. Was the prince wearing shining armor, by any chance?"

"Naturally," Philippa confirmed.

"Near impossible," Wick said. "Scoop a girl"—he pulled back and gave her a quick inspection from head to toe—"who's no lightweight onto a horse while wearing armor?"

"My prince," she said loftily, "would have had no problem with the feat. *He* considered me as light as a feather." She gave him a look akin to the one he had given her. "That was thanks to his physique, you understand."

Wick burst out laughing and then stopped suddenly when Jonas fluttered his eyelashes.

"*You* have no romance in your soul," Philippa said. She leaned back against the sofa and sighed. "It was only very recently that I realized the fairy story had more to do with escaping Rodney than being carried off by an acrobatic prince."

Wick leaned over and peered at Jonas. "Fast asleep."

"I should bring him back to the nursery. I think he sleeps better in his cradle."

"No, he sleeps better in your lap." There was a note in his voice that transformed a simple comment into something altogether different.

She could feel her cheeks turning pink. Maybe he would lean over . . . maybe he would kiss her. She could almost feel his lips on hers.

But not quite.

So she stood up, and together, in the darkness, they made their way back to the nursery. Wick stood next to her, watching silently, as she gently tucked Jonas back into his cradle.

When she straightened and turned around, he was there, just before her. His head bent, slowly, and his lips slipped along her cheek. She stayed still, her heart beating in her throat, willing his lips to touch hers.

"I shouldn't be doing this," he said, low and sweet.

He was looking down at her with velvet dark eyes. He was too beautiful for her, too sophisticated, too princely . . .

"Yes, you should," she said.

Chapter Six

From her first night spent in Pomeroy Castle, Philippa had lain awake in bed and imagined Wick's kisses. They wouldn't be like Rodney's slavering invasions, she had decided. And yet—she couldn't imagine what they *would* be like. What if he thrust his tongue into her mouth, the way Rodney had? Any tongue in her mouth, other than her own, would be disgusting. She knew it.

But now Wick kissed her lightly, just a brush of his lips. A jerk of fire went straight down her body, through her middle. She raised her arms and wound them around his neck. His lips were firm and not at all wet—so how on earth could such a simple motion make her feel so hot and needy?

For a few moments, she couldn't help wondering when he was going to push his tongue between her lips, and what she would feel if he did. But instead, he simply stood there in the dark nursery, his head bent to hers, his mouth brushing hers, over and over. Gradually she forgot her worries; besides, her attention was caught by his hands, roaming over her back, sliding lower, shaping her. Soon enough she could think of nothing but the mesmerizing sensation of his touch; it made her feel quite odd. She shivered and tried to move closer to his warmth.

His lips slipped from hers and dusted along the line of her jaw, down the curve of her neck, leaving a little trail of fire everywhere they touched.

He smelled so good, Philippa thought in a daze. What must he taste like? Impulsively, she opened her mouth and tasted him, her tongue sneaking out to touch the hard line of his jaw.

A rough sound came from Wick's lips, and he turned his face to hers. "Darling," he said, his voice a husky thread in the silence.

Philippa pressed even closer, molding her body to his muscles. She was dimly aware that his hair had fallen from its ribbon, and she reached up, running her fingers through the loose strands. The touch felt almost as intimate as kissing.

His tongue ran along her lips, and then he breathed, "Kiss me back, Philippa. *Please*." She opened her mouth. It was as natural as breathing, as turning one's face up to the sunshine. Wick's kiss wasn't about invasion. It was about the taste of him, and the taste of her, and the way their bodies were trembling against each other.

A groan tore from his throat, then he was kissing her harder than Rodney ever had done, so ruthlessly that she could only hold on, helpless in the firestorm that shot down her legs.

Yet she remained aware enough to know that she wasn't alone in that storm; Wick's large hands were trembling as they slid down her back, rounded onto her bottom, and pulled her up and against his body. Which wasn't a bit like Rodney's doughy anatomy. In fact, he didn't *feel* in the least like Rodney . . .

It was Wick who pulled back, Wick who stepped away, leaving Philippa trying to catch her breath. His chest was heaving too, and she could see the wildness in his eyes. She had never felt more feminine, more desired, and more powerful, in her life.

"I can't marry you," he said, low and fierce. "You're a lady. I cannot marry you."

"I haven't asked you to," she rejoined, her voice catching.

She had to stop him before he said anything, before he said he regretted kissing her. "Good night," she whispered, pushing her hair back from her face.

Wick stepped forward, his hands reaching toward her as if he couldn't stop himself. She turned quickly and walked to her bedchamber door, pausing to glance over her shoulder.

He was gazing after her, just as she'd thought—and hoped—he would be.

"I just want to point out," she said, "that not only am I in the service of your brother, but I gave away my most prized possession, my chastity. As anyone in polite society would confirm, a woman in my situation could never marry a gentleman."

Then, before he could respond, she whisked herself through the door. Because . . . Because she had, for all intents and purposes, just asked him to marry her.

And if *that* wasn't enough to disqualify her as a lady, she didn't know what would.

Chapter Seven

*W*hen Wick appeared in the portrait gallery the following night, he didn't say a word about her implicit proposal. Instead he inquired about Jonas's belly troubles, and then told her a story about his Great Aunt Sophonisba. Philippa nodded and smiled, but inside, she was wild with frustration.

Was he never going to mention what happened between them? She had lain awake half the night searching for magic words that would overcome his comment about her birth, and he wanted to talk of trivialities? Then, quite suddenly, Jonas stopped fussing, gave a little snort, and fell asleep.

And just as quickly, Wick snatched the baby from her shoulder and carried him back to the nursery.

Philippa trotted along behind, her heart pounding. She was having trouble remembering her lines, just like an actress about to enter the stage. What should she say? What should she—should she . . .

In the end, she said nothing, because—the baby having been tucked in his bed—Wick pinned her against the wall and kissed her until she was melting against him, and instead of carefully crafted questions designed to make him realize that he should marry her . . . well, he seemed to like those soft sounds she made when he kissed her, which was good because the way he kissed her, put together with the way he touched her, made her intoxicated. Even more intoxicated than old Fettle, when he was lying in the road singing.

The next night was the same, and the night after that. All during the daylight hours, she mulled over ways to make Wick marry her. Somehow. Because if he didn't ask her soon— well, she really *did* have to write her father. She had begun to feel horribly guilty, certain that he was worried to death about what had become of her.

But when the nighttimes came, and Wick found her in the portrait gallery, their eyes would meet, and all those anxieties would fly from her mind.

The world would shrink to fit that room. She would shiver if his arm touched hers, bite her lip at the look in his eyes.

And then, when Jonas was in his cradle, she would slip into Wick's arms as naturally as the baby had settled down to sleep. Once she was there, the world disappeared entirely, and the only thought in her mind was a dazed wish to know more of him. Wick was like the best present she'd ever received, a gift wrapped in hundreds of different layers. Every night she learned something new, something that the rest of the world didn't know.

He kept vital parts of himself secret, even from his own brother. Yet she'd found the magic key that shook him free of that enormous reserve: she kissed him and kissed him. Slowly, his face would change, move from its implacable cheer into something wilder and fiercer. A look that was for her alone. A look that came close—very close—to revealing a Wick who was no longer in control.

But every time she tried to coax him over that final barrier, allowing her hand (scandalously) to brush his thighs, or even, one night, arching against him like the worst kind of Jezebel . . .

He never broke. She could feel him tremble,

hear the groan in his voice, but his self-control held.

And every time she tried to bring up the subject of their relationship, he withdrew. In a second his face would change to that of a calm and unmoved butler. He would bid her a polite good-bye and leave, closing the door politely, and quietly, behind him. Still . . . he came back the next night, as if he couldn't stay away.

It drove her mad. The only way Philippa could imagine changing Wick's mind was to seduce him. True, she didn't know much about seduction. Rodney had thrown himself in the straw at her feet, after all, and even the memory of him scrabbling at her ankles made her shudder.

One day when Kate took the baby off to nurse, Philippa drifted around the castle until she found Wick inspecting the work of three footmen as they polished some silver. Gathering her resolve, she poked her head in, and said as calmly as she could, "Mr. Berwick, Her Highness would like to speak to you in the nursery."

But when he emerged from the door, she pulled him into the small sitting room next door. They didn't say a word, just came together with a giddiness that made them both shake with silent laughter until the glitter in Wick's eyes became something else, something hotter and more private than mirth.

She kissed him until they were both shaking, until her blood raced, until she could feel him, hard and rigid against her.

And yet, after a few minutes he put her away, looking down into her face with that impenetrable expression that she was growing to hate. There was a frown in his eyes.

"You mustn't do this," he whispered, rubbing his thumb over her lip.

"Why not?"

"I'm not worth it. I'm not worth you. This cannot—*we* cannot—be together."

"We *are* together," she said. "I lo—"

His hand slipped over her mouth. "Don't say it. You must not. I am not a gentleman."

"I love you," she said, pulling her head sharply from his hand. "I *will* tell my father that; I will tell anyone: your brother, Kate, the footmen, the cook."

She could see him swallow. "I could not bear it if you did that."

"Why not?" she asked.

"I would not wish that on my worst enemy."

"What wouldn't you wish?" she asked, genuinely bewildered.

"To ruin the woman he loves," he said.

"I'm already ruined."

He ran one finger down her cheek, and then let his hand drop. "You were not ruined by the loutish Rodney, no matter what you think. There's many a lady who anticipated the marriage bed. But make no mistake, you would be ruined by marrying a servant." He turned and withdrew, leaving her there.

WICK WALKED STRAIGHT out of the castle, down the great marble stairs, and to the lake. He moved blindly, seeing nothing but the disappointment in Philippa's eyes. He felt a queer ache in his heart at the thought of it.

Yet what could he do? He loved her—God, he loved her the way he never imagined was possible. He would step before a raging bull, he would throw himself in—

But he couldn't do what she wanted. Marry her? Make her into the wife of a butler? Never. *Never.*

He was staring at the still surface of the lake, agonized by the turn of events that had brought Philippa to him, and the social conventions that would likely keep them apart, when he felt a touch on his shoulder, turned his head, and found his brother at his side. As brothers do, they understood each other without a word; Gabriel was squinting at him in a way that conveyed to Wick that his private kisses were no longer private.

"Damnation," he said flatly.

"Hmm," Gabriel said, a smile twitching at the corner of his mouth. "Philippa is a lovely girl. Kate adores her."

"I can't marry her."

"Why not?"

It took a moment before Wick could compose himself and look over at his oblivious brother without rage in his eyes. He prided himself on never showing emotion of that sort. "I'm in your service," he said, finally. "As a butler."

"Only because you chose to be so," Gabriel responded.

"Once that choice was made, the decision was irrevocable."

"Rubbish. I can hire another majordomo in London. You only took over because we had no money, don't you remember? Well, now we have Kate's unexpectedly lavish inheritance, not to mention the payment I received for my book on Greek archaeology. In fact, I just bought Kate's father's estate from her stepmother. We could—"

"You could *what*? Make me legitimate? Make

358

me the proper spouse for Philippa?" Wick couldn't help it. The calm front he was so proud of maintaining cracked along with his heart, and bitterness poured like acid into his voice. "You can't give me what I most need: a father who didn't bed a dairymaid and impregnate her. You can't give my mother her marriage lines, nor myself the pedigree that Philippa deserves."

He saw his arguments hit home. "I'm no husband for a lady, Gabe," he said more quietly.

"Philippa loves you," Gabriel said rallying. "A blind man could see that. She doesn't care about your pedigree."

Wick's throat was too tight to answer. He knew that his brother could see raw despair in his eyes because he pulled him into a rough embrace. "She couldn't do better than you," Gabriel said a moment later, thumping him on the back.

He just shook his head. "Bollocks."

"There's just one way in which you fall short."

It didn't seem like merely one way to Wick, but he waited for Gabriel to elaborate.

"You're a coward."

At this slur, a flush of hot rage, the kind that only his brother could inspire, surged up Wick's chest. "You dare not say that to me," he said between clenched teeth.

"You've got the balls to love her, but not the balls to take her," Gabriel said. "And do you want to know why I know that?"

"No." Wick's hands were curling into fists.

"Because I was the same with Kate. I was trapped, thinking that I had to be as rich as Croesus before I could marry. You're not responsible for our father's idiocy. You're afraid to just reach out and take her, even though she wants you."

"I'm no coward," Wick said between clenched teeth.

Gabriel actually laughed. "Luckily for Philippa, she's beautiful enough that another man will come along who has the balls to accept what she's offering."

A muted roar erupted from Wick's throat, and he threw himself at his brother. They fell to the ground with a thump, rolled over in a flurry of blows, rolled over again. Wick found himself on top. "She may want me now but—"

His sentence was derailed by a deft move by Gabriel, who managed to flip him on the ground and knock the wind out of him. It wasn't until they were both lying on their backs panting and gingerly feeling their knuckles, that Wick said it. He said it flatly, because he'd examined it, night after night turning the facts over and over in his mind, and he knew it was true. "Years from now, she will wish she had a man who could take his place next to her in society."

His brother pushed himself to his feet. "How do you know? Maybe she just wants a braver you, a man with the balls to stand up and say he's as good as any other man, regardless of birth."

Wick took the hand his brother held out to him. "I can't be what she deserves," he said, feeling his jaw.

Gabriel looked at him with disgust and turned on his heel. "She does deserve better than you—and I'm not talking about your pedigree."

AFTER WICK ABANDONED her in the sitting room, Philippa slipped back up to the nursery, fully conscious that she couldn't continue to press him for what he told her—over and over—he could not give her. Moreover, Jonas was thriving: he no longer wailed after eating, and his little cheeks were filling out; just that day, he had smiled at Kate for the first time, and later, at his father, and then, at every one of the footmen.

It was time for her to go home.

She would miss the baby and Kate terribly, but it would be a simple matter to engage a new nursemaid. Her heart heavy, she sat down and wrote a letter to her father, sealed it, and gave it to a footman. Her father would have it by evening.

Leaving the castle now, like this, would mean leaving her heart behind. It had been stolen: stolen by a man with immaculate comportment, a quiet and intelligent face, and passionate kisses. She, a daughter of the landed gentry, had fallen in love with a butler.

She was in love with Wick.

But Wick insisted he could not marry her. He respected her; if she loved him, she had to respect him. Even if it meant never seeing him again.

Even then.

But still . . . she had given everything to Rodney—to revolting, despised Rodney. If she could give everything to a lumpen dolt, why could she not give everything to Wick, whom she loved? Setting aside the fact that he kept refusing her, of course.

It wasn't in her to simply give up.

At length, she decided to try once more, just one last time. That night.

The idea grew until her heart was racing with conviction. She *would* do it. She would ask, beg, seduce Wick into making love to her, just once.

So that she knew what it was like, with him. So that, during all those evenings playing chess with her father that lay ahead, she could think back on this one night. It wasn't just chess that loomed in her mind.

There was Rodney. After that letter to her father, there would be no escaping Rodney.

There would be no "happily ever after" for her. Life with Rodney would be . . . whatever it was.

But if she managed to seduce Wick, she would have memories, at least. Still, she would have to be subtle . . . he had a will of iron, and mere sensuality would never break it.

One ethical question kept bothering her. Did she have the right to try to overcome his resolve? Wick's enormous reserve and his adherence to honor stemmed from the same place: his illegitimate birth. If she succeeded in persuading him to make love to her, was she tarnishing that quality he held so dear?

With a wry little smile, she thought about the knight in shining armor her girlhood self had dreamed of. There was no man more born to being a maiden's champion than Wick. He was all that was honorable, good, and true.

In the end, she decided that as long as she didn't cause Wick to break his code of honor, she could not do an injustice to him. And that meant he had to make love to her not because he desired her, but because she needed him—or rather, the act—to save her . . . to rescue her. In making love to her, he would become the instrument of her salvation.

Chapter Eight

That night Phillipa put Jonas to bed and then sat down in the nursery rocking chair, facing the door. If he didn't come by . . . by nine of the clock, she would try to find him. She revised that when nine o'clock came and went. Ten o'clock . . . eleven . . . *Finally* the nursery door opened.

With one look at Wick's face, Philippa flew into his arms like a bird to its nest. Except this bird was in danger of being eaten alive, so perhaps that wasn't a good analogy. His hands were rough, unsteady, and urgent, as if he already knew what she had to say. As if he guessed that it was to be her last night in the castle.

Yet it wasn't long before he pulled back. She would have been angry if she couldn't see raw lust fighting with regret in his eyes. "I'm no

Rodney, taking a maiden in the stables," he said, reminding himself as much as her.

If she was to execute her plan, now was the moment.

"I'm no maiden," Philippa reminded him. And: "I need you."

Every inch of her body was aware of the coiled strength of his. The way he held himself utterly still, not twitching or fidgeting.

"I wrote to my father," she said.

He raised an eyebrow.

"I couldn't allow him to worry about me any longer. It was thoughtless and unkind to give him such anxiety." Jonas made a snuffling sound in his cradle, like a baby piglet. "My father will take me home, of course."

Wick made a sudden movement but stilled.

She swallowed and looked back up at him. "He will come to retrieve me, and take me home to Rodney. That's what he must do, because I—I was fool enough to lie with Rodney in the stables."

"Ah, Philippa," Wick said. And then she was enveloped by his arms.

"I know," she said carefully, "that you would help me if you could."

He held her, warm and close.

"If I had, if I had slept with another man,

perhaps Rodney would refuse to marry me." It sounded absurd. She gave up and started over. "If I—"

He interrupted her. "Philippa."

"I know," she said miserably. "I know you're too much of a gentleman to do what I am asking."

"You are only playing at being a nursemaid, Phillipa. You will go home and be a lady again. But I have never had a gentleman's rank. Servant or bastard . . . either one is ineligible to marry you." His voice was fierce, as ferocious as a wolf in winter. "You ask the impossible."

"I'm sorry! I should never have suggested it." Her words caught on a sob. "I didn't think of it that way. It's just that I thought that you . . ."

"You knew that I desired you and thought I might help you escape from an odious marriage. I cannot have this conversation with the young prince in the room," Wick stated. He walked across the room, bringing Philippa with him, and opened the door to the corridor.

Her heart was breaking. It had all gone wrong. She had insulted Wick. Of course, he couldn't do as she asked. It was as ridiculous as the idea that he should marry her. He was the son of a grand duke. She was a fool—a stupid, naive fool from a small village, and she should have stayed there.

Though if you looked at it another way, he was a servant, and she was a lady. The outcome was obvious.

Besides, her idea was ridiculous, born of desperation. Obviously Wick would never, ever, sleep with an unmarried lady—even if she had begged him.

Her cheeks were burning, as she followed Wick into the corridor and shut the door behind her.

But she came from strong stock, and she would not crumple. "I apologize for asking you to do something so insulting to your sense of honor," she said, keeping her voice steady. And she even managed to summon up a wisp of a smile. "I know you are no debaucher of maidens."

He did not return her smile. "My father was as much. My mother worked in the castle's laundry. I cannot, ever, act as he did."

Philippa nodded. "You are not like your father. And you mustn't think twice about Rodney. I shall explain everything to my father, and I *will* make him understand." She would not burden Wick with the truth: that her father would marry her to Rodney willy-nilly.

"I could kill Rodney, if you wish. Perhaps I should do it whether you wish me to or not."

She blinked and saw that his eyes were entirely

serious. She let out a muffled laugh. "No! Rodney is . . . Rodney is not terrible. I exaggerated the matter when I told you about him. I will tell my father that I don't wish to marry Rodney, and that will be that."

She held out her hand. "I have heard that fine ladies in London shake hands."

He looked down at her hand in the dim corridor. "Are you a fine lady?"

"No, but I wish I were, for your sake."

"So you could buy me?"

Her hand dropped. "*Buy* you?"

"I'm pretty, in my own way," he said neutrally. "Ladies have indicated that they might be willing to support me in a grander fashion than does Gabriel."

For a moment she didn't understand him, then a flash of rage went through her body. "Now you have insulted me, as surely as I did you," she snapped. "I think this conversation has gone quite far enough." She turned to open the door to the nursery.

His hand shot out, held the door shut.

"Wick," she said, staring at his hand against the dark wood, "I must enter that nursery. I should pack. I am leaving tomorrow."

She didn't feel him move, or sense a flash of

his arms, nothing . . . and yet suddenly she was spun around and found herself wrapped in his arms.

"I would let *you* buy me," he said finally, his voice hoarse.

She managed a shaky smile. Then she took a deep breath and put her hands on his face, drawing his lips to hers.

"How much?" she whispered.

"I've been told I'm worth a fortune." His voice had a bleak note.

"I haven't much money." Her tongue stole out, ran along the seam of his lips, tasted that wildness that he concealed with his upright body, his unmoving face.

"There's a special rate on . . . I'm going for a ha'penny," he whispered against her lips.

This time *she* kissed him.

Philippa didn't know how long they stood in the corridor. With her eyes closed, her only sensations came from the press of Wick's powerful body, the drugging sensation of his mouth, the way his hands shaped and teased her.

Then she became aware he was saying something. "I didn't mean to insult you by talking of the women who offered to buy me." His voice was low and rasping. "But I am constrained. I cannot ask you to marry me. The *only* conceivable relationship between a butler and a lady is if she . . . engages his services."

She swallowed, biting her lip when she saw the pain in his eyes. "But I would marry you."

The words had tumbled from her lips. "If you were to ask," she added quickly.

"I am a servant, with a grand lineage on one side but no wealth," Wick said bleakly. "And the truth of it is that I . . . I love you, Philippa." It was his turn to cup her face in his hands. "Which means I cannot make you a servant. If I could marry any lady, any woman in the world, from queen to beggar, I would never choose another than you. And I mean that."

Philippa's lips trembled. "I love you too," she whispered.

"But I cannot marry," Wick said, his eyes searching hers, begging for understanding. "If I were a different person, and this a different place and time, I would have had a wedding ring on your finger a week ago."

"Oh, Wick," she whispered, collapsing forward against his chest. A tear dampened his shirt.

"I would give anything to call you mine." His voice was harsh and true.

"Then I shall have to buy you," Philippa said, brushing away that tear and another that followed it. She pulled back and caught his eye, because this was important. "I am not a child to be handed from one man's hand to another."

His brows drew together. "I do not—"

"You do." She said it clearly, not angrily. "I love you."

He swallowed hard.

"And I am perfectly capable of making up my own mind about the disposition of my body."

"I know."

She opened the door at her back. "Then come." She held out her hand.

His voice emerged strangled from his chest. "Philippa, I *cannot*—"

"If you love me, if you respect me as a person who owns myself and my own body, who is servant to no one and owned by no one . . ."

"A gentleman wouldn't," he said hoarsely.

She smiled at that, picked up his hand. "You just told me, sir, that you are no gentleman."

He followed her, through the darkened nursery, to the door at the far end, through the door.

From a chair at the side of the bedroom, she snatched her reticule, and opened it. "If the only way I may have you is to buy you . . ."

He let out a half groan, half laugh. "Philippa!"

She reached out, caught his hand, and wrapped his fingers around a ha'penny. "Then I own you. And although you didn't ask, my price was very low. I was yours from your first kiss. I suppose you could say that I came for free."

The hunger in his eyes made her feel more beautiful than she had in the whole of her life.

Still, he remained motionless, exercising that infernal self-control of his.

She let the silence grow, then: "I have bought a house, but not possessed it." She was quite sure that the look in her eyes rivaled that of any light skirts on the streets of London. "And *I* am sold, but not yet enjoyed."

There was another beat of silence in the room, during which Philippa's heart drummed in her throat.

"That was a terrible pun," Wick observed. There was something deep and slow in his voice. She bit back a smile.

He put one hand to his perfectly tied cravat. Philippa held her breath.

Eyes fixed on hers, he slowly, slowly lifted a fold of snowy linen, over, up, over, through . . . she saw his hands from the corner of her vision, because she was drinking in his expression, the taut desire that shaped his face.

Then she raised her hands to the cord that held her wrapper together. A moment later, she was wearing only a light muslin nightgown. One glance down at her chest and she felt herself turning pink with embarrassment. Instinctively, she folded her arms over her breasts, hoping to flatten her nipples before Wick saw them.

She couldn't tell if he had. He shrugged off his heavy coat and put it over a chair.

"You," Philippa said, and cleared her throat. "You look . . ."

"Without that livery," Wick stated, "I am a man, nothing but a man."

Joy sparked her heart. "Do you wish me to remove my nightgown?"

He straightened, a shoe in one hand. "If you're having second thoughts, I'll leave."

She gasped *no*, and a smile quirked the corner of his mouth. Then she added: "I think I would feel more comfortable with my nightgown on."

Wick nodded. He dispensed with his other shoe, pulled off his stockings, then paused, hands on his waistband.

Philippa realized her voice had died. It was just that his body was so taut and muscled, like nothing she'd seen or imagined. It was a wicked smile he threw her, the kind that seducers threw maidens . . . though she was no maiden.

"I should probably warn you," Wick said, but she hardly heard him. He removed his breeches, and now his hands were on his smalls.

"What?" she breathed.

"It could be that Rodney and I don't—" Still his hands didn't move.

"Don't what?" she said, unable to imagine what he was getting at.

"Don't resemble each other." His smalls hit the floor, and Philippa's mouth fell open. She instinctively fell back a step, ending up against the wrought-iron bed frame.

"Oh dear." Her voice came out in a squeak. The memory of Rodney's member flashed through her mind: Rodney's little member, she now realized. There was no comparison.

"I gather we don't," Wick said, a wry, yet tender note in his voice.

"No," Philippa breathed. "You don't."

Chapter Nine

*W*ick hadn't known—hadn't dared to think—about what was about to happen, and what it would mean for him. But as laughter gathered in his chest at the look in Philippa's eyes, the helpless, desiring, *appalled* look on her face, he knew.

He meant to have her, to have and to hold, any way he could. Whether that meant becoming a butler in her house, or a gardener in her fields . . . He had to be near her.

This funny, delicious, intelligent woman had walked into the castle and straight into his heart and she would never leave it, as long as he lived.

But that was a problem to be worked out to-morrow. Just at present, he had to pry his beloved off the bed railings.

"Darling," he said, walking closer.

Philippa flicked her eyes to his face, then back down. The agonized doubt on her face almost had him doubling over with laughter, but he couldn't do that. Instead, he swept her up in his arms and lowered her onto the bed.

She lay in the path of the moonlight coming through the window; it flowed across the floor, up and over the bed, spilling on the window and splashing light over her white-blonde hair as it spilled over the pillow and down the side of the bed. She looked ethereal, like a fairy and not an Englishwoman, some sort of fabulous sprite he'd captured and brought to his bed for the night.

He sat next to her on the bed. "Why did you ask me whether you should undress?"

"Rodney didn't, that is, he undressed but he didn't remove my clothes."

"Rodney," Wick stated, "is a fool and a bungler. I don't suppose he used a French letter either, did he?"

"No."

"It will prevent your being with child," he told her. "Our child." There was a little stab to his heart as he said it. He would give anything to have his baby growing inside Philippa, to watch her stomach round, to see her eyes in the face of a little boy or girl . . . But since he didn't know if the obstacles to their marriage could be overcome, the French letter was necessary.

A ghost of a smile touched her lips, but still, she looked strained and uncertain. He lowered himself slowly until he lay on his side, and gently, very gently, leaned forward to touch his lips to hers. His hands tangled in all that gorgeous hair, drawing locks of it through his fingers like silk spun on Jove's own looms.

He kissed her until she opened her mouth to him and turned toward him. He kept kissing her, not moving, letting her body inch toward his, letting her hands take the initiative, slipping from his neck to his shoulders, down his back.

Her touch made him shake with ferocious need, but he schooled himself. He remained still, telling himself that he must not frighten her. Philippa had already had one unpleasant experience; if he muffed this, she'd likely be put off for life.

He waited until her eyes flew open, and she said, "Wick."

"Yes?" He couldn't stop grinning.

"Don't the gentlemen *do* more with the strumpets they buy?"

"What sort of thing would you like me to do?"

"You should know. And stop smiling at me like that."

"I can't help it," he said, leaning forward and

kissing her lips, her cheek, her feathery eye-lashes. "I've never laughed in bed with a woman before."

"That's probably because you were more busy than you are now," she remarked, and he nipped her earlobe, then felt the shudder that pulsed down her body.

"You look like a fairy, a sprite," he said, running his hand down the long line of her leg. She seemed to have a fascination with his chest: she was tracing little patterns on it. "But you sound like a schoolmarm." The last word was strangulated, as Philippa had leaned toward him and was tracing the same patterns with her tongue.

Slowly, slowly, he slid his hand under her night-gown, over her slender thigh, the tender curve of her waist.

"I just want to say one thing," Philippa said, abandoning his chest, much to his regret.

"Mmmmm," he said, his fingers gliding over skin as soft as daisy petals. His heart was thudding in a way he had never experienced before.

"No tiddle-taddling," she said.

Wick's hand was caressing her generous, lush breast, and couldn't think very clearly. Philippa's head fell back against the pillow as he brushed past her nipple and a small moan broke from her lips, so it seemed she wasn't exactly clearheaded

Eloisa James

either. "Is this tiddle-taddling?" he asked, rubbing that sweet raspberry with his thumb.

Another strangled moan, a tiny pulse of air, flew from her throat. "No," she said with a gasp. Then: "You don't know what it is, do you? I should have known only Rodney would try to engage in something so distasteful."

It struck Wick that bedding his beloved was the most delightful, funny, and passionate activity he had ever engaged in. He kissed her again, letting his fingers wander, marking what made Philippa arch her back, instinctively falling into a position to give . . . and take.

Slowly, slowly he inched her nightgown all the way above her breasts. She didn't seem to notice until he replaced one of the hands that was caressing her breast with his mouth—well, she noticed that. And he stayed there, learning her secrets, tasting her sweetness. Savoring her. Every startled gasp made laughter and desire double in his chest.

"Lovely Philippa," he murmured, sometime later, "is *this* tiddle-taddling?" And just to make sure she knew what he was talking about, he leaned down and gave her other breast a kiss, the kind that claimed, that was a little rough and a little wild.

"No!" she gasped and then, "Oh, Wick, that feels wonderful."

Her hands reached out, rather blindly, toward him. "Does it feel the same for you?"

Once they had established to both their satisfaction that, yes, it *did* feel just as good for him, Wick was flat on his back with Philippa lying along his side, one of her legs entwined with his.

"Philippa," he said, dimly hearing the hoarseness in his voice. "May I remove your nightgown now?"

She looked at him, her eyes shining. "If I kiss you *here*, Wick, your whole body jerks in response. Isn't that interesting?"

"Quite," he managed, and whipped her billowing nightgown over her head. "You're so beautiful," he breathed, awestruck.

Philippa followed Wick's gaze down her body. The moonlight had turned her limbs to alabaster; she tried to imagine herself as he saw her. But she would rather look at him.

"Just one thing," she said trying to gather her thoughts. "What I said before . . ."

But his hands were at her waist and his mouth closed over her breast and she lost the sentence, the words, the thought altogether.

"Yes?" he asked.

All the secret parts of her were throbbing, which was such an odd sensation that . . . still, she needed to make the point. "It's just one of Rodney's daft perversions," she said, tugging his shoulders. "He called it diddling, but I know you won't do such a thing."

Wick moved so his body was poised above hers and God save her, the only thing she wanted was that large body to rest on top of hers. She finally understood why women played the strumpet: it was because they caught a glimpse of a man like this one.

"Wick," she whispered, throwing the last of any remaining maidenly caution to the winds, "come to me . . . please?"

"I thought it was *tiddling* that you didn't like," Wick said, his eyes glinting with an unholy mixture of laughter and lust. "Now I find you don't like *diddling* either?"

Philippa rolled her eyes. "You know what I mean."

A strong hand suddenly laid a scorching path up her leg, easing them apart, skating onto the inner flesh of her thigh. Philippa gasped. "That's exactly where Rodney . . . you mustn't!"

"I won't," Wick said tenderly, dropping another kiss on the corner of her mouth. "I'll never do something so ham-handed that Rodney partook in it . . . not unless you beg me to, of course."

And with that, he took her mouth in such a devouring kiss that at first Philippa hardly noticed the hand stroking her legs apart, dancing close to her most secret—but notice she did. She tore her mouth away, and said, "Wick, *no*."

"I would never," he said, his eyes innocent. "On the Continent, we disdain diddling. We do this instead." And without pausing for a response, he pulled open her legs with strong hands, slid down, and before she could even conceive of such a thing, put his mouth—*there*.

Philippa didn't even think of refusing. In fact, she couldn't think at all. Her capacity for rational thought did not reemerge until after she found herself shaking from head to foot, trying to fathom how a scorching wave had burst over her head and dragged her down into its fiery depths.

Wick was there, grinning down at her . . . nudging her.

Her eyes widened. "Is that you?"

"Yes," he said, husky and sweet. "Take me, Philippa. Because I'm the one who loves you, and because you love me. Make me yours."

She knew instinctively that *this* kind of ownership had nothing to do with ha'pennies, or even kisses. And when he was deep inside her, hers weren't the only eyes shining with errant tears.

"You're *mine*," she whispered.

Wick cradled her face in his. "Does it hurt?"

"No," she whispered back, rather surprised. "It did with Rodney, and there's so much more of you. But it feels . . ." She wiggled a little. "It feels good."

"Ah," he said, with such a wealth of satisfaction in his voice that she started to smile, but then he drew back, slowly, and just as slowly, thrust forward, and the smile flew from her mind, along with everything but the wild pleasure, the ravishing feeling that had her arching to meet him, crying out with each stroke.

He kept coming, and coming . . . like the tide washing up on the shore, only not so gentle, then it felt as if the ocean came to her, as if a flood of pure pleasure swept from her toes to the ends of her fingers.

Dimly, she heard his groan, then her own cry.

It was a night of discovery.

SHE WOKE IN the dim light of dawn to find that Jonas had slept through the night for the very first time. Wick was bent over her. She reached up, only to realize that he was, once again, dressed in his livery.

"I must go," he murmured, brushing strands of hair from her face. "And you must return to being Miss Philippa Damson rather than my favorite nursemaid."

She smiled at him drowsily, but she was waking up, and his words coalesced into something ominous. "What do you mean?"

"I expect your father will arrive this morning to take you home."

Philippa sat up, her heart suddenly pounding. "I shan't go."

"You must. Jonas is much better, and young ladies can't serve in the nursery forever. You are no servant, Philippa."

"I don't want—" She stopped. "If you are a servant, I want to be a servant."

"You mustn't say such a thing."

"I don't want to leave you."

"You must." He said it gently, but she heard the stark truth of it in his voice. "There is no place for you here, in the castle. You might come as a visitor, but if I am in livery." He hesitated. "I would rather you did not."

And there it was.

She swung her legs from the bed and stood up, feeling the chill of his words spread through her body. "Please, Wick, don't—don't say this."

He ran his fingers through her hair and pulled

her close. "I will try to come for you," he said, low and fierce. "I will *try*, Philippa. But I could never make you a servant or a beggar at my side. Wait for me—"

"Forever," she said.

"One week. If I don't come for you before one week has passed, I could not manage it. But know this, Philippa." He looked down into her face, as unyielding as the greatest emperor who ever lived. "If I do not come for you, it is not for want of desire for you, nor for want of love for you, nor for want of trying. I would do anything to be worthy of you."

Her breath caught on a sob. "Oh, Wick . . ."

"And I will *never* love another woman above you."

The deep, hungry yearning in his eyes made her knees weak. She caught at him, fumbling for words, the vow that would make him understand that she was his forever. That she would wait a lifetime.

But he was gone.

Chapter Ten

*P*hilippa lay awake until the thin gray light turned pale yellow, and Jonas stirred. She had no sooner washed and dressed herself and Jonas than a footman announced that her father requested to speak with her.

The moment she entered the sitting room, she threw herself into her father's open arms. "I'm sorry, Papa; oh, you *were* worried! I told you not to be."

For a moment, her father merely stood, his arms now tight around her. Then he sat down heavily, pulling her to his knee as if she were five years old. "You told me not to worry . . . and you truly believed your reassurance would be sufficient?"

"I did when I first ran away. But I've learned differently in the past weeks," she confessed. "I thought it would be better for you if I was gone because I didn't want to obey you. But I know now that love is far more possessive than that." She leaned against his shoulder, as if she truly were a little girl again. "I missed you."

"Were you treated well? I spoke to the prince, who seems a very orderly and mannered young fellow. But were you treated well?" He looked around. "I cannot countenance the fact that my daughter has been working as a nursemaid. Thank heaven your mother wasn't alive to see it."

"The prince and princess treated me with nothing but the greatest kindness, Papa."

"I will give them my thanks, but then we must be away. I neglected the house, the estate, everything after you ran away."

Philippa came to her feet and stood as straight as she could. "I will return home with you, Papa, but I will not marry Rodney. I will never, ever marry Rodney." In that long hour before Jonas awoke, while she lay awake longing for Wick she had concluded that it was best not to inform her father that she planned to marry the butler.

"So I gathered from your note," her father said, perplexed. "But why, sweetpea? You've always loved Rodney—"

"No, Papa," Philippa interrupted. "You have always loved the idea of my marrying Rodney.

And Rodney said he loved me. But no one ever asked me how I felt about marrying that fat-bottomed . . . *fellow!*"

Her father frowned. "Fat-bottomed? Is he?"

"Yes."

"I never noticed. Still, you can't make a decision of this nature based on something as unimportant as a bottom. It's a man's character that counts. Rodney is a sturdy lad, in character as well as physique."

That may be true but it was beside the point.

"Would you call him intelligent?" she asked.

Her father gave this some thought. "Well, perhaps not precisely intelligent, but . . ."

"But?"

"A head is like a house," he said. "If it's crammed too full, it's cluttered."

"Rodney's house doesn't have a stick of furniture in it," she said flatly.

Her father's shoulders slumped. "I thought I was doing the best for you."

"Papa," she said, "I will not marry Rodney. Ever."

"Just come home," he said, coming to his feet and taking her in his arms again. "Just come home, please, Philippa. These last weeks have been insupportable."

"I'm sorry," she said softly, realizing the depth of her own unkindness, however unintended it may have been. "I was as bad as the serpent's tooth in the Bible, wasn't I, Papa?"

"Not quite," he said wearily. "And it was Shakespeare's Lear who called his thankless daughter a serpent's tooth. But I haven't felt so distraught since your mother died, and that's the truth. I'll have to speak to Sir George. I told him that you were visiting my brother all this time, but he suspects otherwise, of course. The servants have talked."

"Please not the first day," Philippa implored. "Surely, we can have a quiet day to ourselves. I'll have a posset made, and we'll play a game of chess in your study."

They did just that.

Chapter Eleven

But the very next morning her father looked up from his plate and nodded to the butler, standing at a side table by the fire, ready to provide fresh toast. "That will do, Quirbles."

Philippa put down her fork as their butler closed the door quietly behind him. "What is it, Papa?"

"You're not the same," he said abruptly.

She blinked at him.

"There's something different about you."

"I hope not." She didn't know whether to hope that Wick's French letter had worked just as it ought or not: there was nothing to the outward eye that admitted she'd been ravished—and loved.

"What happened in that castle, Philippa?" her father asked. His voice was kind, but firm.

She picked up her fork again and studiously

pushed her eggs to the side of the plate. "I took care of the little prince. I told you that already, Papa."

"That's not what I mean . . . His father didn't do anything untoward, did he?"

Philippa's mouth fell open. "Of course not, Papa! What a thing to suggest!"

"His Highness is not English."

"He is all that is honorable," Philippa said reprovingly. "And the princess is perfectly lovely. We even became friends. And by the way, she *is* English—though really, Papa, you should not make assumptions about people's characters based on where they come from." In truth, she missed Kate, which was absurd because they had been acquainted for only a few weeks.

"Nevertheless, you have changed somehow. What happened there?" her father persisted.

With a deep breath Philippa took the plunge. "I fell in love."

"Ah, I thought so," her father said, with the satisfaction that comes with having one's guess confirmed. "You know, sweetpea, when your mother was dying, she was very worried about you. She was certain that I wouldn't notice what you were feeling or thinking."

"Well, you didn't, when it came to Rodney," Philippa pointed out, rather unkindly.

"I made up for that now," he said, taking a bite of kipper.

She watched him chew and smile to himself.

But then the significance of it hit him. He put down his fork with a sharp click.

"You fell in love—with whom did you fall in love? Some dissolute scrap of gentry hanging around the prince's knees, hoping for a handout, I'll warrant. One of those glittering court fellows with no more substance or ethics than a tomcat!"

"No." She took a bite of her now-cold eggs though she couldn't taste them.

He frowned at her.

"The butler," Philippa stated; having plunged, there was nothing for it but to keep going.

At this unimaginable revelation the blood drained from her father's face. "You're jesting." His voice was a whisper.

Philippa squared her shoulders. "Mr. Berwick is the prince's own brother. He is the son of a grand duke. He serves as His Highness's major-domo out of strong loyalty and affection."

Her father blinked. "No gentleman would *ever* serve as a butler, no matter what fancy label you give the position."

"He *is* a gentleman," Philippa snapped, in a tone she had never before used with her father.

"Then there's something else wrong with him . . .

Oh, dear God, he's a married man." Mr. Damson dropped his head into his hands. "I should have wedded you to Rodney the day you turned sixteen."

Philippa rose, then slipped into the chair next to her father. "He is not married, Papa."

Her father raised his head. "Poor as a church mouse, I expect. No estate."

"None," she admitted.

"Still, that doesn't explain why he's the butler. The man could marry an heiress if he's the son of a grand duke. There's no need to put on livery; there's many a rich merchant who would love to boast of a son-in-law with that pedigree."

Philippa bit her lip.

It came to him. "Wrong side of the blanket," her father stated, his mouth bunching up with disdain.

She nodded.

"Damnation!" The word echoed harshly in the little room.

"Papa," she said imploringly. "Wick is not—"

"Wick? *Wick?* Like the wick of a candle? I'll be damned if my daughter will have anything to do with a man named after a household necessity." He surged to his feet. "Tell me that the bastard touched you, and I'll kill him myself."

Philippa jumped up as well. "Papa, no!"

He grabbed her arms and stared into her face. "No? No, you are still a virgin?" She didn't answer, and he gave her a shake. "Does that fine prince over there know the consequences of his bastard brother deflowering an English lady? Does he?"

"He didn't deflower me," she whispered.

Her father's face relaxed, but his grip didn't. "Ah." Then, more slowly: "That would explain why he's not here, trying to make his way out of the servant class by marrying you."

"He refused to marry me!" She half shrieked it.

Her father dropped her arms, tottered, and sank back in his chair. "Margaret, Margaret, why did you leave me?" he moaned.

Philippa raised her chin. She couldn't even imagine what her mother would make of the situation. "*I* asked him to marry me."

Her father's only response was a loud groan.

"And he refused on the grounds of his honor."

"Where did I go wrong?" he moaned. "What did we do wrong, Margaret?" He raised his head. "This is all because of Rodney, isn't it? You got a bee in your bonnet about Rodney, and so you fell for a good-looking servant with an interesting tale."

"Wick is a gentleman and as honorable as you are. He means to be a doctor, just like your own brother."

395

"You are not the first," her father said, unheeding. "There's that daughter of the Earl of Southplank, a year or two ago. Everyone knew she ran off with a footman, some say for an entire week. But she's properly married, right and tight now." He stood again. "And that's what you'll be as well. I'll visit Sir George this very afternoon."

"I will not marry Rodney!" A numbing wave of despair broke over her head.

"You will." Her mild-mannered father suddenly took on the look of a bulldog. "You'll do as I say, Philippa. I won't have you ruining your life, pining after a servant who has a better understanding of propriety than you do. I don't know whether I'm more appalled that you played the fool enough to *ask* such a thing of the man, or more grateful that he didn't lunge at the chance."

"No, Papa!" Philippa cried. "You don't understand. You can't!"

"I can," he said. He took her arm and began towing her up the stairs. "And don't think you're going to run away again. I'll tell the baronet that you suffered from a bout of sun-sickness. You will marry the fat-bottomed Rodney on the morrow and count yourself lucky. The last of the banns were said Sunday, just as you were flitting around that castle making a fool of yourself!"

"Papa," Philippa said, her voice catching with tears. "I love Wick. I love him more than—"

"You will forget him," her father stated. They reached the top of the stairs, and he pushed her directly into her bedchamber. "Someday you'll look back on this episode as if it were a bout of fever. I always thought you were a sensible girl, Philippa."

"I am!" she cried. "I loathe Rodney, Papa. I loathe him, and I will not marry him."

"You will," he said, shutting the door in her face. She heard him through the wood, his voice only slightly muffled. "Tomorrow!"

A FEW HOURS later Philippa heard the front door burst open, and she knew that her father had returned, and not waited for Quirbles to open said door to admit him. She hurried down the stairs, her heart pounding. Her father's face was gleaming with sweat, his usual rather mournful expression metamorphosed into pure anger.

Without a word, Philippa ran into the sitting room before him. "That *bastard!*" her father bellowed, slamming the door behind him.

Philippa fell into a chair, judging that the bastard in question was not her beloved Wick. Evidently, Rodney had revealed all.

"He took advantage of you, a maiden, a gently born maiden. And he did so"—her father wheeled and glared down at her—"in a *barn*? In the *straw*?"

Philippa swallowed, but honesty made her admit, "I allowed him to do so, Papa."

Rage twisted the corner of her father's mouth. "That is irrelevant. Irrelevant! You are a gently born damsel, the only child of my house, and you were deflowered in a barn!" He spluttered to a halt. "Your mother," he added heavily, "would kill me for this."

Philippa bit her lip but said nothing.

"Sir George threw his son across the room once that young fool confessed," her father said, seating himself opposite her. He reached up and pulled at his neckcloth as if it were strangling him.

"He did?" Philippa squeaked. "Across the room?"

"The baronet was as appalled as I," her father said, dropping his head back on his chair's high back. "That donkey didn't even seem to realize what he'd done. Of *course* you ran from the house. You, a damsel, taken without the benefit of marriage, my daughter—in a *barn*." That seemed to be the worst detail. "I shall never recover from this, never."

"Papa," Philippa began, hardly knowing what to say.

Her father jerked his head upright. "I want you to know, dear, that Sir George and I understand entirely why you fled. Entirely. It must have been an awful experience for you. Terrible. Like those suffered by women in wartime, I have no doubt. In the Egyptian campaign, for example—" He stopped and shook his head. "Irrelevant to the present situation."

"I'm sure it wasn't nearly as terrible as that," Philippa said tentatively, as her father had never instructed her on the plight of women in wartime.

"No gently bred lady should be introduced to a situation that she instinctively finds distasteful except in the most acceptable circumstances."

Philippa frowned, and her father frowned back. "In the dark," he clarified. "In a proper bed, within the sanctity of matrimony, and with the knowledge that your husband respects and admires you, even though the act itself—to wit, consummation of the marriage—is necessarily distasteful to you, if not painful."

"Oh," Philippa said. That would have summed up her probable marital relations with Rodney. But it had no relevance for intimacies with Wick.

"As I said, neither of us blames you," her father repeated.

"Thank you," Philippa said.

"Your mother would have fled as well." Her

father pulled off his neckcloth and mopped his face with it. "I simply cannot countenance the idiocy of that young man. Idiocy!"

Philippa waited, a sick feeling in her stomach.

"But be that as it may," her father said, "you have made your bed, albeit in the stables. Did you confide to this Candlewick what happened to you?"

"His name is Berwick, not Candlewick." But she nodded.

Her father wiped his face again and threw the neckcloth to the floor. "I shall send the man a gratuity. One hundred pounds. In refusing you, he showed the breeding of his paternal lineage. Obviously, he realized that you were slightly cracked because of the horrendous experience you endured. And he responded as a gentleman must. Two hundred pounds," he added.

"Be that as it may, you're to marry Rodney immediately," he continued. "We'll forget that episode with the castle and the butler ever happened. Rodney is not the man I should have chosen for you; I see that now. And I am sorry. But you know as well as I do, my dear, that all other doors are closed to you at this point."

To Philippa, his voice seemed to take on a brassy sound, like someone speaking a foreign language. "Papa," she pleaded. "I cannot marry him. *Please.*"

"Do you think that your mother wished to remain married to me after our wedding night?"

There was no possible answer to that.

"She did not," her father said heavily. "The act is horrifying to a delicately bred creature. But we managed, and we loved each other, and there's no one else in the world I would rather have married."

"*She* didn't have to marry Rodney!" Philippa cried.

"I want your word of honor that you will not run away again, Philippa."

"Wick might come for me," she blurted out.

Her father's eyes softened. "Oh, sweetheart. Didn't you just say that he refused to marry you?"

She nodded miserably.

"He truly is a gentleman," he said gently.

"But he might come for me," she said, tears running down her cheeks. "He—He knows how much I detest Rodney, and he *loves* me."

"He can't support you," her father said, standing up and pulling her into his arms. "Were I he, I would loathe the idea of lowering the woman I loved, a lady, to the level of a servant. Did he say anything of that sort?"

A sob rose in Philippa's breast.

Her father held her even closer. "I see he did. Well, my dear, the truth of it is that you have met

two young men. One of them is a true gentleman, though perhaps his birth is not the best.
And the other is no gentleman, though he's a
baronet's son."

"P-Please don't make me marry him," Philippa
managed.

"There's no choice," he said, rocking her a little. "You know that, Philippa. There's no choice.
You'll forget your noble butler in time. Rodney
genuinely loves you, for all the boy's a fool. You
could do much worse."

"I can't bear it," Philippa said, sobbing.

"You mustn't run away," her father said. "It
broke my heart. I aged ten years, sweetpea. I
couldn't bear it if I didn't know where you were.
Please."

Silent tears seeped into his coat.

"And you're a lady," her father said, pressing
forward where he obviously saw an advantage.
"You must marry Rodney." Then he played his
strongest card.

"It's what your mother wanted."

She knew it was the truth.

"Margaret's heart would break to think of you,
her only child, as a servant, or withering into
an old maid," he said. "I promise you, child, I
promise that you will learn to love Rodney. He's a
fool, but he's not vicious or unkind. He genuinely

loves you, in a way that I've rarely seen among gentlemen, to tell the truth. He will always care for you, and for the children you will have."

The weight of his words felt like heavy brambles, rooting her in Little Ha'penny, in Rodney's arms, in Durfey Manor.

"I—" She swallowed, made herself say it. "I will marry Rodney, but only if you give me a week. If you force me to marry him tomorrow, Papa, I will run away tonight. I will crawl out my window if I have to."

Her father sighed. "Waiting for the butler?"

"He's a gentleman," she said stoutly. "You acknowledged it yourself. He *loves* me. He told me so. He'll find a way, some way, to come to me."

Her father turned away, but not before she saw raw sympathy in his eyes. "As you wish," he said. "I owe you that at least."

Chapter Twelve

$\mathcal{H}$our by agonizing hour, day by day, the week of Philippa's temporary reprieve crept past. She tried not to look out the window in the direction of the castle. Wick had promised her a week. He would try. He would . . . try. She kept repeating that to herself though she went to sleep sobbing at the possibility that he wouldn't come.

Or at the possibility he would come to ask for her hand, but a day too late, a week too late, a year too late.

On the fifth day in the early afternoon, her father found her, sitting in a back room without a view of the dusty road leading in the direction of the castle. She was tired of leaping to her feet every time she heard the slightest sound that might be a carriage.

"My dear," he said, "would you do me a great kindness and take this book to the vicar? I borrowed it sometime ago, and I expect he'd like it back."

She took the book from his hand. "*The Hellenica*, by Xenophon," she read. "What on earth is it?"

"A most interesting account of military prowess," her father said. "Xenophon was an ancient Greek warrior."

"Of course, Papa," she said. "I'm trying to finish hemming before suppertime, but I'll take it to the vicarage first thing in the morning."

"No, the vicar is waiting for the book," her father stated. "Please do so at once."

Philippa saw that her father's jaw was set. He seemed to be vibrating with a kind of wordless excitement, one that she instantly interpreted.

"You're having another argument with the vicar, aren't you?" she asked, with a sigh. "And I suppose *The Hellenica* proves your point."

"Exactly," her father said with satisfaction. "Riggs will be quite surprised."

"Must I go this very moment?"

"You could . . . do your hair," her father said, waving vaguely at her. "After all, no one has seen you since your return."

Philippa made her way upstairs, thinking about that. No doubt the villagers were agog

405

with excitement. Certainly by now they knew all about her stint as a nursemaid in the castle. The realization made her put on her second-best gown, a fetching pale blue one caught up under her breast with navy ribbons. She had a bonnet to match, a silly little thing that emphasized the color of her hair.

Once in Little Ha'penny the first person she saw was the baker's wife, delivering hot rolls to the Biscuit and Plow. "Aye, so you'll be a baroness as of Saturday," Mrs. Deasly said comfortably. "When I think of you as just a little scrap, coming in here with your nursemaid, I can hardly believe you're all grown-up. Your hair was like sunshine, even then, and you were the prettiest little thing I'd ever seen. It's a lucky girl you are, Miss Philippa!"

"Yes," she said, smiling at Mrs. Deasly. Even if she had to marry Rodney, she had loved and been loved, and that was more than many a woman could say.

As she approached the village square, she saw the vicar in front of his church, chatting with the blacksmith. Father Riggs was a gentle, stooped man, as dear to her as a grandfather. He was standing under an oak tree. The sun was slanting through the boughs, and his black cassock was dappled, as if it had been spotted with rainwater.

"It is a pleasure to see you again, my dear Miss Philippa. And it will be my honor to perform your wedding ceremony on Saturday," he said, rocking back on his heels.

Philippa couldn't quite manage a smile, but she nodded.

The vicar drew a little closer and scrutinized her face. "My dear, are you . . ." He stopped and began again. "Often those of the fair sex feel a trifle reluctant to marry, but I assure you that the rewards of being a dutiful and loving wife are remarkable, and realized not merely in heaven."

Philippa nodded absently. She was wondering whether a broken heart ever scarred over. She returned her attention to the vicar when she saw that his face had grown soft and regretful, as if he were consigning her to the gallows rather than the altar.

He put a consoling hand on her arm. "I will certainly—" But at that moment she heard the clatter of horses' hooves on cobblestones and her heart bounded. Surely it was Wick at last! She spun about so quickly that the priest's hand fell from her arm. It was—

407

It was Rodney.

As soon as he saw her, he jerked his head to the two young men riding with him. They withdrew to the opposite side of the square, and Rodney swung off his horse. For a moment, he simply stood before her, his face tight, before by an effort of will, it seemed, he regained his habitual sleepy look.

At last, he bent into a bow. "Miss Philippa." At the bow's lowest point, she saw that he would be bald quite soon. Bald as an egg, likely.

She curtsied, and held out her hand to be kissed. "Mr. Durfey."

"Ah, the dear betrothed couple!" Father Riggs chortled beside her.

They ignored him.

Rodney took her hand in his, raised it to his lips, and didn't release it. "Philippa," he said, with a windy sigh. "Ah, Philippa."

Philippa said nothing. Instead, she looked at Rodney as a naturalist might examine a specimen, cataloging the thinning hair, the arrogant yet indolent slope to his chin, the genuine—yes, genuine—affection in his eyes.

"I am sorry," he said finally, still clinging to her hand.

Philippa forced her mouth to curve upwards, but pulled her fingers away. "It's quite all right."

"I—I didn't understand. I was slightly mad, I think. Your beauty is intoxicating."

Philippa didn't think he was mad. She thought that he was simply lustful, and that he would always be lustful. It was part of Rodney, together with his fleshy thighs and his warm eyes. She knew in that second that he would not be faithful to her. Not Rodney, not once he was a baronet. He would rove on, cheerfully deflowering maidens in barns, or perhaps even inns.

But at the moment, he was all hers, for good or ill. He snatched up her hand again, and held it tightly. "I love you," he said, turning his shoulder on the vicar. "I love you, Philippa. I'll do whatever you wish."

She could see that he meant it. Rodney would frolic now and then with a willing woman—in a barn or otherwise—but at night he would return to her, with that love shining in his eyes.

For a second she felt as if she couldn't breathe, as if she were trapped behind a pane of glass, looking out at a world she couldn't touch. Panic filled her, the suffocating fear that she would spend the rest of her life without ever being in the arms of the person she loved.

And all the more suffocating for being always in the arms of a person who loved *her*.

Dimly, Philippa became aware that she was

swaying, her heart clenched at the thought of the life that lay ahead of her. Father Riggs squealed something, began fanning her with his hat.

Rodney pulled her to his chest, smashing her nose into his coat. She smelled starched linen and sweat. She was held there for several moments, lights playing behind her closed eyes, like the dappled sunlight on the vicar's cassock. Her heart was beating in her ears as loudly as if a hunting party was pounding through the forest.

No . . .

It wasn't her heart.

She pulled away sharply and turned to see a great party, all on horseback, slow to a walk at the beginning of High Street. They were gaily dressed in the brilliant embroidery and silks of nobility. There were grooms in scarlet livery, and even a coach following, its scarlet trim glittering in the sunlight.

"Lord Almighty," Rodney muttered beside her.

The horses pranced down the street, their riders smiling and nodding to the villagers trotting from the cobbler and the smithy.

"It's better than the fair!" she heard someone say shrilly.

But Philippa's eyes were fixed on the rider in front, a man who was not wearing the exuberant embroidery of his royal brother nor the scarlet livery of the groomsmen. Nor was he wearing shining armor.

He was riding a snowy white horse. His costume was one her own father would have chosen: a dark, dark green coat with a snowy neckcloth. It was not ostentatious, but it proclaimed the wearer a gentleman.

Perhaps, even, a member of the gentry.

Perhaps, even, connected to a royal family, albeit a non-English royal family.

She stepped out from the shadow of the oak, her arm sliding from Rodney's hand.

As Wick's horse paced toward her, Philippa didn't even smile. Her heart was too full for that: full of song and laughter and the love that would sustain her to the end of her life.

And Wick didn't smile either. He was as grave as a king as he brought his mount to a trot, leaned down at just the right moment, swept out an arm, pulled her onto his saddle—and then galloped straight down the street and out of Little Ha'penny.

When they reached the edge of the town, alone now, since the royal party had stayed in Little Ha'penny, the better to dazzle the villagers, Wick jumped from the horse again and reached up.

She fell into his arms with a sob of pure joy.

Wick dropped to his knees there, in the dust of the road. "Miss Philippa Damson, would you do me the very great honor of becoming my wife?"

"Wick, oh, Wick," Philippa said, reaching out a shaking hand to bring him back to his feet.

But he waited. Had there been an observer standing in the ditch, that observer might have found his face impassive, unreadable. But to Philippa, his eyes spoke of deep love, a fierce passion, and just the tiniest amount of uncertainty.

She fell to her knees and wound her arms around his neck. "I was so afraid you wouldn't come!"

His arms were warm and strong about her. He kissed her ear and whispered something, but she was sobbing too hard to comprehend. At last he tenderly picked her up and carried her into a field of buttercups, well away from the road. There he sat her down and began kissing every part of her face he could reach until she simply had to stop crying.

When he reached her mouth, he kissed her until her breath was quick, not with sobs but with a quite different emotion.

Finally, he pulled back and said, "May I ask you again?"

"Of course I will marry you," she said, turning to catch his mouth again. "Yes, yes, yes!"

"My name," he said, sometime later, "is Jonas. Jonas Berwick."

"My *husband*," Philippa said with great delight, "is a man named Jonas Berwick."

He shook his head.

"No?"

"He's a future doctor named Jonas Berwick. And he owns an estate called Yarrow House, which was the gift of his brother."

Philippa swallowed. "Oh, Wick."

"*Jonas*," he said. "Wick was a majordomo at a castle once upon a time. Jonas is a gentleman of unknown birth but obvious gentility, who lives in England with his entirely English and altogether beautiful wife. He is apparently connected to a royal family, but because they are from a strange and small country, no one pays much attention to that."

Tears were again sliding down her face, not from fear but from the deepest happiness.

"I love you," he whispered. "I love you so much, Philippa, my future wife. The imprint of you is on my heart and will be there the day I die."

"You sound like a doctor, diagramming your body," she whispered back.

Eloisa James

"I think you will not complain when I diagram *your* body," he said, soft and low. The flame rose between them instantly, and when Jonas rolled his future wife over, sinking into a patch of buttercups so they couldn't be seen from the road, indeed there were no complaints.

Epilogue

Several months later

$\mathcal{W}$ick looked down at his bride with a surge of joy that came to him every time he saw her face.

Philippa was supine on their bed. They had retired to their bedchamber after luncheon, and now she lay in a patch of sunlight, her cheeks pink and her chest still heaving.

"I like our house," he said, picking up a few strands of silky hair and curling them around his finger. "I like this bed. I'm sorry we're leaving for Edinburgh."

"I'm not sorry," Philippa said, squinting at him. "You're driving our poor butler out of his mind. I know *you* were an astonishingly competent majordomo, Jonas, but you can't expect the poor man to ascend to your heights."

"All I asked was that the silver be thoroughly polished on a regular basis."

Philippa closed her eyes. "I cannot imagine how you did all that you claim a butler should manage in one day, and neither can poor Ribble. At this rate, you will know all there is to know about medicine in six months rather than a year."

"Did you see that your father sent another letter?" he inquired.

She nodded. "He has launched into a ferocious battle with a benighted professor from Cambridge who had the temerity to disagree with his reconstruction of Napoleon's first campaign."

"I like your father," Wick said. "He is a model of perseverance."

"He's too rigid," Philippa said. "He will never accept that anyone else is right, even about the trivial details."

Wick grinned down at her. "And yet . . . here I am."

"Well, that's true," Philippa said. "He did change his mind about you. And I still smile every time I think about his insisting that I go to the village merely to return that silly book. It was very unlike him to participate in your charade."

"What you should smile about is the image of

me practicing that horse business," Wick said. "I could have been at your side a full two days earlier had it not been for the hours and hours I lost, sweeping the knife boy up before me in the saddle."

"Oh dear," Philippa said sleepily. "I hope you didn't drop him."

"Often," Wick said. "But he didn't break anything. I came to you the moment I felt reasonably certain that I wouldn't drop *you*." He touched her nose lightly. "You are the most precious thing in the world to me."

The corner of her mouth quirked, and she whispered, "Love you," then she was asleep.

Wick lay beside her, watching as the sunlight shifted across the bed, making stripes over the bare skin of his exquisite wife. The doctor side of him cataloged the tiny swell in her stomach, and the way she dropped asleep at any time of the day. The man side of him noticed that her bosom was even more enthralling than it had been when they married, three months ago.

And the child side . . . the small boy inside, who was never quite sure of his place in life . . . That small boy had vanished.

He belonged *here*, next to a woman whom he loved more than life itself.

Though how that happened he didn't know. In

fact, he didn't really understand his own luck until years later when his eldest daughter Clara grew old enough to discover fairy tales. Then, with stories of knights, dragons, lovely maidens, and magic beans swirling through the house, Wick realized who he was. Not an illegitimate son of a grand duke. Not the best doctor in the country. He was the stable boy who won the princess.

The stories never said much about the stable boy's birth. They just said that the princess was as beautiful as the sun and the moon.

But most importantly, those stories all end the same way.

They lived happily ever after.

Do you love historical fiction?

Want the chance to hear news about your favourite authors (and the chance to win free books)?

Suzanne Allain
Mary Balogh
Lenora Bell
Charlotte Betts
Manda Collins
Joanna Courtney
Grace Burrowes
Evie Dunmore
Lynne Francis
Pamela Hart
Elizabeth Hoyt
Eloisa James
Lisa Kleypas
Jayne Ann Krentz
Sarah MacLean
Terri Nixon
Julia Quinn

Then visit the Piatkus website
www.yourswithlove.co.uk

And follow us on Facebook and Instagram
www.facebook.com/yourswithlovex | @yourswithlovex

PIATKUS